TOURNAMENT OF SHADOWS
II

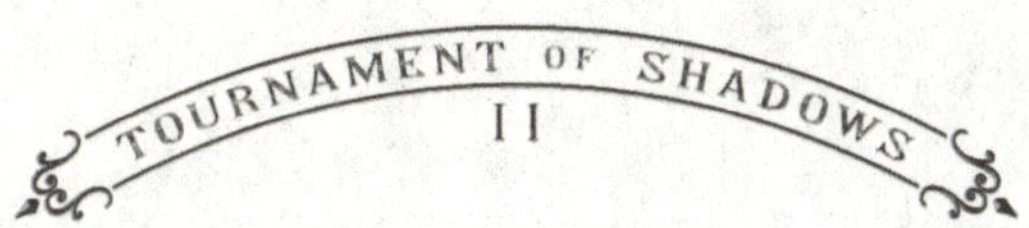

A DANGEROUS RUSE

TILLY WALLACE

v13062022

ISBN: 978-0-473-64014-9

Published by Ribbonwood Press

To be the first to hear about Tilly's new releases, sign up at:

https://www.tillywallace.com/newsletter

ONE

L*ondon, August 1788*

"L*ADY* W*INYARD*, M*ISTRESS OF* D*RAINS*." Elliot read the headline aloud as he carried the newspaper into the room. He dropped it at her elbow on the desk, where Seraphina Winyard sat regarding the street out the window.

She placed her pen in its holder and pushed the newspaper away. "I cleared three drains and now I'm the sorceress of sewage."

The footman snorted. "There was a lost opportunity for the newspaper. I'd like to see *sorceress of sewage* across the front page. What was blocking the latest one?"

"A thigh." She watched the children outside

bouncing a bright red ball among themselves. Had the owner of the leg once raced around with his friends without a care in the world or an inkling of the fate that awaited him?

Elliot leaned against the wall and crossed his arms. "A thigh with nothing else attached?"

"From the knee joint to the hip ball. I was told it's not unusual to find body parts down the drains in that part of London." Three times now the Mage Council had sent her out to aid the poorest area of the city, and she didn't imagine that was a coincidence. Since she had thwarted their attempts to retain control of her, they dispensed horrid jobs with a petulant glee. Kitty's father and his supporters were doing their bit to overturn the amendment to the Mage Act, but until the Mage Council was defeated in Parliament, she lived under a cloud.

Elliot raised his eyebrows. "Makes you wonder what goes on behind some doors. It's not like a fellow just loses his entire upper leg."

A rap at the door saved her from having to speculate on the origins of the body parts liberated from the narrow channels sweeping waste out to the Thames.

A familiar murmured voice came from the hall and Elliot reappeared, followed by the surgeon Hugh Miles. He clutched a battered leather satchel in his hands. On seeing her, he dropped it to the floor and slid off his hat.

"Good morning, Sera." His tongue stuttered over her name, which, unlike *Lady Winyard*, was still unfamiliar territory to him. Sera thought *Lady Winyard* sounded like a dour old matron who never smiled.

"Good morning, Hugh. What a pleasant surprise. Elliot, do see if Rosie can rustle up a tea tray for us." She waved at the footman.

Elliot grinned behind Hugh's back, then the impertinent man puckered his lips and made a kissing motion. Sera moved to the settee and wriggled her fingers, sending an invisible smack to the back of Elliot's head. A muffled oath from the footman made Hugh turn and frown.

"What brings you to this neighbourhood?" Sera asked, distracting her companion from the antics of her staff.

"I was visiting a patient nearby and thought I would call on you. You must be relieved to no longer have the accusation of murder hanging over your head." He took the armchair before the fire, as had become his habit.

"The accusation has been withdrawn, but the taint remains." Some would always believe she had supplied the poison to Jake Hogan, even after Lord Tomlin had unexpectedly come to her defence and said a gifted apothecary might have brewed it.

"You proved wrong those who accused you. Do you think the Mage Council will accept you now?" He leaned on the arm of the chair and fixed his warm gaze on her.

She heaved a sigh. How she wished it were as simple as proving a few stuffy men wrong, and being left to live her life as she pleased. Unknown secrets whispered over her skin and darted at the corners of her vision. *Their plan is abhorrent...* She would unearth what truth lay behind those few words.

"I always wondered why the Mage Council let me live, when for centuries they quietly disposed of any girl mage. I used to have to perform at mage tower while they sneered at my attempts. As though parading me about as an inferior specimen somehow justified their horrific actions in the past."

Hugh rose from his chair and the settee sagged as he sat next to her. He took her left hand in his and rubbed his thumb over the fading scar left by the magical bracelet that had been the cause of her humiliation. "No one who ever met you could think you in any way inferior. You crackle with power and potential."

The magic flowed freely through her veins now. But for many years, the river had been dammed and strangled to a mere trickle. "The pretty bracelet I wore for all those years suppressed my magic. I would know why. Branvale did not act alone. Someone instructed him." She met his gaze. "I found an ensorcelled page he used to correspond with someone, and on it was written, *Keep her with you, however you can. To ensure her safety, the council must believe her feeble, with little power, and of no consequence.*"

She found it easy to confide in him, with his solid and comforting presence. He would no more reveal her secrets than a snow-covered mountain would. She still puzzled over the last part of that secret message, which made no sense to her.

There cannot be another Nereus.

"That sounds as though someone has been trying to protect you. But why put you through what you have endured when they could have acted openly?" A frown pulled his brows together and his thumb stilled on her skin.

That was just one of the many secrets she sought to uncover. "I don't know. Perhaps it is someone not in a position to speak against the council?" An ordinary concerned citizen, perhaps? No. Branvale would never have listened to a busybody. For him to follow instructions, the person had to possess magic, power, or wealth. Or possibly all three.

Hugh cleared his throat and clasped her hand between both of his. The furrow remained on his forehead, but his eyes brimmed with concern. "Do you think there is someone within the council who might try to move against you? Even though you have proven your worth?"

"I am convinced of it. There are layers of secrets here that stretch back to when I was born. That afternoon in Jake's rooms, his last words to me were, 'You don't know, do you? How deeply you're caught in his web.' They thought me a feeble girl, but I have shown them a competent woman. That might prove my undoing. But I am not afraid of them. I *will* know the truth."

For most of her life, an unknown hand had placed her on a game board. She had shaken free of that grip, and would make her own moves. If only she knew the identity of her opponent. They kept themselves hidden in the shadows.

The name *Lord Ormsby* flew to the front of her mind, but was he too obvious a candidate? The Speaker of the Mage Council barely hid his contempt for her. At least with him, Sera knew exactly where she stood. No, the greater risk came from those who murmured quietly and sharpened their knives behind her back.

"I would assist you in your search for truth and will do anything you require of me. You have only to ask." The worry at his brow lessened a little, but he did not dissuade her from her path. How wise of him.

A clatter from the hall preceded Elliot's return with the tray. "Scones fresh from the oven." He didn't need to tell Sera—the delicious, warm aroma enticed her nose and she leaned towards the tray.

Hugh's eyes widened, and Sera wondered if he had eaten yet. She dropped two fat scones on a plate and handed it to him, inviting him to help himself to the clotted cream and jam, both gifts from country clients. Then she poured tea.

A rap on the front door elicited a sigh from Elliot. "Who is it *now*?" he muttered as he left the room to perform his actual duties.

Muffled voices came from beyond, then Elliot returned followed by two men wearing the purple and gold livery of the Mage Council. Each man clutched the rope handle of a wide, flat crate hoisted between them.

"Delivery for you, milady," Elliot murmured, sounding almost like a real footman.

Sera rose from the settee, and Hugh leapt to his feet, clutching his plate in one hand and half a scone in the other. She wrapped the tea tray in magic and lifted it out of the way. "Place it on the table, please."

The men lowered the object to the low table, and Sera resettled the tray on her desk. Then she turned her attention to the delivery. It stretched two feet long, a foot and a half wide, and several inches deep. The men bowed and shuffled out without speaking.

"Talkative fellows," Elliot remarked.

She only half listened, her attention on the crate. Sera laid both hands on the rough wood. A spell tickled across her hands. An enchantment ensured that only the intended recipient could open the lid. Anyone else would receive a nasty shock. She picked at the spell, trying to find the point where it would unravel, rather like possessing a bunch of keys but not knowing which one fitted the lock.

"Have you thought about adding some sparks while you're working, or swirly colours? Or some light music for those of us watching? It's all a bit boring," Elliot said.

Sera cracked open one eye and sent an arc of harmless blue sparks towards the footman. He jumped back and glared at her. Hugh grinned and ate the remaining half of his scone in one mouthful.

The lid emitted a *crack*, but otherwise the crate appeared unchanged. Sera grabbed it and levered it away to reveal a tightly packed mass of straw.

"Bedding for a donkey?" Elliot tugged a flake of straw free.

"Nothing quite as stubborn." Clearing away the straw, Sera found a large book with a worn leather binding. In the middle of the cover was stamped the number six in faded gold. The number corresponding to her seat in the council chamber. "The mage genealogies."

After she lifted free the book, Elliot and Hugh took a handle each and removed the crate, depositing it by the door. Sera set the book on the table and knelt on the floor before it. She rested her hands on the cover. Once, this had belonged to her predecessor, and like his magic and seat, it now became hers.

She opened the book and flicked through to the more recent entries. At the top of each page was written the name of a mage, and underneath, their date of birth. Below, the book kept track of the mage's offspring. Once a mage was born, and except for their own children, the five generations that followed, called aftermages, were touched by magic and inherited different gifts. In some, like her friend Lady Abigail Crawley, magic manifested in a gift for music. No one knew what form the gift would take, only that it appeared the strongest in a mage's grandchildren—the third generation. Then it faded, until the seventh generation barely possessed any magic at all. After that, it disappeared entirely and a mage never reappeared in that family line.

Near the middle of the book she found her name. Apart from three younger mages born after her, the rest of the book was blank, its pages yet to be filled by mages and their progeny.

Seraphina Elizabeth Winyard

15 July 1770

THE PARENTS of a mage were never recorded. History deemed them unimportant.

"How does it work?" Elliot peered over one shoulder, Hugh at the other.

"A magic so old, I don't think anyone knows how it came to be. The book knows when a mage is born, marries, or their children produce an aftermage. Their names simply appear on the page. When a book is full, twelve new copies appear in the library—one for each living mage." She turned back a few pages and found Lord Branvale. The date of 15 July 1788 was now recorded under his name as his date of death. Crisp black lines led from his name to those of his two children and a scattering of grandchildren.

"What if it's wrong, or out of date, or a child dies?" Hugh leaned closer, his words scented with jam.

"As long as a child draws a single breath, their life is captured in the book, and it is never wrong." With a fingertip she traced a line from her former guardian to his newest grandchild. A girl who, according to the book, could see the dead.

Hugh's sleeve brushed her shoulder as he reached out, but he stopped short of touching the magic paper, perhaps lest he leave a buttery smudge. "Something there has been rubbed out."

"What?" Sera followed the line of his finger.

He gestured sideways. "The way the light hits the book from here, I can see a line going to the right of Lord Branvale's name."

Sera stood and carried the book with her to the desk. Setting it down in front of the window, she picked up one side and angled the page. Sure enough, a faint line and the impression of letters appeared to the side of Branvale's name.

"That's impossible." With the book laid flat, the erasure was invisible. A horizontal line meant a marriage, or was used to denote the mother of a mage's child. Such things were never undone. Was it as simple as a mistake by the book? Or had Hugh stumbled upon one of Branvale's secrets?

"How many hundreds of years has the book been recording all gifted mage descendants? Is it that surprising it made one mistake out of thousands of entries?" Hugh gestured to the page.

Elliot held his silence, and took the opportunity to pocket a scone from the plate. Sera rolled her eyes at him, and the footman discreetly slid out the door.

"I will consult the book held in mage tower. It's the original genealogy—these are all its copies. Or descendants, I suppose. It is not impossible that in duplicating the entries, an error might have been made, but I have never heard of such a thing before." Sera closed the book.

Hugh picked up the last scone and cast a longing look at the one with a small nibble out of it on her plate. "Do you think this is one of the secrets that Lord Branvale's valet referred to?"

Sera tore off a piece of scone and popped it into her mouth. They were too delicious to let the surgeon eat them all. "I don't know. But that still doesn't explain why the book recorded something and then erased it. It's not like we can submit corrections or alterations to it."

The clock in the hall chimed ten times, and Hugh grew taller as he stood to attention. On the last chime, he grabbed his hat and bag. "Blast. I have a meeting with Lieutenant Powers at half past. I am sorry, Sera. I did not mean to linger so long."

"Rosie's scones are quite the temptation." She followed him out to the hall.

He clapped on his hat with one hand and paused on the doorstep. "I meant it. Anything you need of me, you have only to ask."

"Thank you, Hugh." Then an idea occurred to her. "If you like, I could ask Contessa Ricci if you could join us for our monthly dinner?"

His eyes lit up, whether at the thought of a well-laid table or a chance to examine the elegant vampyre, she did not know. Likely both. "I would not wish to impose, but neither could I decline if such an invitation were made."

After she closed the door on his broad back, Sera returned to the parlour. The faint line next to Lord Branvale's name in the mage genealogy was a puzzle for another day. There were two other names she needed to pursue first.

Sera opened a drawer in the desk and pulled out a square of paper. She rotated it between her fingers, sliding it along her palm on one edge and then flicking it over to the other. Two names and a place name were written in the middle of the square. Enough for her to start a journey of discovery. But did the people want to be found?

When she turned eighteen, Sera had requested the

names of her parents. Lord Pendlebury had supplied the details on one of her visits to the tower. Taken from her mother at age five, she had few memories of the woman who had borne her, and none whatsoever of the man named as her father.

Nora Jones.
Benjamin Cohen.
Oswestry, Shropshire.

THE PEOPLE HAD DIFFERENT SURNAMES. The most likely explanation was that her father had died, and her mother remarried. And yet...the hollow in her stomach made her wonder if there was another reason. One tied to why her parents hadn't bothered to contact her since she'd come of age. Nor had they stayed in touch. Some parents kept up a steady correspondence with their magical offspring. The Mage Council removed a young mage at five to begin their training, but in one aspect at least, they weren't monsters. Mothers and fathers could write, and receive replies. That decision lay entirely in their hands.

Why had her parents remained silent?

Sera knew little about Shropshire except that it bordered Wales and had, at times, changed hands between the two countries. An ancient area, steeped in magic—with a portal to the Fae realm. Currently, time did not allow her a trip to the area to knock on her mother's door. Instead, she had made a request of Mr

Napier, father of her best friend, Kitty, to ferret out any information he could about the couple.

With one last look, she returned the paper to its drawer. Kitty's father had sent a man to Oswestry a week ago. Surely that was ample time for him to discover whether her parents were alive or dead?

Two

Sera dashed off a quick note to Kitty using her ensorcelled paper, asking if she might visit. The Napier family carriage collected Sera just before noon and deposited her outside the Mayfair home of her friend, next door to the house in which Sera had grown up. Sera strode up the path and through the door, opened with impeccable timing by the family's butler.

"Lady Winyard," he murmured. Onward she swept to the front parlour.

"Any news of my parents?" Sera asked, hope a clenched fist in her chest.

Kitty set aside her book and shook her head. "Nothing yet."

Sera's posture slumped. "What is taking so long?"

"It's been thirteen years, Sera. People might change location in search of work. Your parents might have moved elsewhere. Give Papa's man a little time to find them." Kitty patted the settee next to her.

Sera dropped onto the brocade seat as instructed. "Yes, that must be it."

Or possibly her parents didn't want anything to do with their magical offspring and had relocated so they couldn't be found. Or a roving band of pirates might have kidnapped them, and they now scrubbed decks out on the ocean, wondering what had happened to their child.

Or they were dead.

"Stop being so miserable, it will not do. You have Papa and me—we are your family." Kitty nudged her with her shoulder.

"You and Abigail are both like sisters to me." She possessed friends and family, and considered herself blessed in them. But at night, when she lay awake in bed, the small voice in her head wanted to know about her origins. What songs had her mother sung when she couldn't sleep? Had she a favourite toy or game, or any siblings? Did she resemble her mother or father? Why did her parents have different surnames?

"Has the council not found another blocked drain that requires your delicate touch to keep you occupied?" Kitty murmured.

Sera straightened with a snort and stared at her friend. "*Et tu, Brute?* It's bad enough the newspaper is calling me *mistress of drains*, and Elliot, my footman, prefers *sorceress of sewage*. But to answer your question, no, they have not. Due to my efficiency, I have the sewers all cleared and the Thames is flowing up and down them as it should."

"They are certainly making you earn your stipend.

Speaking of which, Father left some papers for you to read." Kitty rose and collected from the sideboard a deep red folder tied with a black ribbon.

Sera took the folder and plucked at the bow with one hand. She couldn't concentrate on financial matters at the moment, apart from worrying about how to find an income source to supplement her entitlement from the Crown. She'd made a deal to supply Contessa Ricci's brew for free, so that wasn't going to fund her plans for the future. "I'll read these tonight."

She spent a pleasant hour talking with Kitty, then her friend moved to the rosewood writing desk to work on her correspondence. Sera tried to read, but found the novel lacklustre and the heroine somewhat insipid. Dropping the book to her chest, she lay back on the chaise and stared at the ceiling rose. To amuse herself, she sent a gentle waft of magic to animate the plaster vines and flowers as though a breeze stirred them. Then she added a fat bumblebee droning from one creamy bloom to another.

"Whatever is bothering you?" Kitty folded her letter and selected a stick of wax.

"I received an invitation to a ball this week. Queen Charlotte says I must attend." Sera wasn't sure what bothered her more—the fact she would have to behave, or that so many eyes would be watching and judging her every move. After her *faux pas* at Abigail's musical evening, she worried about making such a mistake again. The rest of the *ton* were far less forgiving than her friend.

"If the queen commands, then you must obey."

Kitty held the wax to a candle and melted a drop onto the letter. Then she stamped it with her seal. "What event is being inflicted upon you?"

Sera sat up and slipped off her shoes to tuck one foot up under her. "The Duchess of Edgecombe's ball."

Kitty walked to the bell pull by the door and gave it a tug. "Cheer up. We all have to go to that one—even Father and I are invited. Apparently the duchess is hosting on behalf of the king and queen. It's a diplomatic thing for some Austrian nobles and we all need to put on a good show."

The footman entered and bowed. Kitty handed over her letters and he left again on silent feet. Then she dropped to the chaise next to Sera and pointed to the silver pot on a tray. "Could you warm what's left, please?"

Sera rolled her eyes. Her one true calling in life. *The witch of warm beverages.* She wrapped a tendril of magic around the pot and soon steam puffed out of the spout. Kitty murmured her thanks and poured the remaining brew into their cups.

"I thought you didn't like balls?" Sera plucked her cup from the tray and cradled it between her hands.

Kitty picked up her cup and took a tiny sip. "I have nothing against balls. What I dislike are the nincompoops who, emboldened by the size of Father's fortune, drool over my hand. Honestly, it simply confirms their idiocy. They can't figure out that, due to our comfortable position, I have neither the need nor the intent to marry."

"Not at all?" Sera leaned on the rolled arm of the

chaise to regard her friend. Kitty had never expressed any desire for marriage, unlike Lady Abigail, who was duty bound and pressured by her parents to marry well. Sera was ambivalent about the subject. She supposed marriage might be tolerable with the right person. But if the council pushed the subject, she would dig her heels in and live a scandalous life as a merry spinster. Or she would take lovers and possibly produce her own unmagical offspring. If men could do it outside the sanctity of marriage, then so could she.

Kitty blew out a snort. "I suppose if I found a man who could hold an intelligent conversation, and who had the good sense to know he would never get his hands on Father's money...then I might consider an offer."

Sera's sentiments exactly. Not the fortune bit, since she lacked one of those, but a partner who stimulated her mind. "The evening will be bearable with all three of us there."

"Do say you will dress here and go with us." Kitty's eyes sparkled with mischief. "I hate the way everyone stares at these things, but if you accompany us, no one will notice me."

Sera laughed. "I am a mere penniless mage. How can the *mistress of drains* compare to the embodiment of the magnificent Napier fortune?"

Kitty's brows pulled together in a serious expression, but her lips twitched with suppressed mirth. "If you weren't holding hot chocolate over my favourite chaise, I would smack you with a pillow."

With a wave of magic, Sera sent her cup to sit on

the table so she could grasp Kitty's hand. "You do yourself a disservice, Kitty. You have a loyal heart and a keen mind. Any man who cannot see that is, as you observe, too dense to appreciate you. Also, I shall turn any man who offends you into a toad."

Kitty tapped a finger on her chin. "Perhaps we could circulate that rumour in advance. It might save my best gloves from all those sweaty hands. Some of them squeeze my hand so hard I am sure they are trying to make coins pop out my ears."

THE NEXT DAY, Sera worked at her desk. The papers Kitty gave her contained information of those who would vote against the amendment to the Mage Act and her plan slowly took form. A faint scratching caught her attention, as though a bird struggled to find a foothold against the brick outside. Leaning forward, she glanced out the window to find not a bird, but a hooded figure on the doorstep.

"How intriguing," she murmured. There being no sign of Elliot, she rose and opened the door herself. "May I help you?" she asked the woman in the soft green cloak.

"Lady Winyard?" a timid voice enquired. The uncertainty matched the hesitancy of the knock.

"Yes. Why don't you come inside? My parlour is

small, but private." She stood aside to let the visitor enter.

In the hall, the woman pulled back her hood. Dark brown hair was knotted at her nape. Hazel eyes regarded her from under dark brows. The woman twisted her hands together, and Sera noted a wedding ring. "I am Lady Noelle Tinwald and an acquaintance of Miss Napier. She always speaks of you with the highest regard."

"Any friend of Miss Napier is welcome here. Might I take your cloak?" Sera held out a hand and wondered where Elliot had gone. Not sensing him nearby, she set off a ding in the kitchen to alert Vicky and Rosie to the fact that they had a visitor. Hopefully one of them would boot the footman up the stairs.

"Oh. Um...yes." Lady Tinwald undid the clasp and passed it over, all the while staring through the parlour door and along the short hall.

Elliot finally appeared at the top of the kitchen stairs. He stopped on seeing Sera with someone and smoothed two palms over his hair. "Tea, milady?" he murmured with a quirked eyebrow.

"Yes, thank you, Elliot." Sera gestured to the small parlour. "This way."

Curiosity gnawed at her insides as to what had prompted the noblewoman to seek her out. How she wanted it to be some scandal or intrigue. From her appearance, her visitor didn't appear much older than she, perhaps somewhere in her mid-twenties. The gown under her cloak was plain, but well made and of an expensive fabric.

Sera took one of the worn leather armchairs and left the equally aged settee to her visitor.

"This is a rather modest home for one of your station, is it not, Lady Winyard?" Lady Tinwald couldn't help staring with wide eyes.

Little had changed in the weeks Sera had lived in the terrace house. She'd rather spend her money on books and food than furnishings. "It suits me for the time being." Folding her hands in her lap, Sera decided how to discover whatever had driven the other woman to her doorstep. "I suspect you sought me out for a particular reason, Lady Tinwald. How might I be of assistance?"

Lady Tinwald produced a lawn handkerchief and twisted it around a finger. Whatever bothered her, Sera suspected it would involve tears. "I have been married some five years now. Lord Tinwald is a kind man and I am content with the match. But, there is something... that I fear requires...a helping hand."

Sera couldn't even guess at what the other woman needed. It could be an embarrassing rumour she wanted suppressed or a cloaking spell to smuggle a lover into the house. "I might be young, Lady Tinwald, but I can assure you of the utmost discretion. I worked beside Lord Branvale for many years in creating potions and salves for his noble clients."

The other woman nodded and her lips moved, but nothing came out, as though she were rehearsing her lines in advance. "My husband will inherit the title of earl one day from his father. As his wife, it is my duty to provide an heir to continue the family name. But...our endeavours so far have not been...*fruitful*." She whispered the last word and then blushed furiously. Her gaze dropped to her hands.

Ah. Mother Nature could be fickle in whom she blessed in that regard. Sometimes those who wanted a child the most were left with empty arms, while some poor woman who craved a moment of quiet to herself birthed a dozen in quick succession. A fertility potion and the cooperation of Mother Nature would assist in populating the Tinwald nursery. "I can brew a tonic for you that will enable you to conceive."

A sigh heaved through Lady Tinwald. "Thank you. But I fear that is only one part of the possible problem. Lord Tinwald—he...ummm...sometimes cannot—" With one hand covering her now beetroot-red face, Lady Tinwald held out her other hand, wriggled her pinkie and then the little finger...drooped.

Sera had heard of such an issue among men. Especially those who liked a few drinks before retiring at night. The footmen used to tease each other that their members were incapable of performing the act under discussion when they had consumed too much ale on their rare nights off. "I can provide a potion for both of you that will be tailored to the particular needs of each."

Lady Tinwald heaved a sob. "Thank you, Lady Winyard. To fulfil my duty would bring me the greatest joy. I have not been able to seek any assistance in this matter. Our doctor and the local apothecary are both men, and I would never mention such an issue in their company. Further, Lord Tinwald refuses to discuss it, and has stated most vehemently that there is no fault on his side."

Sera bit her tongue. If his lordship's flag was never raised (a euphemism she had learned below stairs), then the fault most definitely could be laid at his door. "Once they are ready, I could deliver the items to Miss Napier and you may collect them from her without anyone's knowledge. The potion will need to be drunk on a regular basis, and anything to assist Lord Tinwald will need to be taken before he retires for the evening."

Her guest perked up. She dabbed at her eyes with the handkerchief before tucking it away in her reticule. "Oh, I always take him a coffee on my way to bed. It's our little ritual. I can do it then."

"Excellent." How easy to be a poisoner, if people were so eager to slip a magical remedy into someone else's cup.

Jake. Her guardian's former valet appeared in her mind. *Did you act alone, or did someone instruct you to pour poison into Lord Branvale's nightcap?* Those events still bothered her and unanswered questions kept her awake at night. Not to mention the secrets that proliferated like lazy flies during a humid summer.

Lady Tinwald leaned forward and her eyes simmered with happiness. "I will pay most generously for your assistance, Lady Winyard. Shall we sweeten the pot? If I conceive in the next three months, I believe a bonus would be in order."

The job at hand would improve Sera's finances and perhaps she could buy a new settee after all. Especially if she delivered the desired result for Lady Tinwald and was paid a bonus. That made Sera wonder how many other ladies had problems of a delicate nature they couldn't discuss with their family physician or local apothecary. Nor would they go to one of the male mages with feminine issues. An exclusive niche opened before Sera. All she needed were some satisfied clients to spread the word, and she'd soon increase her bank account and holdings.

Elliot appeared with the tea tray and paused in the doorway. Sera waved him forward and changed the conversation to less personal matters. "You must tell me, Lady Tinwald, how long you have known Miss Napier?"

"Oh, many years. My mother was a dear childhood friend of Mrs Napier and she has kept watch over Mr Napier since his wife's passing. He in turn was a strong shoulder of support when Papa died three years ago." She perched on the edge of the settee, her back ramrod straight in a manner Sera often tried, and failed, to emulate.

Sera tightened her grip on the teapot's handle. Kitty's mother had died when she was a child and her father had raised her alone. A sad story and yet one that resonated with love and devotion for his wife. Was it time for him to loosen his hold on grief and find someone with whom he could enjoy his remaining years?

"You must tell me of Mrs Napier. I am sure your mother had many stories of their time together."

Lady Tinwald let out a sigh. "I heard so many tales,

I often don't know which were true and which Mother embroidered to entertain me."

"Pick the most outlandish." Sera poured and decided that yes, it was time for Mr Napier to find someone who would ease the ache in his heart.

THREE

Later that afternoon, Sera journeyed out to mage tower at Finsbury Fields. In the barren outer ward stood a young oak. She reached out to stroke a vibrant green leaf. The oak continued to thrive and its vitality rubbed off on the grass planted below it by previous mages. The once brown blades grew lusher and greener under the protection offered by the sapling, and from the amendments Sera had made to the soil.

"Keep growing, my friend," Sera murmured to the tree. Its base grew thicker as its roots drove deeper into the soil. The spell Sera had crafted nurtured the dirt and encouraged worms to return. Unseen by the mages walking back and forth above ground, bit by bit the earth would repair itself. She imagined the area around the tower transformed into a glorious green space of trees and shrubs. Fat bumblebees would fly from one bright flower to another, and perhaps in time she might add a water feature to lend a peaceful air.

Inside the tower, Sera took the stairs down to the library nestled deep in the ensorcelled earth. The tower was home to two very different libraries. One was freely accessible to enquiring minds and frequented by young mages, students of magical phenomena, or other interested parties wanting to read the histories held by the mages.

The other library was kept secret. Only those mages who had proven their worth by growing a blade of grass —or in her case, a tree—in the desolate yard were allowed to enter. Here, the shelves held books and scrolls on innumerable magical topics, the mages' shadowy history, and the hand they had taken in world events. And dark enchantments used in times of war.

A metal gate some eight feet high and wide guarded the entrance. In the very middle of the gate was what at first glance appeared to be intricate knotwork three feet in diameter. Only on closer inspection did it reveal itself as two snakes—one silver and one brass. Their bodies wound around each other as they grasped the ends of their tails in an eternal cycle of being eaten and reborn.

The snakes created an effective lock and the gate could not be opened without their co-operation. The next part of the process unnerved Sera. She stood before the gate and extended her hands, palms stretched towards the joined snakes.

"I seek entry," she murmured.

The silver ouroboros came alive and let go of its tail. Its tongue tasted the air and flicked close to her palm. A sibilant hiss filled the corridor as it communed with its sibling. A brass head broke free of the central panel to brush against Sera's skin. Two snake heads swivelled to commune with one another, then they unravelled their bodies to allow the gate to swing open.

"Thank you," she said as she walked through.

Behind her, the door swung shut and metal rasped over metal as the snakes' bodies knotted together once more and locked her inside.

She had two missions on this visit. One was to find the recipes for the potions needed for Lord and Lady Tinwald. The other was to examine the original genealogy ledger to see if the faint line appeared next to Lord Branvale's name on the master copy.

Just inside the entrance of the library, with a softly glowing lantern suspended above, was a podium bearing a map of the library. Areas were marked by different colours depending on the umbrella topic. Yellow for history. Red for war. Black for the dark arts. Green for issues relating to the human condition. Purple for books about other creatures.

Tapping a green area with a fingertip, she glanced up to orient herself and determine a direction. With the location in mind, a green strand appeared in the air, and she followed it along the stacks and down an aisle to a far corner. She ignored the anatomy texts and read spines looking for anything about reproductive concerns—a topic that appeared to be poorly represented in the otherwise well-stocked library. After a while, a title stopped her finger's exploration.

"Ah! *For the Bearing and Birthing of a Child*." She pulled the book free and a cloud of dust puffed out and made her sneeze. The book looked as though no one had consulted it in over a hundred years. Would the advice be of any use to Lady Tinwald, if some crusty old man had penned it centuries ago?

A glance at the author's name restored her faith: one Goody McTavish. No wonder the tome had languished on the shelf for decades—a woman had written the advice it contained. She wondered if the gender of the author had kept the book on the shelf, or the fact it was about *feminine issues*. Clutching the heavy book in her arms, Sera walked back to the study area. A single long, narrow table with padded chairs on either side sat beneath pendant lights shaded in amber glass. A few armchairs were scattered for more casual reading. The middle of the table held baskets containing fresh writing supplies.

Setting the book on the table at one end, Sera pulled out a chair with a deep red cushion and sat. Opening the book, and leaning away from the resulting dust cloud, she began. The author proved to have a well-organised mind and the contents were set out in a logical fashion. Somewhere towards the middle of the book, she found a section about what to do when an otherwise healthy woman failed to conceive.

"*A brew to nurture conditions of the womb,*" Sera murmured as her finger moved along the old text. Most of the ingredients were familiar to her, such as black cohosh and chaste berry. She would need to gather the supplies necessary to make the potion, but it was easily within her abilities, and she could add her own magical touch. From the thorough approach of the book and the pragmatic advice it contained, Sera guessed that in life, Goody McTavish must have been a gifted aftermage who practiced midwifery.

"How many women and babies did you save, I wonder?" Motherhood was the most fraught journey a woman could undertake, and sadly many did not survive. Why did mages not use their skills to discover ways to ease childbirth for mother and babe? Instead, they focused on ways to make cannon more accurate or bridges less likely to collapse.

Ideas circled in her mind as Sera copied the recipe on a clean sheet of paper. For too long women had no voice on the council. She could change that. She vowed to do something to address the conditions that affected women and children, whatever their station in life.

With one brew recorded, she considered the second half of the problem—Lord Tinwald. It wouldn't surprise her if the hidden library contained an entire section devoted to the male member, and most likely not a single word would mention its failure to perform. With a snort, she imagined all the poetry books and sonnets proclaiming the marvellous properties of that piece of flesh. Probably with embellished illustrations.

"Do not fail me, Goody McTavish." Sera pulled her mind back to her task and continued to read.

Thus far, the book provided detailed coverage of many aspects of conceiving and birthing a child. Along the pages she scanned, picking out key words and phrases. She was about to give up on finding what she needed, when a sentence made her choke back a laugh.

Women nurture and protect for nine months, yet men think their few seconds the pivotal contribution. Men are unable to see the defect hanging limp beneath their bellies...

Sera stopped reading aloud on hearing footsteps coming along the stacks. Goody McTavish had a rather scathing view of men who, due to their own indulgences or health concerns, blamed their wives for any failure to conceive. A number of potions were given to address a range of ailments, including one to make *the lazy soldiers stand at attention.* Sera noted down the steps involved and added the necessary components to the list of things to purchase at the apothecary.

The rustle of garments made her look up. Lord Tomlin approached the long desk with an armload of books. Today he was dressed more like a scholar, with a brown jacket and hastily tied cravat, rather than his flamboyant mage robes.

"Lord Tomlin." She nodded, her gaze wary. Friend or foe? She had not yet decided. He had lied to cast an accusation of murder upon her, whether of his own accord or due to pressure from Lord Ormsby. But then he'd spoken up to say that an apothecary might have provided Jake with the poison that took his master's life. He had provided reasonable doubt, and she had been set free.

"Lady Winyard." At a point three chairs along from her, he dropped all the books but one, which he clutched to his chest, long fingers wrapped around the spine. "Given we must work together for the king's banquet, I wanted to say I am sorry for any...misunderstanding during recent events."

"Thank you. It was an unfortunate turn of events, which I am relieved is now resolved. Have you had time to gather your thoughts about the performance we must put on?" She wouldn't dwell on the matter. It was now behind them.

He placed the last book on top of his pile and pulled out a chair. "I thought something that never fails to please—light against dark."

No need to guess who would be the dark force. Then an idea sparked in her mind. Yes, she rather liked the idea of being a dark goddess pitted against Lord Tomlin. If dark should triumph, that would upset the world view of many observers. "A favourite battle throughout the ages, is it not? Perhaps we could add a Greek theme, as I rather fancy representing Nyx, the goddess of night. If you have no objection to taking the side of the light, of course?"

His eyes widened. Apparently he had expected an argument from her. Then he nodded. "If you wish. I shall play Apollo, god of the sun."

Already Sera imagined her costume. A gown of midnight silk, scattered with glittering stars. She could darken her hair and set fireflies to glow among her locks. How satisfying it would be when Apollo's light was diminished by her greater ability. "A night among the gods. I am sure that will please our audience and the king."

"Indeed." He smiled and it appeared genuine.

"Shall we call it *A Night on Olympus*? We could cast King George as Zeus, overseeing a number of challenges that we would perform."

They discussed ideas for the evening, and Sera wrote a few notes to herself. Using Greek mythology as her inspiration itched at a name lying concealed in her brain. *Nereus*. Could the reference be to something from a myth? She added a note to pursue that later.

Then, she smiled and nodded as Lord Tomlin outlined how he saw the grand finale unfolding—with Apollo defeating Nyx as the new day's sun banished the night. With an outline for the evening settled, Sera gathered up her notes and murmured a farewell. After returning Goody McTavish's book to its rightful place, Sera stalked the aisles to where the original editions of the mage genealogies were shelved.

The current volume rested on a carved rosewood lectern. A single lantern hung above it, the magical light encased in amber glass shaped like a teardrop. Unlike its copies, the original was bound in a thick, dark brown leather embossed with a design of intertwined circles and knots. The gold lettering was raised and glinted under the soft light.

Wondering what she would find, Sera opened the large volume and stuck a finger in the approximate location of Lord Branvale's record. After flipping a few pages, she found the entry. Over the coming years, the lives of his descendants would fill the page and continue his magical legacy.

Sera squinted at the blank space beside Lord Branvale's name.

"Nothing," she muttered and tapped a fingertip against the side of the book. Was it the lighting? She had only seen the faint line when she angled the book towards the sun streaming in her parlour window. The muted glow cast by the amber teardrop was more like an eerie sunset. What if she brightened things up for her examination?

Whispering a spell under her breath, she then snapped her fingers and a bright white orb no more than an inch in diameter burst into life. The tiny sun hovered over the page, and Sera pushed it to a better position. With her knees bent so that her gaze was level with the page, Sera tried again.

"There," she breathed.

Sure enough, the orb of sunlight revealed a faint line extending to the right of Lord Branvale's name, then a few scratches that looked like a name that had been written and erased. The shapes taunted her, but her brain couldn't wrangle them into actual letters. Snapping her fingers, she extinguished the light and the impression vanished.

A line to the side meant a marriage, yet in all her years under his roof, Lord Branvale had never mentioned a wife. Even if she had died, the union would still appear in the genealogies, for benefit of the children. That left her two options. Either the genealogy had been mistaken and corrected itself, or someone had deliberately erased evidence of Branvale's marriage.

"I will keep scratching until I reveal the truth," Sera

whispered to the book. Then she closed the volume and left the hidden library.

On her way back to Soho, she stopped at the apothecary shop recommended by Hugh Miles. The bell tinkled over the door as she entered, clutching her basket. She drew a deep breath of the rich, herby aroma of the shop. Notes of soft lavender and crisp mint filled her nostrils. A woman leaned on the counter and held a quiet conversation with the owner, a man with bushy grey sideburns and a distinct lack of hair on his head, who glanced up at Sera. He acknowledged her with a nod, then returned his attention to his customer.

Sera paced the room, peering at bottles on a shelf. Above her head, bunches of herbs dangled upside down as they dried and waited to be ground up for potions and lotions. After a few minutes, the bell tinkled and the other customer left.

"What can I do for you today, Lady Winyard?" the owner asked from behind her.

Sera turned. "You know who I am?"

He winked. "Mr Miles talks of you often, and while the drawings in the newspaper aren't that accurate, they do capture a certain something about you. I'm Leon Fleece, and right pleased I am to make your acquaintance."

"How do you do, Mr Fleece? Mr Miles recommended your apothecary to meet my needs, as I have no garden of my own yet. I have quite a list, if you could assist?" Sera extracted the sheet of paper with the required herbs and infusions.

The apothecary scanned the ingredients and then

stared at her with wide eyes. "I do brew a similar potion to assist women wishing to conceive."

"I hope you don't think I am poaching your customers. The person concerned sought me out, as I believe she felt more comfortable confiding in another woman." Hugh spoke highly of the gifted apothecary, but he was no mage. The magic in his veins was a diluted legacy from his mage ancestor. Sera could offer a more potent brew touched with her power.

He waved away her concerns. "There's enough sickness in London to keep dozens of apothecaries and mages busy." He took her list to the shelves behind the counter and began plucking down baskets and bottles. "It's not often a woman ventures in here to seek this sort of help. There are many concoctions I sell that can ease a number of feminine ailments, if only we could talk about them without blushing or stuttering. I'm right glad to finally see a woman mage, my lady. You'll have a steady stream of customers with delicate problems. I'm more than happy to steer customers your way and supply the ingredients you need."

She hoped word would spread and more customers would seek her out. It would benefit both her finances and the overall health of womankind. "Have you thought of hiring a woman to assist in the shop and to serve other women?"

He chuckled as he began measuring out quantities into smaller containers. "I'd still have to train her in such womanly matters, and I'd be right back at my original problem."

Sera pondered that for a moment. How did women

learn about such things if they couldn't speak to men who held the knowledge? "It seems a waste, if a girl has an aftermage gift for medicine or herbology and cannot use that skill to benefit her sex. Someone has to be bold and grasp the knowledge for themselves."

"The medical schools won't take girls, my lady." He tapped a stopper into a small vial of ridged brown glass.

Sera snorted. "A ridiculous situation, is it not? We cannot have true equality until education is freely available to all."

Even when a physician attended a woman, some still refused to touch her, or had a sheet raised and they fumbled behind it so they didn't cast eyes on their undressed noble clients. Something had to change.

The advice from Mr Miles washed through her mind. *Do one thing.* Small changes built into bigger changes. Educating one woman was an excellent place to start. Mr Miles seemed the sort to nurture a young and eager mind, and a book such as that written by Goody McTavish would provide invaluable insight. She would raise the idea with the surgeon—the medical training of young women to assist other women.

FOUR

Sera returned to her terrace house with a loaded basket and handed over her cloak and hat to Elliot.

"Fancy a cup of tea?" he asked with a grin as he hung the items on their hooks.

"Yes, please, and whatever it is Rosie is cooking that smells so divine." A sweet aroma wafted up the stairs and reminded her how long it had been since breakfast.

"She's made some fancy cake and banned me from the kitchen. I'm sure that now you're home, I can creep in and steal a slice." The footman set off down the stairs with a bounce in his step.

Running her hands through her hair and pulling it free of its pins, Sera walked to the rear of the house. Day by day, the small study transformed into a diminutive workroom. The empty bookshelves now housed liquid ingredients in vials, bottles, and jugs of various sizes and hues. Dried herbs and other concoctions sat in open bowls or closed boxes for the more unusual items

The desk before the window had become her work-bench. On one corner sat a set of brass scales, the weights stacked beside it.

Setting down the basket, she surveyed the empty containers and selected what she needed for the day's tasks. Next she smoothed out Goody McTavish's instructions for her potions. Ingredients were measured, ground, and distilled over a magical flame. To the simmering pot, Sera added a spell. Closing her eyes, she reached out to Mother Nature and sought a blessing to enhance the brew. She asked for help to fill the arms of a woman who only desired to fulfill her purpose in her aristocratic life.

A gentle touch brushed along Sera's arms and from her fingertips, a deep green mist flowed into the pot and mingled with the berry-coloured liquid.

"Thank you," she murmured.

With one potion completed and cooling, she turned her attention to the next—the tincture for Lord Tinwald. That task required a much smaller vessel. It simmered over the flame and emitted a pungent, acrid odour.

"Bloody hell! Smells like old socks and fish in here," Elliot exclaimed as he carried in a tray.

"It won't smell like that when it's finished. It should be coffee scented." Sera peered at the mix and then reread her notes to double-check her work.

"Coffee that's been strained through socks, maybe. What's it supposed to do?" The footman placed the tray on the sideboard within easy reach.

"A few drops in a gentleman's coffee of an evening

will ensure he can...um...function as his wife requires."
Sera wiggled her pinkie finger for effect.

Elliot's eyes widened, and he glanced at the deep
brown liquid. "Poor sod. You sure it doesn't kill him and
that's what makes him go stiff?"

Sera glared at him. No one who consumed one of
her potions would die. If she *were* to intend such an
outcome, poison would not be her preferred method.

"Sorry, Sera. Poor choice of words, after Branvale
and all." He raised his hands, as though expecting a
magical outburst.

She waved his apology aside. He meant no harm
and the concoction did possess a horrid odour. It
required no small amount of faith to wait for the
process to finish and trust it would have the required
coffee flavour. Otherwise, the earl would never imbibe
the drink and Lady Tinwald would bear the brunt of
her family's and society's disappointment.

"I would rather be known as a healer, not a
poisoner. Or the sorceress of sewage."

"I imagine there's good money in being a death
dealer. Everyone has somebody causing problems in
their life that they'd like to quietly disappear." He broke
off a chunk of cake crammed with currants from one of
the slices on the plate.

How many women struggled with demons, both
Unnatural and all too human, they could not seek help
to overcome? Most women in society were powerless.
Only the magic coursing through her veins put Sera in
the unique position of being able to govern herself. And
even then, she'd had to fight hard for it.

As ideas drifted through her mind, Sera took a piece of cake before it disappeared, and bit into the moist mix. She closed her eyes and savoured the faint hint of almond and then the pop of sherry-soaked fruit. "Rosie is the true magician in this house."

"She's been practicing some fancy recipes for when you entertain. Right cruel it is to not let me sample them all." The footman snuck another chunk from the plate.

"I'd rather fewer visitors and more cake for us." She popped another bit of cake into her mouth. She stood at the beginning of her career and imagined all the adventures ahead. Her position would strengthen and one day, Rosie would have charge of the kitchen in a much grander house, where visitors would call daily.

Elliot laughed and tucked the empty tray under his arm. "Anything else?"

"No, thank you." Slurping a mouthful of tea, Sera contemplated her next course of action. Labels were carefully written for the two bottles bearing detailed instructions, and she would paste them on once the brew was ready.

Opening a drawer, she drew out a rumpled sheet of paper. This contained the instructions for casting and working with mage silver. The rare metal allowed a mage to reach out to someone close to them. From the little she had learned from Lord Branvale, a ring formed from mage silver worked somewhat like a door knocker. One person could alert the other to their presence, or the need for a conversation. She intended to create enough of the mercury-like silver to present a ring each to Kitty and Abigail, and one for herself.

The process was long and arduous, with ingredients that needed to be weighed exactly and then combined through her magic. Long hours of concentration passed as the sun dropped outside her window. Finally, the mix was stirred into a pot and left to bubble over a magical cool flame that flickered blue and silver. At least this brew didn't smell offensive—it even had a touch of lavender. Its appearance, however, was off-putting, being a deep purple with octopus-like tentacles that waved from within as though some creature sought to escape.

"You had better stay put." She wagged a finger at the cast iron pot and its captive. Between the pot's three stout feet burned her special flame.

The spell required a number of days before the metal would be suitable for forming into a shape. To ensure her house didn't burn down, Sera cast a protection spell around the pot to keep any stray draft from fanning the tiny flame.

THE NEXT DAY, Sera dressed for the monthly meeting of the Mage Council, choosing her dark green riding habit. It conveyed a somewhat serious and businesslike air, in her opinion. In the barren yard around the tower, she took a moment to appreciate her oak sapling once more as she passed.

Within, she nodded to the others present and took her seat at the circular table marked with the numeral six. Lord Ormsby was last to arrive, carrying a large book under his arm with papers sticking out. He dropped it on the table with a *thump*, and sat. Then he shuffled papers and cleared his throat.

Most of the business was mildly interesting, like the discussion of significant magical activity by mages in other countries. Then a brief report on the work being done to create various weapons to aid in the defence of England in the event of war or civil unrest. Next, the Speaker asked how planning was proceeding for the upcoming diplomatic dinner.

"Lady Winyard and I have decided on a Greek theme," Lord Tomlin said before she could reply. "We are calling it *A Night on Olympus*, with the king as Zeus, and shall put on a display of Apollo battling Nyx." As he spoke, Lord Tomlin conjured a tiny scene of toga-wearing gods lounging on sofas and eating grapes, while Apollo and Nyx threw a silver orb at one another, rather like a tennis match.

Lord Gresham rapped his knuckles on the table. "A fine idea, Lord Tomlin. I'm sure Lady Winyard will put up a good show before the god of light defeats the darkness."

Sera forced a sweet smile to her lips. Oh, she would most certainly put up a good show. "We have yet to discuss the finer details of the entertainments, but I am sure the king and his guests will be delighted with the evening. Perhaps we could also project it out on the clouds or the Thames, so all of London might watch?"

"A marvelous idea," Lord Pendlebury said. "I shall work on a way of doing that."

As the meeting drew to a close, Lord Ormsby cleared his throat more often and clutched his papers more tightly. Finally he announced, "This leaves only one matter to discuss. We must settle on an appropriate suitor for Lady Winyard."

Fortunately Sera had her hands resting in her lap, so no one could see the way her fingernails dug into her palms as anger surged through her body. "Excuse me?" she managed to ask in a somewhat calm tone. She drew a long, slow breath as sparks ignited under her nails and skittered over the green wool of her skirts.

Lord Ormsby glanced at her while the other mages fell silent. He dropped the bundle of papers to the table. "It is the responsibility of this council to fulfil the role your father would naturally have assumed, had you still been in his household. After seeking appropriate consultation, we have four candidates for consideration. All are aware of your obligations to this council and England, and will permit you to continue performing your duties." He extracted one sheet from the pile in his hand and slid it to one side. The pages not required were piled on top of the ledger.

Tight writing covered the sheet and only a brief pang of curiosity flared through her, wondering who they considered *suitable*. Then anger at the council's continued insistence on treating her like a child burned away the curiosity.

"No." The word spat from her lips. "I do not require your governance or your matchmaking. I thought I had made that quite clear."

"This situation is unprecedented. We are only concerned for your welfare and that an appropriate gentleman is found to guide you in the coming years." He smiled, but it didn't reach his eyes.

"Guide me? You mean act as my puppeteer, and pull my strings as you dictate?" She pushed back her chair and stood with her hands resting on the table.

"I think what Lord Ormsby is trying to convey is that we do not wish you to fall prey to someone who might use your power to their personal advantage," Lord Dench said.

Fury washed cold through her body. No one would control her. "Let me reassure you on that point, then. No one will have dominion over me."

"The king has spoken of his desire to see you well settled, Lady Winyard, and by the end of the year. We thought it better if you were to have a say in the chosen candidate." Lord Pendlebury spoke with a measured tone from closest to her.

The king? If he commanded her to wed, what would she do? A lump formed in her throat and she swallowed it down. Abigail would help her petition Queen Charlotte about it. The amendment to the Mage Act continued to be debated in Parliament, even as Mr Napier worked with his noble friends to have it struck down entirely.

"Then I shall thank the king for his concern about my welfare and assure him that I am quite capable of managing my own life. If that is all, gentlemen?" With a terse nod, she swept from the chamber.

Lord Pendlebury rushed after her, the piece of paper clutched in his hand. "Lady Winyard, if I might have a moment."

She halted and waited for him under a tall, narrow window. A shaft of light played over her hands as she clasped them together.

He glanced over his shoulder and lowered his voice. "Lord Ormsby is most determined in this. While I do not agree with his approach, you might wish to consider the advantages of an arrangement where a gentleman could offer protection against interference in your life from the council."

A number of angry retorts flew to her tongue and she bit them back. Lord Pendlebury always treated her fairly and the rational part of her mind realised he made a valid point. A husband would stop the council's meddling. Conversely, she would then have some man trying to dictate her actions and she could never stomach that.

What to do? She could see the attractions of widow-hood. Then at least she could say she had followed their advice and *whoops*, her husband had died.

"Thank you, Lord Pendlebury. I know you mean well. But I will not wear a collar, no matter who holds the leash."

A small smile touched his lips. "I understand. At the risk of having you consider me an interfering old mage, might I suggest you look to Queen Elizabeth as your guide in this situation?"

Sera's mind took a detour as she wondered what the Tudor queen had to do with her current predicament. "I don't understand the reference, my lord."

"Queen Elizabeth faced similar pressure to marry from her people and her privy council. Many believed a woman could not wield such power without a man to govern her. The queen received their suggestions of suitors and spent some time—years, in fact—in reviewing them. While she gave the names the full and careful scrutiny they deserved, she continued to rule and live as she chose. Not by the dictates of others."

Ah. Now she understood. By playing their game and being seen to consider their applicants, she had time to figure out her next move. She couldn't see any harm in reading their list.

The other mages emerged from the chamber behind Lord Pendlebury. Plastering a smile on her face, she reached out and took the sheet of paper. In a louder tone so they all overheard, she said, "You are right, Lord Pendlebury, and thank you for your wise counsel. I spoke in haste. I would be only too happy to consider those nobles the council believes appropriate for the role of husband to a mage."

He winked and bowed his head. "Always happy to assist, Lady Winyard."

She took her leave of the tower. She needed some fresh air to clear her mind.

————◆————

ONCE AT HOME, Sera changed from the riding habit into a plain gown with an apron to protect it. She needed a solution to the council's insistence she wed, so as advised by Lord Pendlebury, she would follow the example set by Queen Elizabeth and pretend to review their names. Once their attempt to alter the Mage Act was defeated, she would be free of them—or so she hoped—and she could tear up the sheet of paper. A conversation with Mr Napier should allay her fears on that head.

In her study, she poured the finished potions into their respective containers. A large bottle for the tonic for Lady Tinwald. A small vial with a dropper for his lordship's tincture. The labels were pasted on, then they were packed in a box surrounded by straw. Pressing a few coins into Elliot's palm, she dispatched the footman to deliver the parcel to Kitty.

Then, Sera pulled out her ensorcelled piece of paper and dashed off a note to her friend.

Parcel for Lady Tinwald on its way. She will collect it from you discreetly. Looking forward to tomorrow.

The last was a small falsehood. The following evening was the Duchess of Edgecombe's grand ball. What would the night bring? She couldn't decide whether to be excited or to dread it. Whatever unfolded, at least her friends would be at her side.

Another thought popped into her mind and she added a postscript.

Do you know the name Nereus? Is it from mythology?

Her friend replied while she was reviewing her other correspondence. Words appeared in Kitty's neat and pragmatic hand and marched across the page Sera had left lying in a shaft of sunlight.

Nereus is Greek. Son of Gaia, Mother Earth, and Pontus, god of the sea. No much to say about him, often called the Old Man of the Sea. A shapeshifter with the power of prophecy who aided Hercules. Why do you ask?

Sera turned over the scant information. A child of Mother Earth. That resonated through her veins. She considered herself a child of Gaia. Her spells and castings grew in power when she dug her feet into the earth and sought the assistance of Mother Earth. Was there a clue in that, as to what Branvale's secret message meant? *There cannot be another Nereus.*

Will tell you tomorrow. Much to discuss.

Sera couldn't unravel all of Branvale's secrets on her own. She needed the help of her friends. By putting their heads together, perhaps they would find the truth.

THE NEXT AFTERNOON, Elliot and a Napier family footman carried a trunk down the stairs and out to the waiting carriage. Within were Sera's gown, undergarments, and headpiece for the evening.

Rosie and Vicky stood on the step. "Oh, I wish I could see you all dressed up for the ball." Rosie heaved a sigh and Vicky had a dreamy expression on her face.

"I'm sorry you will miss it. But perhaps Vicky can help me dress in that gown another day, and we will hold our own grand dinner, just for us?" The more she thought on it, the more Sera liked the idea of a special evening just for her little family to celebrate all they had achieved so far.

"Brilliant idea. Especially if Rosie makes more of that cake with all the currants," Elliot called as he loaded the trunk onto the rear of the carriage.

"I'd like that, too, milady," the shy Vicky chimed in.

"Then it is settled. We shall have a celebration just for us and we will all dress up for the evening." Sera kissed Rosie's cheek and then took Elliot's hand to step up into the vehicle.

Once she alighted at the Napier home, Sera pulled Kitty into the parlour while the staff swung into action to prepare the family members for the grand ball. As an extra precaution, Sera crafted a spell to keep their hushed conversation secret and to deflect any listening ears.

Kitty raised one eyebrow at her safeguards. "I assume this relates to your Nereus question?"

"Yes. Remember the copper bracelet I always wore and could not remove?" Sera moved away from the soaring window and stood closer to the solid wall.

Kitty tapped Sera's wrist. "I had noticed its absence since you turned eighteen, and the scar it left."

"It drained my magic." As her friend's eyes widened, Sera narrated the little she knew of the bracelet and the secret correspondence between Branvale and an unknown person.

FIVE

At the end of Sera's story, Kitty remained silent for several moments before she spoke with quiet deliberation. "The message implies there is a link between you and this Nereus. That might explain this unknown plan. We must dig deeper into history to discover more."

"You will help?" The only vague connection Sera could grasp was that of Mother Earth. She had no great affinity for the ocean and had never ventured to the seashore, except when her mind flew with an avian friend.

Kitty huffed a quiet laugh. "Of course. How could I resist such a tantalizing mystery? Like you, I would know why they dared to suppress your magic, and torture you into thinking you were feeble. All in the name of keeping you safe? I cannot understand it."

Sera hugged her friend and whispered a thank you against her hair.

"But now we really must go upstairs to bathe before

the water cools." Kitty's amber eyes sparkled with humour.

Sera let out a groan. "You want me to heat baths now? I suppose it is similar to warming chocolate. The only difference is in the scale."

In the sea-green tiled room used for bathing, Sera and Kitty sat in matching copper tubs draped with linen as they were washed and scrubbed. While Sera preferred to dress herself and fought a wave of discomfort at being treated like a doll, she did enjoy the company of her friend and the chatter of the maids. Besides, she told herself, it was a rather special occasion.

Having adopted a peacock feather as her symbol, Sera took the inspiration for her gown from the vain bird. A deep blue silk served as the base, then long feathers reached up from the hem of her dress and wove together close to her waist. The embroidered eyes were enhanced with a touch of magic so that the design appeared to wink. A stomacher embroidered with metallic swirls of deep green, rich blue, and iridescent bronze completed her outfit.

As usual, Sera refused to don a wig and a ridiculously large hairpiece. Instead, the maids swept her hair into a simple updo and three peacock feathers were secured with a jewelled pin.

"You look stunning," Kitty said.

"As do you," Sera replied.

Kitty chose her usual autumnal tones of burnt orange and deep red, with a caramel brown. The pattern swirled over her dress like feathers. A tiny kestrel perched in her hair, its claws clutching a branch woven into her locks. Sera thought the bird a fitting companion for her friend.

Mr Napier awaited them in the foyer, resplendent in his formal attire, a deep charcoal jacket and matching waistcoat and snowy cravat. His legs were displayed to advantage in knee breeches and white stockings, and on his feet, gleaming black shoes with silver buckles. He grinned as they descended the stairs. "I have the pleasure of being accompanied this evening by the two most beautiful and eligible young women in the kingdom."

"I do worry about your eyesight, Father," Kitty replied as they reached the bottom step.

He took Kitty's hand and tucked it into the crook of his arm. "Your mother was the most beautiful woman I ever laid eyes on, and you are much like her."

"Oh no, Sera. Old age has robbed Father of his mind and not just his vision," Kitty teased.

Sera bit the inside of her cheek to stop from laughing. "Thank you for the compliment, Mr Napier. Kitty and I consider our minds our best attribute, although that seems to be the most intimidating trait for most men."

Kitty sighed. "Remember our promise, Sera. I'll not have my good gloves ruined by fortune hunters drooling over Father's money who think I'm as witless as a squirrel."

"Any man would be lucky if either of you so much as looked in his direction." Mr Napier took Sera on his other arm.

Sera winked at her friend. A squirrel might be a

fitting addition to the evening if it proved boring. Perhaps one equipped with wings that could leap from chandelier to chandelier?

At the duchess's residence, a parade of carriages waited to discharge nobles under the portico. A silver-liveried footman handed down Sera and Kitty and they linked arms to walk up the stairs. Mr Napier was waylaid on the steps as nobles sought a quick word and his advice on financial matters.

Raised voices made them pause and step aside as two solid footmen half escorted, half carried a protesting noble out the front door.

"My betrothed is in there! I must be with her!" The young man struggled to free his arms and kept looking back at the house.

"You weren't invited, sir," one footman said as he used both hands to hold on to an arm.

They moved past Sera and Kitty and the footmen released their prisoner at the edge of the path. Nobles whispered and drew themselves away from the trouble-maker. The young man made one attempt to dash back in, but a threatening move from the footmen made him reconsider and slink away.

"I'll wager that was the most exciting part of the night," Kitty sighed.

Inside, the two women followed the flow of people towards the ballroom. They paused in the doorway and surveyed the room.

"Oh, my," Kitty whispered and her grip tightened on Sera's arm.

"I am not the only peacock here tonight," Sera murmured.

The room swirled in colours from the palest pink to a green so vivid it made one wince. It wasn't just the women in bright displays; many of the young courtiers attempted to outdo each other with heavily embroidered coats. A woman walked past and her hair chirped. An entire birdcage was crafted into her towering wig, and a songbird clung to a wildly swinging perch.

"Poor thing." Sera formed a quick spell in her mind and set it free with a swipe of her finger. A tiny gilded door popped open and the bird, needing no other encouragement, took flight and headed straight for an open window. She closed the little door behind it.

"The bird or the woman? Can you imagine carrying that weight around on your head all night? How will she dance?" Kitty pulled Sera to one side as another couple swept into the room.

Sera craned to look over the tops of heads, seeking Lady Abigail. A whispered finding spell, aided by conjuring her friend's face in her mind, created a strand of pink smoke that drifted across the room.

"Found her!" The smoke curled into itself and created a vertical spiral dangling from the ceiling above the third member of their trio. Sera steered Kitty through the crowd and towards the sign only she could see.

Tonight, Lady Abigail resembled a blushing rose, her gown in tones of pink, beige, and the softest green. Even her hair was powdered a delicate shade of pink and then garlanded in blush-pink roses. The three friends conducted the odd ritual their social standing demanded. Kitty curtseyed to Abigail, who dipped her knees to Sera. In return, Sera nodded and took her friend's hand.

"I feel better equipped to navigate these treacherous waters with your help, Abigail," Sera said.

Abigail squeezed her hand. "You will do fine. Just remember all I have taught you."

"I intend to find the library as soon as I can," Kitty muttered.

"Oh, no you don't. Both of you will dance this evening. Kitty, I have selected a number of appropriate partners for you. Before you curl your lip at me, I am aware of your preferences. One is Lord Huntley, who has some radical approach to managing his tenant farmers you might find intriguing. Another gentleman who would claim your hand for a dance is the Marquess of Loburn. I believe he wishes to discuss workhouse reformation with you. Is that not so, Lord Loburn?" Abigail raised her voice as the lord in question made a beeline for them.

Lord Loburn's eyes widened and his gaze sparkled. "Workhouse reformation? Oh, yes. A subject dear to my heart." His attention slid to Kitty as he bowed before them.

"The treatment of widows and orphans in this country is quite appalling. As a nation, we should strive to implement a minimum standard of care for all our citizens." Kitty held out her gloved hand, and Lord

Loburn took it as though she offered him a great treasure.

Sera noticed the distinct absence of drool, since Lord Loburn possessed a fortune of his own and obviously enjoyed Kitty's company. The two quickly fell to discussing some proposed piece of legislation with their heads bent together, and barely noticed Abigail leading Sera away.

"Do not think to escape, my friend. I have several dance partners in mind for you, too," Abigail murmured as they strolled the edges of the room.

"You need not go to any trouble on my behalf." As much as Sera loved Abigail, she didn't like this new development of insisting they all needed to marry. An idea took form in her head, one in which Sera and Kitty established their own household and hosted dinner parties where everyone conversed about topics that affected all of society. Once they found someone to keep Mr Napier company, of course. Like a dear friend of his departed wife, perhaps?

"Do you know which lady is Lady Tinwald's mother?"

"Lady Tinwald?" Abigail tapped her bottom lip with her fan. "If I remember correctly, it is Lady Plimmerton. Why do you ask?"

"Oh, no reason." Sera tucked away the name. She would send Elliot to find out what he could discover before she raised the topic with Kitty.

"Here is the Austrian delegation. There is a key member I wish to introduce to you." Abigail gestured with her fan towards a loud group of men and women

Many of the women had highly elaborate and tall hairstyles, but rather than the white powdered style favoured by many nobles, the Austrian pieces were powdered in pink, purple, and blue. The men were more subdued in their hair and clothing, although not by much.

Abigail circled the group, then approached a man who looked to be in his early thirties. He fell silent as they neared but had a curious expression on his face.

"Seraphina, Duchess Winyard, may I introduce the Margrave Otto Zedlitz from Austria. A margrave is similar to our marquess."

Of a similar height to her, Zedlitz sported a fine moustache of a light brown that curled at the ends, and thick brown curly hair. He wore a deep blue jacket with white trim that gave him a nautical air. Intelligence gleamed in his hazel eyes. He snapped his heels together and bowed over her hand.

"I am honoured to meet you, Lady Winyard." His continental accent made him appear all the more charming.

"Lady Winyard is the newest mage to come of age in England and she is much sought after in company," Abigail said, giving her friend a little push towards the Austrian noble.

Interest sparkled in Lord Zedlitz's eyes. "I am honoured to converse with a mage. They are not seen much in our country, and are either found at the emperor's side, or hiding in their towers. But we have heard of *you* even in Austria, Lady Winyard."

Sera doubted good news would travel that far. The

Austrians had probably been told her magic amounted to little more than parlour tricks.

"I shall leave Lady Winyard in your care, Lord Zedlitz. If you'll excuse me, Seraphina, I have spotted Lord Methven and I must speak with him." Abigail rolled her eyes at the Austrian, winked, and then took her leave.

From reading the not-so-subtle clues, Sera gathered she was supposed to make a good impression on the margrave, although his name hadn't appeared on the short list prepared by the Mage Council. She probably shouldn't turn him into a squirrel should he prove terribly boring. She would play along with Abigail's game in this instance. Wouldn't it be fun to torment the Mage Council into thinking she had decided on a foreign husband?

The thought made her smile. "I hope you have been made welcome to our shores, Lord Zedlitz. Will you be with us long?"

He stepped closer to her side. "*Ja.* For some three months. The emperor has tasked me to negotiate a treaty between England and the Hapsburg empire regarding wool, which I am sure will be very tedious and boring. I am accompanied by my mother, who thinks an English rose might make a fine wife for my rather lonely castle."

That explained Abigail's interest—a noble on the hunt for a bride. "A castle? Well, I am sure many an English gentlewoman will find a castle hard to refuse. I imagine it must be a particularly beautiful one nestled in the Austrian scenery." How she longed to travel and see not only England, but the world beyond her borders.

"I believe it is the most beautiful, especially when it snows. Then it looks like a picture from a storybook. Frightfully cold, though. I do wish mages could conjure up some way of heating draughty old castles." His eyes crinkled as he smiled.

"I shall make a study of it. I'm sure many of us would prefer warmer homes during the depths of winter." How hard could it be to find a more efficient way to heat a home than an open fire? Especially in rooms with no fireplace. Every winter she had worn mittens in Branvale's windowless workroom.

"I would be most interested in what you discover. I am sure many nobles would pay handsomely for such magic." A few around them nodded and shared stories of ice forming on the insides of their windows in winter.

"Otto!" A shrill voice cut through the conversation and Lord Zedlitz winced. He pressed his thumb and forefinger to the bridge of his nose.

"Is everything all right, Lord Zedlitz?" Sera cast around for the owner of the voice, who seemed to think the duchess's ballroom a fish market, and that the Austrian lord should run to her side like a lost dog.

A short, stout woman with white powdered hair and a gown of pale yellow, covered in what appeared to be embroidered birch branches, bustled towards them. "Otto!" She waved her hand at him in a *come here* gesture, even as she neared the edge of the group.

The younger people parted to allow her through.

One woman muttered, "*Die vettel*," in her wake and the man next to her muttered agreement under his breath.

Sera wondered what the words meant, but found she had a more immediate problem.

The older woman stopped before them. She possessed a downturned mouth, as though she found life a perpetual disappointment. Her top lip curled as she narrowed her gaze at Sera. "Who is this, Otto? This is not one of the women I approved."

Lord Zedlitz drew an audible long breath, and Sera had the distinct impression he was counting to ten in his head. "Lady Winyard, may I present my mother, the Dowager Margravine Zedlitz."

Ah. An overbearing mother who was used to yelling along draughty castle corridors. Sera inclined her head. As the equivalent of a marchioness, the older woman was below Sera's new rank.

The older woman glared. "You must curtsey to me."

"I am a duchess, Lady Zedlitz, and curtsey only to the queen." Sera pulled her lips into a tight smile.

"Not by birth. You are a commoner. *My* blood runs blue in my veins." The words spat from the other woman like small cannonballs. Now that Sera considered her, she did have the stoutness of a cannon.

"*Mutter*." Lord Zedlitz uttered the single word as a sharp retort. "Do not be rude to England's only female mage."

"She is rude and must curtsey." She snaked out a hand, grabbing Sera's wrist. A gasp rolled off those around them.

Sera's knees shook and of their own volition, started

to buckle. Where Lady Zedlitz clung to her, a thin silver thread wormed between them and dug into Sera. A flash of sickening recognition flared inside her stomach. She wrenched her hand back and slapped her palm over the thread.

As she lurched from side to side, both to fight the compulsion and rid her body of the sliver of magic, Lord Zedlitz caught her elbow and steadied her. "Lady Winyard, are you well?"

Muttering under her breath, Sera froze the strand and pulled it from her body. Dropping it unseen to the floor, she ground it under her shoe while she regained her composure. "Thank you, Lord Zedlitz. I caught my heel in my gown."

Rage coloured Sera's vision. The older woman sought to compel her with a method similar to the ensorcellment that had once dampened her magic! But from what Sera knew, Lady Zedlitz did not possess any magic in her blue-blooded veins. That meant she must have an item about her person that exerted a magical influence. Sera examined the other woman, searching for what had almost forced her to curtsey. Red light glinted from under several strands of diamonds on her left wrist.

"My, what an unusual bracelet." Sera brushed a strand of magic over Lady Zedlitz's arm and pulled back the diamonds to expose a cuff of copper some four inches wide and carved with an ornate swirling vine. Each tip held a small bud set with a tiny diamond chip. If the other woman would tell her where she had acquired it, Sera could discover what mage had constructed the bracelets—for surely both had been cast by the same hand?

The margrave's mother brushed the diamonds back over the plainer item. "It is nothing. A pretty design, that is all. Foolish, but I forgot to remove it when dressing this evening."

Lord Zedlitz huffed. "I have never known you to take it off, *Mutter*, since it passed from *Oma*. I think it must be of great sentimental value to you."

"Come, Otto. I have found a meek woman who would fit into our household and who knows her proper place." She took her son's arm and practically wrenched him away from Sera. A glint of silver betrayed a thread that disappeared through Lord Zedlitz's jacket under his mother's firm grip.

The Austrian lord's demeanour changed. His shoulders sagged and the smile fell away from his face. In a dull voice, he intoned, "*Ja, Mutter.*"

A shudder raced down Sera's spine as the margrave was sapped of his own free will. She pitied the meek woman upon whom Lady Zedlitz had set her mind, who might likewise be forced to do the older woman's bidding. In England, the Mage Council had strict rules against meddling in people's minds. Lady Zedlitz needed to learn that such behaviour would not be tolerated on English soil.

Sera could solve two issues with a few quiet words whispered into the receptive ear of Queen Charlotte. The queen could rebuke Lady Zedlitz for forcing people to act against their wishes. And she could also demand to know the origins of the bracelet.

Six

Spotting Sera standing alone after the Austrians dispersed, Lady Abigail sent over another candidate to dance with her. Sera failed to see Lord Zedlitz again that evening. She pleaded sore feet in order to remove herself from the dance floor and set off to find Kitty, who didn't appear to be availing herself of Abigail's carefully selected partners, either.

At length she came upon her friend in the library with a group of men. Lord Loburn stood on one side, and the half-Fae Arwyn Fitzfey, natural son of the king, on the other. The group appeared to be engaged in a heated discussion.

"What are you afraid of, gentlemen, that you keep the vote from your fellow Englishmen and women?" Kitty asked.

"The country will go to ruin if the uneducated are allowed to make ill-informed decisions," a lord replied with such passion he waved the glass in his hand, spilling a little liquid on the floor.

"Then is not education the answer?" Kitty shot back.

A titter of laughter ran around the group. Lord Loburn cleared his throat. "I believe Miss Napier makes an excellent point. Would not our society and economy improve if every child were educated?"

"Imagine if all men were equal, in both education and wealth," Arwyn said.

"Careful, Fitzfey, you're sounding a lot like those revolutionaries over in France," another noble warned.

Laughter erupted and Sera took the chance to tuck her hand into Kitty's elbow. "Gentlemen, I'm afraid I must steal Miss Napier away for a moment."

"Of course, Lady Winyard. Always a pleasure to hear your opinions, Miss Napier. I hope it is not too long before our next meeting." Lord Loburn raised his glass to her and the circle echoed the sentiment.

"Are you inciting a revolution?" Sera whispered as they slipped away.

Casting a backwards glance, she noticed two gentlemen in particular watched her friend leave, despite the way she undervalued herself.

Kitty snorted. "As unfair as it is, men like those are the ones who hold the vote. I need to convince them first of the need for change, if we are to claim any power in this country. Unless you can do it with magic?" When Sera shook her head, Kitty went on, undaunted. "I can't tell you how refreshing it is to find a bunch of nobles who can hold a decent conversation and overlook the fact that I'm wearing a dress."

"I need to call upon the power of your mighty mind

with a question about the Hapsburg nobles. What can you tell me about the Margrave Zedlitz?" Sera asked.

"From what I recollect Father saying, he has a large tract of land in Austria and a rather beautiful castle perched upon it. High up in their nobility and favoured at the emperor's court, he is wealthy and considered quite the catch." Kitty leaned away to study Sera. "Not considering leaving our shores for the delights of schnitzel, are you?"

"Schnitzel?" Sera's tongue stumbled over the unfamiliar word as the conversation took an unexpected turn.

Kitty grinned. "A few of the ladies are whispering about it. Apparently it's a fried and breaded Austrian dish and quite the treat, if he offers it to you."

Sera wondered if Rosie would like such a recipe. Elliot would no doubt volunteer as taste tester. "No, I was not pondering the margrave's schnitzel delights. Rather, the bracelet his mother wears. It is very similar to the one I used to wear and is likewise imbued with magic."

Kitty pursed her lips. "Jewellery is not my area of expertise. We could consult Lady Abigail—her grandfather might know something of magical jewellery?"

Sera knew little of the old mage. He had retired from the Mage Council some years ago, preferring to spend his time in quiet study. With Abigail by her side, she could seek an audience with the elderly gentleman to ask his advice.

But locating their friend in the overcrowded ballroom and overflowing mansion proved more difficult than she expected. Even Sera's finding spell failed, and the pink smoke clung to the ceiling like a frightened child hugging its mother's leg. Eventually, Sera and Kitty arrived back at the main entrance hall as a clock struck twice.

Sera stifled a yawn, and an ache took up residence in her feet. "I shall ask next time I see her. As much as I want to sate my curiosity, it is a matter better suited to a private discussion."

"I don't know about you, but I have had quite enough of people for this evening. Why don't we leave word for Father and return home to our beds?" Without waiting for a reply, Kitty gestured to a footman.

SERA TRIED TO SLEEP LATE, but the Napier household stirred early regardless of when the occupants had crawled into bed. At ten of the clock, she threw back the blankets and dressed. Mr Napier sat in the dining room, sipping coffee as he read the newspaper. For a man in his late forties who must have had less sleep than she, he looked amazingly refreshed and alert.

"Good morning, Sera. How did you enjoy the ball?" he asked in a chipper tone.

A footman held out her chair, and she took a seat. Waving him away, she poured hot chocolate herself from a silver pot. "Lady Abigail took it upon herself to select a number of dance partners for Kitty and me.

One of them thought that if he married me, I would turn the tin in a mine he owns into gold and make him ridiculously wealthy. It took some effort to escape his clutches and retreat to the library."

Mr Napier chuckled. "I hear Kitty has made rather an impression on Lord Loburn."

"He does become quite animated in her company. I think she enjoys verbally sparring with him." It gladdened Sera to know that her friend had found a gentleman who challenged her intellect. Although no one could mistake the way Kitty regarded Lord Fitzfey. Few women were immune to the half-Fae's ethereal beauty, but Sera's friend enjoyed his conversation more than his appearance. To his credit, like Lord Loburn, Arwyn appeared to seek out Kitty for her opinions and for the fact that she did not display the shallowness of those who swooned over his good looks. Though Sera had to admit that his views were more extreme and raised alarmed whispers among many nobles.

The newspaper snapped as Mr Napier turned it to a fresh page. "Loburn seems a good sort. He takes his seat in the Lords seriously, unlike many other nobles, who regard it as a place to nap. Not that Kitty is under any pressure to marry. I have no objection should she wish to remain unwed and continue to sit near me at the table. My daughter is free to make whatever decision she wants."

Sera studied her friend's father as a hint of sadness crept into his voice. If Kitty ever married, she would leave their home and establish her own household. That would be a difficult move for a father and daughter who were so close. "Do you know Lady Plimmerton?"

The lines at his eyes deepened as he smiled. "Oh, yes. She was a dear friend to my Francesca. Harriet is a lovely woman who has been a great support to us over the years. At least I could offer her a similar service when she lost Lord Plimmerton three years ago. Why do you ask?"

"No reason." Sera smiled into her hot chocolate.

Kitty joined them, stopping to stretch and yawn in the doorway. As they chatted over breakfast, a summons arrived for Sera, requesting her presence at court.

She tapped the card against her palm. "I wonder what entertainment I will be asked to provide for them today."

"I hear the queen put in a brief appearance last night while we were elsewhere. Perhaps she wants to ask what you thought of the Austrian delegation? I know Abigail introduced you to the charming Lord Zedlitz." Kitty buttered her toast and then reached for the pot of marmalade.

"He seemed delightful, although we only managed a brief conversation. His mother practically dragged him away by the ear to throw him at some poor woman she deemed more appropriate." Sera replayed the odd interaction in her mind, the margrave's response clearly influenced by the bracelet his mother wore.

Mr Napier huffed in laughter. "Lady Zedlitz has a formidable reputation. She came to England some fifteen years ago. There are those still smarting from the experience and licking their wounds. There was one noble who locked horns with her over a cow or a bull or some such, and I seem to remember was quite ruined afterward."

That piqued Sera's curiosity, but it was a conversation for another day. She pushed back her chair and stood, glancing down at her simple gown to ensure no jam had spilled on the light fabric. "I had better make sure I am presentable for court."

"I will have our carriage brought round for you, Sera. Best not keep the king and queen waiting." Mr Napier gestured to a silent footman, who hurried from the room to convey the request.

When she reached the palace, a subdued atmosphere clung to the walls and Sera wondered how many nobles had been roused too early from bed by their monarchs. The guards at the presence chamber door remained mute as she walked inside. A far cry from the first time, when they had tried to bar her entry.

Through the crowd she passed, spotting Hugh's tall figure at the back of the room conversing with a group of four older men. His head turned and he flashed her a wide smile. She returned the silent greeting before continuing on. Knowing Hugh lurked behind the nobles and courtiers settled her nerves and reminded her, should the need arise, to control her temper.

Today King George sat upright on his throne, a noble before him making some plea about another who encroached on his land. The king looked bored, the toe of his shoe tapping the floor. Queen Charlotte ignored the noble entirely and conducted a quiet conversation with her ladies to the side. Behind the king's throne stood Lord Pendlebury, who represented the Mage Council when Lord Ormsby was not available.

Sera stopped beside the noble and curtseyed, waiting to be acknowledged.

"Excellent! The pretty one is here. Go away, Davenport, I've heard enough from you," the king said.

Sera bit her lip. As the only woman mage, it wasn't too hard to be the pretty one. She was also the smartest, tallest, and most tired one.

"How may I be of service today, Your Majesty?"

"I liked those fish you did that time. Do it again and Pendlebury here will assist." King George waved a hand and Lord Pendlebury stepped forward.

"I believe His Majesty wishes to turn the presence chamber into an aquarium, or what he believes the deep ocean to be like. Having worked with the army for some years now, I am somewhat rusty at creating such delicate entertainments," the older mage murmured.

"Perhaps you could conjure our surroundings and the larger fish, while I add the smaller, more colourful ones that delight His Majesty?" Sera rolled her hands together, picturing in her mind a brightly striped fish she had once seen in a book.

Lord Pendlebury nodded and pushed up the sleeves of his robe. Standing back to back, they sent forth magical creations. Those assembled gasped as the presence chamber was turned into an underwater scene.

Sera released a school of yellow-and-black-striped fish and then considered what to create next. King George clapped his hands as seaweed wound around his throne and turtles swam back and forth across the ceiling.

A courtier raced into the presence chamber, and then stumbled to a halt upon being confronted by a large sea bass. Ducking around the fish, he approached the king at a more sedate pace, although his gaze darted back and forth.

"What is it?" King George said without looking at the man.

"There has been an unfortunate incident involving the Dowager Margravine Zedlitz," he replied.

Sera perked up, wondering what the Austrian peeress had done. Had she sought to influence the wrong person and been shoved into a privy? One could only hope.

"Whatever has she done now?" King George tapped a mackerel and leaned forward, his eyes clear and, one hoped, his mind lucid.

"She has died, Your Majesty, most unexpectedly." The courtier whispered from the side of his mouth, but given the hush that descended on the room, everyone within twenty feet heard him clearly.

The king clutched the arms of his throne. "Died? How?"

Now the courtier fidgeted, his weight moving from foot to foot. "The margrave says that it was not by natural means and is demanding that you investigate."

Gasps raced around the room and a hundred eyes bored into Sera. She clapped her hands together and the illusionary fish turned into droplets of rain that fell to the floor and dissolved.

"Am I to be blamed for every death that touches this court?" she muttered.

"Apparently," Lord Pendlebury quipped. "Let us hope this one is easily resolved."

"We can't be upsetting the Austrian diplomats—treaty negotiations have only just begun. Where's that army chap with the moustache? Where's our surgeon?" King George snapped his fingers and cast around him as though he possessed magic and the two gentlemen should materialise before him.

The murmurs of nobles turned into snippets of conversation. Then the crowd parted and Hugh Miles strode forward and bowed. "Your Majesty, I do not believe Lieutenant Powers is at court today."

"Well, somebody fetch him. Go find out what happened to Lady Zedlitz, Miles. Perhaps she simply ate too much strudel and her heart gave out." The king's eyes drifted in two different directions and he slumped back in his chair. The queen took his hand and murmured orders to those nearby.

"I will notify my contact at the army camp, and have him dispatch Lieutenant Powers," Lord Pendlebury offered.

Sera attached herself to Hugh's side. If yet another death was to be left at her door, she was entitled at least to know what she had done this time. Besides, her skin itched to think of the silver thread that Lady Zedlitz had loosed on her flesh. This presented an opportunity to examine the copper bracelet.

The courtier led them along palace hallways and up a flight of stairs. Their journey paused outside a set of doors that stood next to a window overlooking a court-yard below. The courtier rapped once before pushing inside.

"Yes?" The margrave spoke without turning. He stood by the window, his body facing the view. One fist was clenched at his side. He wore a deep green velvet banyan with two thick gold tassels dangling from the ends of the knotted cord around his waist. Fluffy cream slippers covered his bare feet. Given his state of undress, he must have been roused from bed to tend his mother.

"Lady Winyard, milord, accompanied by Mr Hugh Miles. He is a renowned surgeon and the king has ordered him to investigate as you requested." The courtier bowed and then retreated, almost as though he didn't want to be in Lady Zedlitz's presence even if she no longer breathed.

Sera glanced at the bed, where the coverlet was pulled up over its permanently slumbering resident. Then her attention drifted about the room. The panelling was painted a deep blue, with silver flocked green wallpaper above the chair rail. Rugs in grey and muted blue covered the floor. The heavy brocade drapes around the bed were a silver and green similar to the wallpaper. The room had the feeling of being underwater, rather like her recent performance for the king.

Hugh approached the noble. "With your permission, Lord Zedlitz, I would like to examine your mother."

The margrave half turned, but still did not face

what had happened inside the chamber. "Very well. But she is not to be disturbed, if we understand each other?"

Hugh clasped his hands behind his back. Sera wondered if by *not to be disturbed*, he meant no one should go rummaging around inside his mother.

"I shall endeavour to discover a cause of death by visual examination alone, then." With a nod of permission from the margrave, Hugh walked to the bed and pulled the coverlet down to Lady Zedlitz's waist. She wore a long-sleeved, high-necked nightgown, with a bow tied at her throat. On her head, a lace cap was pulled low on her brow. Hugh picked up one hand and raised her arm to inspect her fingernails.

Sera turned to Lord Zedlitz. "Who discovered your mother?"

"Inge. Her maid. *Mutter* did not rouse for her breakfast tray. When Inge opened the curtains..." He placed a hand to his forehead and closed his eyes. A deep breath caused his nostrils to flare.

"I am sorry. I did not mean to upset you." Sera touched his arm. From what little she had seen the previous night, Lady Zedlitz kept a rather firm grasp on her son. But whatever their relationship, she had been his mother nonetheless.

Behind them, feet shuffled and fabric rustled. Hugh coughed to attract their attention. "Was she found like this, my lord? By which I mean, is her current repose *exactly* as she was discovered?"

"No. I closed her eyes and mouth. There was something fearful in her expression and I did not wish to leave her like that. That is why I do not think she simply died in her sleep. Would that not have crept peacefully over a person?" Lord Zedlitz's hand dropped to his side and curled.

"With your permission, my lord, I must remove your mother's nightgown to examine her fully," Hugh said.

"No," Lord Zedlitz snapped.

"I cannot make a determination from looking at her head and hands alone, my lord. With the information you have just given me, I am concerned there might be an injury under her nightclothes. Your mother also has a number of recently broken fingernails on each hand." Hugh kept his voice low and calm. "Perhaps the maid could assist?"

The margrave shook his head. "I will not subject Inge to any more than she has already endured."

Sera glanced to Hugh, then back to the bereaved noble. "If you will allow me, Lord Zedlitz, I will assist Mr Miles."

The Austrian drew a series of long breaths through his nose before he nodded. "Very well. If it is necessary."

Hugh returned to his patient and reached out for the nightcap. The removal of the soft lawn and lace revealed a balding head underneath. Short tufts of hair clung in patches, like a dying greensward during an unnaturally hot summer. Between them lay angry red peeling spots.

"A scalp condition, perhaps brought on by an allergy," Hugh murmured.

Next he untied the laces at her throat. He had already rolled the blankets down to the bottom of the bed. Hugh reached for the hem of the gown and an involuntary shudder ran through Sera. The two of them manhandling his mother might further distress the margrave. Was there a way to easily remove the night attire?

"Wait." She held out a hand and Hugh paused. "Let me try first."

She drew strands of magic from her torso and set them zinging along her arms to her hands. Then she held her palms outstretched over Lady Zedlitz's legs. On its own, the fabric of the gown wriggled its way up the woman's body. All they had to do was carefully slip each arm out of the billowing sleeves, and it came free over her head.

"Thank you," Hugh murmured once the body was fully exposed to view.

As the surgeon continued his examination, Sera's gaze slid to Lady Zedlitz's left wrist. The bracelet was gone and scars decorated her wrist instead. Sera pondered its absence. A jewellery case sat on the dresser, its lid shut. Did the copper piece rest inside, rubbing up against the diamonds and other jewels? Or had Lady Zedlitz kept it somewhere safe and close to hand, perhaps tucked under a pillow?

Or was it, as Sera's had been, only removed by force?

SEVEN

Not wishing to violate the dead woman's privacy by rifling through her possessions as the surgeon scrutinised her physical form, Sera returned to Lord Zedlitz.

"Do you require anything, Lord Zedlitz? A cup of tea, perhaps?" Sera wracked her brain for anything relevant Abigail had taught her during their etiquette lessons. The topic of how to console someone after the sudden death of their mother didn't bring forth any memories. There was one thing Abigail had imparted, though—the English thing to do in any crisis would be to offer a cup of tea.

He shook his head. "What I want most is to know who did this. You may find this hard to believe, Lady Winyard, but my mother was not much liked."

One lesson from Abigail leapt to the front of her mind. *If you have nothing nice to say, it is better to remain silent.* Sera lifted her gaze to the ceiling rose.

Lord Zedlitz let out a long breath. "*Mutter* was not

always as...forceful as you saw at the ball. Once, she possessed a lighter heart and often used to dance along the draughty halls of our castle, singing." He turned and leaned on the window frame, crossing his arms over his chest. "When *Oma* died, she changed. As though the joy had seeped from her life."

"I am sorry to hear that. Some women are very close to their mothers. Perhaps losing hers dimmed the enjoyment she found in life." Saying the words made a pang spear through Sera's heart. She had never had the opportunity to develop a close bond with her mother. If she ever had a daughter, Sera would treasure their connection and give the child the friendship and guidance that had been missing from her own life.

A frown drew lines in the margrave's forehead. "No. From what I remember, they were never close. *Combative*, I would have called their relationship, for they argued often. It was most odd, how utterly she changed afterward. *Mutter* used to love music and our home was filled with laughter and song. She lost that joy so suddenly it was as though someone had cast a hex over her."

"A hex?" Did he mean some form of magical transformation? Sera's attention returned to the bed, where, having finished his inspection, Hugh pulled the sheet up and over Lady Zedlitz. Before she could pursue the topic of curses, Hugh approached them.

"I do not believe your mother died of natural causes, Lord Zedlitz," he said in a slow, measured voice. As though he selected each word with care. "I fear that something more sinister has happened here."

Lord Zedlitz drew a deep breath. He glanced to the sheet-covered shape and wet his lips. "She was indeed murdered?"

Hugh clasped his hands behind his back. "The capillaries have burst in her ladyship's eyes, indicating a sudden lack of oxygen. There is some bruising around her lips, as though she struggled to breathe when a hand or some other object was pressed there. On each hand, as I said, there are recently torn fingernails. I cannot be entirely sure without an autopsy, though, to see what her internal organs have to tell me."

"No. She will not be violated so." Lord Zedlitz choked out the words.

"There is one more thing that might shed light on these sad events." Hugh walked to the bed and picked up and examined the pillows one by one. When he finished inspecting the ones on the bed, he stepped back. With a cry of "Aha!" he bent down and retrieved one from under the bed. The white corner was all that poked out from under the draped coverlet. Turning it over, he revealed a damp and chewed segment of cloth roughly in the middle. He held the pillow up. "The murder weapon. It appears someone smothered Lady Zedlitz."

"You believe a madman took my mother's life?" The margrave returned to the large bed with Sera at his side.

"Or madmen." Hugh moved to the end of the bed and lifted the blankets away from the cold feet. Encircling each ankle was a line of telltale bruises. "It would appear someone held her feet, as bruising only appears while a heart still beats. Another covered her face with the pillow."

Silence thickened in the already quiet room. Sera held in a sigh of exasperation. There went her chance to learn more about the odd copper bracelets. Had the unknown murderer also known about the innocent-looking piece, or had Lady Zedlitz's life been taken for another reason?

"The king has summoned Lieutenant Powers. He is a fine investigator and he will discover who has done this." Sera sought to reassure the bereaved son, who was now free of his domineering mother's unnatural influence.

A thought flared hot through her mind, and she bit her lip so she would not exclaim out loud. What if *he* had permanently silenced his mother? From the little Sera had seen the previous evening, Lady Zedlitz treated her son like a feeble child. Sneaking up on her while asleep would be the only chance to silence her, without her using the bracelet to alter his actions.

Leaving the margrave to return to the window and his quiet contemplations, Sera crept closer to the bed. The matter of the bracelet preyed on her mind. Scanning the draped body, her attention lingered on the arm protruding from under the sheet. On the left wrist was etched a familiar patterned scar. Instinctively she wrapped her hand over the one on her own arm. The red lines were fading to silver with time, whereas the scars on Lady Zedlitz appeared laced with old silver lines and fresh, bright ones.

"Does this not remind you of something?" she murmured to Hugh as he moved to her side.

He picked up her left hand and rubbed a thumb over the scar. "Yes. I noticed the similarities. Do you know what it means?"

She nodded. "Not here. When the lieutenant joins us."

While they waited, Sera used her magic to clothe Lady Zedlitz in her nightgown once more. Then they tucked the blankets around her and tugged the sheet over her face. She appeared almost peaceful, only a slight tension in her jaw giving away the sudden nature of her death.

A sharp rap on the door preceded Lieutenant Powers entering the room in his red uniform and polished black boots. He nodded to Sera and Hugh, and presented himself to Lord Zedlitz with a smart bow. "My lord, I am Lieutenant Powers. The king has charged me to discover what has transpired in this room."

The margrave turned tired eyes to the newcomer. "Mr Miles has discovered that my mother met a foul end. You must discover the fiend who did this."

"It is indeed murder?" The lieutenant's eyes sparkled and he twisted one end of his moustache.

"Suffocation by means of a pillow," Hugh murmured. "I believe there were two assailants, as there is recent bruising around her ankles."

Powers huffed. "If someone held her feet to minimise her struggles, that makes my task easier. A lone murderer is harder to find. Two people will have difficulty keeping their terrible secret. How long has she been dead?"

"The body is still warm and there are no signs of rigor mortis. Three hours, four at most," Hugh said.

Powers extracted his notebook and jotted down notes. "But first, who discovered her? I must know all that happened."

Lord Zedlitz gestured to one side of the room. "Inge discovered her. Her maid. She is in her room. She is quite distraught."

The lieutenant smoothed his moustache. "I am not an inquisitor. I shall tread gently in my questions to her. Please ask her to come out."

Lord Zedlitz approached a section of wall and pushed. The panelling popped open to reveal a tiny maid's room beyond, so she would be close at hand should her mistress require her. A murmured conversation drifted into the main chamber and then the margrave emerged with a young woman trailing behind him.

With an auburn light in her hair and fair skin, she was short of stature but well formed, like an exquisitely created doll. She moved with elegance, as though trained in dancing. Her hands wrung a handkerchief, but her hazel eyes were clear.

"I did not do it, sir," she announced in a sure tone, her gaze going immediately to the regimentals of Lieutenant Powers.

"Please, sit." Powers gestured to the chairs before the fire. "You are Inge?"

"Inge Wassler, sir." She perched on the edge of the chair.

"Tell me what you remember." He opened the little notebook on a bent knee and held the pencil poised over the page.

"Lady Zedlitz instructed me to wake her at ten. I woke early and did mending in my room. At nine, I crept out to prepare her tray." Inge spoke in a steady tone, with no tears or trembling.

The lieutenant fixed his attention on the young woman. "Was she awake then, or asleep?"

The maid shook her head. "The room was dark, sir. I walked quietly so as not to wake her. The curtain was mostly drawn and I saw only the shape of her under the bedclothes."

"When you left, did you leave the door locked or unlocked behind you?" He gestured to the door to the corridor.

With no hesitation she replied, "Unlocked."

An eyebrow quirked. "What happened next?"

"I went to the kitchen and asked for her tray. It is such a long walk. I did not return until close to ten." Her words came shorter and in gasps as she reached the climax of her story. Her gaze darted sideways to the margrave.

"And then...?" Powers murmured.

"I put the tray on the table." She gestured to the abandoned tray not far from the bed. The toast uneaten. The tea never poured. "And opened the curtains to let in the day. Then, when I pulled back the drapes around the bed—"

Silence fell and the maid bowed her head to dab at her eyes with the handkerchief.

The lieutenant waited until she had regained her composure. "What did you see?"

Inge drew a deep breath and straightened her spine. "Her eyes and mouth were open wide, as though yawning. When I touched her shoulder, she did not rouse. Nor did she blink. I rushed immediately and woke Lord Zedlitz."

Powers glanced to the margrave and back to his notebook. "Do you recall the placement of the blankets and the pillows?"

The maid gestured with her hands, touching them to her shoulders. "The blankets were pulled up to here. The pillows were on the bed much as you see now."

"Did you like Lady Zedlitz?" He asked the question with a soft tone, but it had an immediate reaction.

The maid sat taller, her spine rigid. "I am fortunate to have this position with a good family, sir. I am always paid on time and allowed one day off a week. Others are not so lucky."

The answer sounded rehearsed to Sera, or as though Lady Zedlitz had impressed it upon the maid on a frequent basis.

"That is not what I asked." Powers kept a steady eye on the maid.

Inge huffed and glanced sideways. "Lady Zedlitz could be...demanding. She liked things done in a particular way."

The pencil scratched across the page of the note

book. "Do you recollect anyone in the hall when you left the room?"

"Yes. There was a guard or footman, in that red and gold uniform." A frown pulled on her pale brow. "He was gone when I returned."

The lieutenant's hand froze. "Do you remember what he looked like? Young or old? Tall or short?"

She sucked in her bottom lip, and her brows pulled low. When she released the lip, they bounced back up. "Not so old. Perhaps in his thirties. Of average height and build with brown hair."

Such a description could fit dozens of palace staff.

"Was anything about him remarkable? A limp, or an accent if he said anything to you?" The lieutenant must have shared Sera's observation.

"Oh, he had a scar here, that ran from his lip all the way down his chin, like this." She held her finger across her chin in the appropriate spot. "I asked him how he came by it, and he said he tripped on a stair."

"Thank you, Inge. That is all for now." Powers slid the pencil back into the spine of the book and closed it.

"What will become of me now?" She stood, her hands stilled on the handkerchief.

Sera wondered if the clutching at the handkerchief was more about the shock of finding a dead body, rather than any real grief for her mistress.

The lieutenant tucked the notebook into his jacket pocket as he rose to his feet. "I do not know. That will be up to Lord Zedlitz, I imagine."

"My mother no longer commands you, Inge. You can decide your own future," Lord Zedlitz said.

"Could one of the other nobles in your party offer her a bed with their servants? It might be best if she stays with her own people," Lieutenant Powers suggested.

Lord Zedlitz stared at the maid for a long moment, then he rubbed the stubble forming on his jaw. "Inge is no servant, but from an old and noble family. When her parents died—"

"Lady Zedlitz said she would take me in. I thought she meant as a companion. Instead, she made me her servant." Inge spat the words and fire flashed in her eyes.

Sera raised her eyebrows. Here was an interesting turn of events.

"I do not know if the king will let you stay here, Inge. Nor would I imagine you wanting to, after Lady Zedlitz met her end in this room." The lieutenant gestured to the bed.

Inge held her ground. "I do not want to stay at the palace. May I not take lodgings elsewhere?"

Powers narrowed his eyes and touched his moustache, as though reassuring himself it maintained its ornate curl. Sera could hear the unvoiced objection. The noblewoman turned maid was the closest person to Lady Zedlitz and had slumbered not far away as her life was stolen. Or might even have stood at the foot of her bed as it happened. The lieutenant probably imagined her fleeing, never to be seen again.

Since Sera had inserted herself in the investigation by accompanying Hugh, she might as well dive in deeper. "If I might offer a suggestion? Inge is welcome to stay at my home. We are a small household, and would make her welcome. Although we are not as grand as a castle."

The young woman angled her head and then nodded to Sera. "Yes. I would prefer to be with Lady Winyard, the mage."

"Thank you, Lady Winyard. It is settled. I entrust Inge to your care." Lord Zedlitz nodded to Sera.

"I will pack my belongings and be ready to leave with you, my lady." Inge returned to her small chamber and closed the door.

Powers approached the margrave, who stared at the closed door. "Where were you last night, my lord?"

"At the ball, where I met Lady Winyard." He smiled in her direction.

"And afterward?" The interrogation turned from the victim's maid to her son.

The margrave gestured to the door and the hall beyond. "Asleep in my chamber across the hall, until Inge roused me."

"Can anyone vouch for that?" The question was murmured in such a quiet tone, Sera had to strain to catch it.

Lord Zedlitz's eyes widened. "I was alone. My valet slept in a room much like the one Inge has off this chamber. Are you suggesting that I did away with my mother? For what reason, given I have already inherited my title and fortune on the death of my father?"

The lieutenant gave a noncommittal shrug. "Families are complex. Often it is those we love most who drive us to distraction."

"Are you suggesting I would travel all the way to England and murder my mother at your court, where all eyes scrutinise our every move? If I were so inclined, I would wait until winter when we are snowed in at our castle, the only potential witnesses our loyal servants, and not a whisper would ever escape those stone walls."

Sera could see his point. If she wanted someone quietly removed, how convenient if they should fall from a castle rampart. Who would be brazen enough to commit the act in a foreign palace?

Someone who had to seize what opportunity presented itself, a voice whispered in the back of her mind.

"Of those in your delegation, do you know of any who bore ill will towards your mother?" Powers changed direction.

Lord Zedlitz shrugged and spread his hands. "She was a difficult woman. Many went out of their way to avoid her. You would have to ask them for their personal opinions."

The lieutenant crossed his arms and tapped a finger against the sleeve of his uniform.

While he gathered his thoughts, Sera dropped her own question into the conversation. "Lord Zedlitz, where does your mother keep the copper bracelet she wore last night when she removes it?"

He frowned and glanced at his mother's still form. "She never took it off."

"Never?" Cold fingers traced down Sera's spine.

"The day *Oma* died, *Mutter* picked it up from the bed and clicked it around her wrist. I never saw her take it off from that day to this." As he spoke, he walked to the dresser and tried to open the wooden jewellery case. "It is locked. One moment while I find the key."

He searched the drawers and soon found a tiny golden key. Once the case was unlocked, he pulled out bracelets and necklaces set with diamonds and precious stones, but nothing made of copper. "It is not here. Is it not still on her wrist?"

"No. Only a mark where it resided," Hugh said.

Sera blew out a sigh. *Bother.* If Lady Zedlitz never took off the bracelet, it was most likely because she couldn't. Much like her own that, once closed, had no visible seam or catch.

"Then I do not know where it might be." He flipped the case closed and locked it again before slipping the key into the pocket of his banyan.

"Is there anything else missing? Other jewellery or precious possessions?" Lieutenant Powers asked.

Lord Zedlitz conducted another search of the dresser. "Not that I can see. Inge would know best. Now, could I return to my room, so I might dress?" He gestured to his velvet-trimmed gown and slippers.

"Of course, my lord. Perhaps Mr Miles would oblige by finding someone with whom to discuss appropriate arrangements for your mother?" Powers nodded in Hugh's direction.

"Certainly I can assist with that," Hugh murmured.

The margrave nodded to the surgeon. "Thank you. I shall return."

When the door snicked shut on Lord Zedlitz, Sera drew the two men closer to her with a gesture and then placed a finger to her lips. Closing her eyes, she crafted a protection spell in her head to ensure their conversation remained private. When the device was fully formed inside her, she opened her eyes and drew an arc with her hands. Light shimmered around them for a moment, and several loud popping noises sounded.

Eight

Sera huffed as the last *pop* faded away. "Someone was listening, but no ear will penetrate this barrier. We may talk freely now."

"You have something to tell me that you wish to remain a secret?" Powers leaned one shoulder on the wall and waited.

Hugh regarded her with curious brown eyes. "It's about the scar on your wrist. Lady Zedlitz bears a similar mark."

Sera raised her wrist so that the lieutenant might see. There were so many unanswered questions about the cuff she had worn. Who had sought to protect her? What ancient magic had they used? And what did *the child of earth and sea* have to do with it?

Pushing all those questions aside, she concentrated on the matter at hand. "Lady Zedlitz wore a copper bracelet that is ensorcelled. I believe it creates a compulsion inside someone to do her bidding. At the Duchess of Edgecombe's ball last night, we had a disagreement over who should curtsey to whom. I outrank Lady Zedlitz, but she held a different opinion. She grabbed my wrist and said I must curtsey to her. Against my will, my knees buckled. As a mage, I recognised the spell worming its way under my skin and forcing me to obey. When I glanced to where she had hold of me, a gossamer strand, like a single thread of cobweb, had snaked from the bracelet and burrowed into my skin. I froze it, removed it from my body, and flung off her coercion."

Lieutenant Powers narrowed his gaze. "Miles said a moment ago that you bear the same scar on your wrist. Does that mean you likewise possess a piece of jewellery that can compel a person to do your bidding?"

"No. The piece I wore worked against me, somewhat like a shackle. It had no effect on anyone around me. The cuff Lady Zedlitz wore worked for her and against whomever she targeted." Its workmanship told her the same hand had crafted both items, but now she doubted that. Lord Zedlitz had said his mother came into possession of the piece when his grandmother died. And she had worn it for as long as he could remember. The bracelet could have been in their family for generations. Was the cuff that had suppressed Sera's own magic also decades old?

"Lord Zedlitz did not see it in her jewellery case, but she might have kept it somewhere closer to hand," Powers mused.

"I don't think so. Besides, the margrave said she never removed it, which I believe means she *could not* take it off." Sera recalled the night she had removed her own bracelet and the effort it had taken. At times, she thought the pain would force her into unconsciousness. "If her bracelet is what I believe it to be, it can only be removed by magic or death. Lady Zedlitz does not possess any magic, but the bracelet would have clicked open when she passed."

"Which fits with his lordship's recollection of her picking it up after her mother died," Hugh said.

"If indeed there is nothing else of value missing, it would appear that someone killed her solely for the bracelet. There is a motive that needs investigating. What would someone do to obtain a bracelet that compelled others to do one's bidding, even against their will?" Powers stroked his moustache and a speculative look entered his eyes.

Hugh let out a soft whistle between clenched teeth. "There are diplomatic negotiations in progress. Imagine touching one of our nobles, or even the king, and having them change their mind to favour the emperor."

"I don't know who might have been aware of the bracelet's power," Sera said. "I perceived the spell, others would not. But anyone she touched must surely have been aware that their words and actions were not their own." Forcing people to act in a certain way would create numerous enemies. Had she meddled in people's lives, tugging their strings as she had those of her son?

"Given how recently they arrived in England, we will start with the Austrian delegation. I doubt she had sufficient time on our shores to enrage an Englishman enough to strike out at her." The ends of his moustache bounced as Powers chuckled.

That made a memory surface in Sera's mind. "She has been here before, many years ago. Mr Napier said some were still smarting from that visit—and some incident involving a cow."

"Indeed?" The moustache waggled in surprise. "An old dispute might be a possibility, but let us start with more current events and work our way outward."

Hugh glanced at his silent charge, as if he checked she still lay under the sheet and hadn't been roused by their discussion of her. "Surely it is more likely someone with a long association with the family. Someone who would know of the bracelet and what it was capable of."

Powers murmured his agreement. "Like her son. What is your opinion of him, Lady Winyard?"

"I think he was a man controlled by his mother, who is now free." She had to voice the concern eating at her insides. While her initial reaction had been to like the margrave, had he murdered his mother to rid himself of her magical interference? "He might have had no other way to escape her."

"What of Inge, the erstwhile maid?" Hugh lowered his voice even though Sera's spell kept their words audible only to their small group. "She made it sound as though Lady Zedlitz had tricked her into being a maid —certainly a most demeaning thing for a noblewoman to endure."

"Indeed. So we have a magical bracelet that compels people to do another's bidding, a son much under his mother's control, and a noblewoman thrust into the role of servant. What an interesting investigation you have found for me." Powers twisted his moustache as he thought aloud. The ends of his facial hair curled upon themselves and he sharpened the very ends until they resembled round pencils.

Copper bracelets and their abilities were much on Sera's mind. Investigating the origins of one might help locate the other. "I will learn what I can of the bracelet and its origins. I fear what will happen now. No one will be able to resist any command made by whoever wears it."

"Can you tell when it is being used?" Hugh asked.

"I will craft a spell to assist me with that. If a noble took it, they might even now be prowling parlours and ballrooms, forcing their will upon others." Sera could experiment with her own now harmless bracelet, and create a spell that activated when the other copper piece was near.

"Or whoever holds it might be sitting in a closed room, negotiating a treaty with an unfair advantage," Powers murmured.

"You could cause mischief and misery, or bring down a country." Sera pondered what Lord Zedlitz had said about his mother changing from a carefree woman who loved music to the dour and angry woman Sera had met at the ball. Had the loss of her mother altered Lady Zedlitz so much, or had the bracelet changed the wearer?

"Let us inform the king that Lady Zedlitz has been murdered. Then, I need the Austrians roused from bed. Third, I must find which footmen were in this area this morning." Lieutenant Powers laid out his plan and indicated they should be on their way.

"I will remain here and wait for Lord Zedlitz, so we might discuss the next journey for his mother," Hugh said.

Sera hadn't considered that part. What happened when someone died so far from home? Assuming Lord Zedlitz wished her shipped back to Austria, a mage would be needed to finish any embalming and preserving process to ensure she didn't rot before being entombed on her family lands. What a shame Lord Branvale had died. He had been renowned for making the deceased appear in the flush of life, and they stayed that way for years. One bereft lord had his wife's coffin fitted with a glass lid so he might continue to gaze upon her visage. Branvale had boasted to Sera that some twenty years after he had cast his spell, the dead woman still had a dewy complexion and lush red lips.

Sera accompanied the lieutenant back to the presence chamber, where the court had broken into clusters to gossip and entertain themselves. Queen Charlotte read dispatches to her husband, who leaned heavily on one arm of his throne.

King George perked up on seeing them. "What have you discovered, Powers? The Austrians are muttering about Lady Zedlitz's death and we don't want to upset the Hapsburgs."

Powers bowed to the king. "Mr Miles has ascertained that Lady Zedlitz did not die of natural causes. He believe she was smothered in her sleep by persons unknown."

Conversation erupted around them, the gasps and

twitters flowing from one side of the room to the other like an undulating wave.

"Another murder, eh?" The monarch turned his gaze to Sera.

Was this her life—to be accused of every crime committed at court, simply because she didn't conform to the rules society dictated for women?

"I can assure you, Your Majesty, I am in no way connected to this one. Death comes for many citizens of London every single day. I am not his handmaiden, plucking souls and offering them up to the dark lord as though they were ripe grapes."

"Well, possibly not." The king's brow furrowed and he didn't look convinced. "But life at court has certainly been *enlivened* since you came to us, Lady Winyard."

Lieutenant Powers took another step forward to draw the royal attention back to him. "With Your Majesty's permission, I will talk to the members of the Austrian delegation and whoever directs the household footmen and guards. I need to ascertain who was in the hall outside their rooms this morning."

The king waved a hand, then pressed it to his forehead as though a headache threatened. He screwed up his eyes, and the queen leaned closer to his side. "Yes, yes. You carry on and report back when you have something interesting."

A courtier bustled forward and indicated they should join him at the side of the room. "I can provide the names of the household staff you need, Lieutenant Powers. I only need time to consult the work schedules.

Most of the Austrian delegation are here and I can have them escorted to a private sitting room, if that suits?"

"Yes. Thank you. With somewhere adjacent where I can talk to each person in private," Powers said.

"Of course. I shall assemble what you require and then have a footman fetch you." He bowed and retreated beyond the door, where he issued commands to his underlings.

"I will join you, if you do not mind. There is a chance that the suspect might have snapped the bracelet around their wrist." Sera wrapped her words in a drift of magic to ensure they reached only Lieutenant Powers's ears.

He huffed. "Of course, but surely I would be able to see it, if one of them possesses the bracelet."

"But you might never be able to mention it or remember it, if they touch you." All it would take was the light brush of a hand, and the command to either be silent on the subject or to forget about it entirely. The lieutenant would never know he had had the murderer within his grasp as the person left the room. With Sera present, it would be more difficult for the guilty party to influence them both.

"Ah. I had not considered that possibility. That would be mighty inconvenient." His eyes sparkled and he seemed to be enjoying himself with another murder to investigate at the king's request.

"I will not interfere with your questioning. I promise to be as quiet as a mouse," Sera said.

As they waited out in the hall, Powers paced with the pent-up energy of a man used to action. Sera replayed her brief meeting with Lady Zedlitz in her mind. Over and over, she saw the matronly woman yelling at her son and the way the Austrian nobles parted to let her charge through the middle of their group. One woman had muttered under her breath, and while Sera didn't understand German, the tone had been clear—dislike.

"The Austrian party is assembled for you, Lieutenant Powers. If you'll follow me." The courtier gestured along the hall. "I will have a list of staff for you by the time you finish."

"Good. Make sure to include a list of all members of the Austrian party, including their staff and servants. I don't want to miss anyone." With a nod, he stood aside to let Sera enter the drawing room first.

Conversation fell away as they entered. Some of those assembled appeared curious, others annoyed. Another door stood open to reveal a smaller parlour that would be used for interviews. There, Sera selected a chair away from where the lieutenant gestured for the first noble to sit.

Interviewing people about their whereabouts was frightfully boring. One by one, a noble was ushered into the room. Each told a similar variant of the same story— they had been asleep in their room (either alone or accompanied) and neither saw nor heard anything. While they talked, Sera examined their arms. If the person wore long sleeves, a whisper of magic tugged on a cuff to reveal each wrist.

Then a woman who looked familiar entered and took her seat. An elegant woman in her thirties, with light brown hair piled atop her head. The one who had muttered under her breath.

Her eyes narrowed as she stared boldly at Sera. "Why is she here?"

"Lady Winyard will weigh your words and inform me if you are lying." Lieutenant Powers gestured to the chair opposite him.

The woman's eyes widened, then she swept her skirts to one side in order to seat herself.

"Your name please, madam, and your role in the party," Powers asked, his tone kind.

"Lady Liesel Haas. I accompany my husband who, alongside Lord Zedlitz, is charged by our emperor to negotiate the trade treaty." She clasped her hands in her lap and darted a glance at Sera.

Lady Haas wore a pale green gown with three-quarter sleeves whose Brussels lace brushed her forearms. No glint of copper came from either wrist. No sparkle came from any part of her exposed body, as the lady wore no jewellery apart from a wedding ring and a green velvet ribbon tied around her throat.

The lieutenant's attention drifted to the woman's hands and then back to his notebook. "What time did you return from the ball?"

Lady Haas shrugged. "I am not sure. After three, I think. We sought our bed and did not roam the halls, if that is what you are asking."

"When did you wake?" A tired tone entered the lieutenant's voice. They were nearing the last member of the delegation and they had yet to unearth a single useful nugget to aid the investigation.

"It was after eleven. My maid rushed in and told me Lady Zedlitz had died. A maid heard Inge scream, and when they ran into the hall, they saw her rush to Otto's room. Soon, all the servants were talking about it."

Nothing travelled faster than a juicy bit of gossip. Had she truly heard about the death from her maid, or had Lady Haas more firsthand knowledge?

"You didn't like Lady Zedlitz—that was obvious last night," Sera interjected when her curiosity couldn't be contained any longer. "What did that phrase mean, that you uttered when she swept past you?"

Lady Haas fell silent in a long pause, then she pursed her lips. "I do not remember saying anything. It was a loud party, was it not?"

Powers leaned forward in his chair as he caught the scent of an interesting tidbit. "What were your feelings towards Lady Zedlitz?"

"She is from an old and noble family and is much respected." Her lips pulled back in a smile, but it resembled a grimace and her eyes were cold.

"I didn't understand the phrase you uttered, but your tone was clear." Sera met the other woman's gaze. While she couldn't peer into the woman's mind to determine the truth of her words, she gambled on Lady Haas not knowing that.

Lady Haas swallowed and a slight tremble ran through her clasped hands. "I did not like her. She was unkind. Spiteful. Nor am I alone in that opinion." Having said her piece, she clamped her lips shut and stood. With a nod, she swept from the room.

"We have learned nothing," Sera said.

Lieutenant Powers huffed under his breath. "We learned many did not like Lady Zedlitz, but that is not sufficient motive for murder. I shall dig deeper. I need to talk to the servants to find the one who saw Inge cross the hall. She may remember any other staff about at the same time."

"If you have no further need of me, I shall introduce Inge into my little household." Sera would not ask the noble-turned-maid to share an attic room with Vicky. The small bedroom on the same floor as hers seemed the better solution.

"Do keep your ears open, Lady Winyard." Powers tapped the side of his nose.

"Oh, I intend to. I need to find that bracelet." Sera pinned her hopes on uncovering some clue as to the origin of both bracelets if she could compare them. Perhaps somewhere in the ornate carving would be a tiny maker's mark, such as silver bore.

With relief, Sera stepped from the palace into the coal smoke–tinged air of London and the palace court-yard. Footmen lingered in groups, and one broke away on seeing her and rushed to fetch a carriage.

Inge waited on the cobbles. Sitting on a valise, she sketched in a notebook perched on her knee.

"I am sorry to keep you waiting so long." Sera tried to see what the other woman drew, but she snapped the book shut and dropped it into a satchel at her feet.

"I do not mind. Lady Zedlitz gave me little time for my own interests." Inge picked up the valise in one hand and the satchel with the other.

At least Sera didn't have to make the woman walk

home. The king allowed his mage the use of a carriage to return to her home and the footman had summoned one for her. They rode in silence, each taking the measure of the other. Sera longed to ask her new lodger how her parents had died and what else Lady Zedlitz had compelled her to do. But she held her tongue. Inge seemed encased in a hard shell and gave no signs of wishing to converse. If the other woman chose to remain silent, the next few days would be uncomfortable.

NINE

At home, Sera led the way up the front steps. Elliot flung open the door as they approached. He raised an eyebrow as he peered over Sera's shoulder at the newcomer. Then he bustled down the stairs and took the valise and satchel from Inge's fingers. "Let me take these, miss."

In the foyer, Sera peeled off her gloves and dropped them on the narrow side table. Next, her jacket was shrugged off her shoulders. Then she made introductions. "Elliot, this is Miss Inge Wassler. She will be staying with us for a while. Please take her bags to the bedroom next to mine."

Both eyebrows shot up, but he kept his silence.

"Once you are settled, Inge, come down to the parlour and we'll have some tea." Sera pointed to the doorway to their right.

The other woman nodded, then followed Elliot up the stairs. Sera headed in the opposite direction and hurried down to the kitchen. Rosie and Vicky sat at the table, preparing vegetables for dinner.

"There will be one more for dinner," she said.

"There's plenty to go around," Rosie said as she chopped parsley.

Sera snuck a peeled carrot from a bowl and chewed the end. "Also another mouth for breakfast and luncheon. Inge will be staying for a few weeks. She is Austrian, and the lady she served has just been murdered."

Vicky gasped and the potato in her hands dropped to the table. "Another murder of a noble? Did she do it, then?"

Sera drew a breath to answer, and then realised she didn't know how to respond to that exact question. "I don't know, Vicky. Lieutenant Powers is investigating and I am sure he will get to the truth of the matter. Inge is a noblewoman in reduced circumstances and she didn't want to stay at the palace with the others in her party."

Rosie shot a glance at Sera. "She's been through much, then."

"How much, none of us yet knows," Sera murmured. From the few exchanged glances between Inge and Lord Zedlitz, she suspected there was more to uncover in the former maid's tale.

"We'll keep our ears open and our mouths shut." Rosie winked and scraped chopped herbs into a large bowl.

"Thank you, Rosie. I hope she isn't too much of a bother for you." Only now did it occur to Sera that Inge might be left to her own devices for most of the day. Sera couldn't exactly drag her around London as she undertook magical tasks or hunted for the bracelet.

"I'd rather cook for ten than just one, and between the three of us, we'll keep an eye on her. Now, will you be wanting a tray sent up?" The cook picked up an onion from a basket and sliced it in half with one stroke of her knife.

"Yes, please. I had better return to the parlour and prepare to play hostess." With reluctance, Sera left the cozy and delicious-smelling kitchen and headed to the parlour. A pile of invoices waited for her on the desk. She had learned her lessons from Mr Napier and settled her bills as they fell due. No creditors would be banging on her door; on the contrary, they would be more likely to supply her household first.

A half hour later, feet shuffled out in the hall. "What's up with that one?" Elliot rolled his eyes to the ceiling as he carried a tray into the room with a light repast upon it.

Sera sent a trace of magic up through the floor to ensure her guest was still in her room and not lingering on the stairs. "Her mistress was murdered sometime this morning. Naturally, all eyes at court fixed on me, but thankfully I spent last night with the Napier family and went straight from there to the palace. Then, it was revealed she is a noblewoman of reduced circumstances who had become the murdered woman's maid."

Elliot's eyebrows shot up. "Sounds like the plot to a novel."

Sera waved the footman and his tray to the table

between the settee and the armchairs. Pushing aside her account ledger, Sera moved to the armchair favoured by Hugh. "Lieutenant Powers wants us to keep an eye on her. She is not yet cleared of any involvement." How much strength did it take to hold a pillow over someone's face while they struggled for their life? Lady Zedlitz had been a solid woman and Inge was small of stature. Or had she held her mistress's ankles while another held the pillow? From what little Sera had seen of Inge's hands, she didn't have any scratches, while Lady Zedlitz had broken fingernails. Although they could have snagged in fabric and never broken flesh.

The footman rubbed his hands together. "You can count on me to keep one eye on her. I'm glad to finally have an interesting job to do." He placed the plates, teacups, and teapot on the table. When all was arranged to his liking, he slid the empty tray under his arm. "What if she does a runner when you're not here?"

Sera could create an enchantment to keep Inge tethered to the Soho home, but she baulked at doing that to another after her years on Branvale's leash. If the young woman had committed the crime with an accomplice, better to give her space to either seek that person out or even to find the bracelet if it were hidden somewhere. "I will cast a location spell over her that will assist should she go out and not return."

A casting could be hidden at both the front and rear doors, and would attach to Inge when she passed through. Satisfied with the solution, Sera waited for her guest.

As Elliot left, Inge ventured into the parlour and

looked around. Curiosity burned in her eyes. "This is not where I thought a duchess would live."

Sera gestured for Inge to be seated. "It is modest, I know. But I am very new to being a duchess and I find my little home far more cozy than a grand mansion."

The woman made a noise in the back of her throat as she sat. Perhaps, having lived in a castle, she had much higher expectations.

"What do you like to do for entertainment? I don't have many books at the moment, but intend to enlarge my collection when space allows." Sera stared at the sad bookshelf to one side of the room. She had a few volumes, but wasn't sure any would appeal to the serious woman now sharing her home.

"I like to draw. I will not be any bother to you. Do you think Lord Zedlitz could visit me here?" She asked her question from under lowered lashes.

"Of course he can. I am sure you would like to see a familiar face." Sera poured tea for Inge. Elliot would keep his ears open should the margrave visit while Sera was elsewhere. Not that she could imagine what the two would discuss, unless they found solidarity in exchanging tales of how Lady Zedlitz had oppressed them both.

Or how they had done away with her?

Sera tried to engage Inge in conversation, but found the other woman reserved, either because of the day's events or because it was her natural character. As things became stilted and she was beginning to wonder how on earth to extricate herself, Elliot reappeared.

"Where will milady and Miss Wassler be dining this evening?" the footman asked from the doorway.

Bother. Sera ate in the kitchen with her below-stairs family. That might not go well with the noblewoman used to living in a castle.

Inge solved the issue by standing and fidgeting with a pleat in her skirt. "I will take a tray in my room, please. If you do not mind. I am rather tired and would like to lie down before dinner."

"Very well. I'll have Vicky bring you a tray this evening if you are awake. I shall see you in the morning." Sera nodded a good-night to her guest, even though it was only early afternoon.

Elliot moved to allow her to pass, then leaned on the door jamb. The stairs creaked as she trod up to her bedroom. After a moment of silence, Elliot asked, "What will you do about meals? I doubt she'll want to eat in her room for weeks on end. We'll all understand if there is a change for a while."

Sera let out a sigh. There were some things about being a duchess she disliked. Such as having to let go of the cozy intimacy of the kitchen table. At least the small townhouse had an equally small dining room. "Ask Vicky to clean and tidy the dining room, please. We shall have to use that while Inge is with us."

His dark eyebrows shot up. "It's gloomy in there."

Gloomy was something Sera could cure. "We shall inject some cheer into it with some paint or wallpaper and a few decorations. We will have our celebration dinner in there. I have not forgotten my promise of a night to dress up for us all." Sera beckoned him along the hall to the room in question. If they were to redecorate by morning, they had better set to work. Luckily, one of them possessed magic.

SERA, Vicky, and Elliot worked all afternoon to transform the dining room. The first task was to clean the grime from the window to let in the sunlight. Next, they painted walls and trim a pale cream. Sera added a thin golden line around the panelling and ceiling. As a final touch, she used her magic to paint the likeness of a peacock with tail spread across one wall. A luminous hint in the blues and greens added sparkle as the lamplight caressed the bird's feathers.

A sense of satisfaction washed over Sera as she took breakfast the next morning in the dining room. Pale sunlight filtered through the window that overlooked the rear garden and the room could almost be called cheerful—if it hadn't been so small and its furnishings so shabby.

Inge appeared and nodded in her direction as she took a seat at the other place setting.

Sera steeled herself for another awkward conversation until one of them could leave. "Good morning, Inge. Did you sleep well?"

"No. I woke throughout the night." She yawned before reaching for a piece of toast.

"Oh. Was your room not comfortable?" Had Sera

already failed as a hostess? Lady Abigail would be so disappointed if she ever found out.

Next Inge selected the pot of marmalade. "It was not that. Lady Zedlitz used to wake me during the night. Her scalp itched terribly and I had to rub lotion on it."

"Couldn't she do that for herself?" Sera couldn't imagine summoning a sleeping maid to do something her own two hands were perfectly capable of doing.

For the first time in their acquaintance, Inge bestowed a smile upon Sera. "She could do it herself, yes. She chose to wake me instead."

"Had she suffered an itchy head for long?" When Hugh had examined the deceased woman, they had found the sores and tufts of hair hidden under her lace cap.

"For as long as I worked for her, but it became worse in the last year or two." Inge selected a sausage from the plate being kept warm by one of Sera's magical flames, and dropped it next to her toast.

"How unfortunate for her." Sera sipped hot chocolate and mused over the implications. Magic took a toll on mages and aftermages, drawing on their physical energy. The bracelet might work differently on a non-magic user. Lady Zedlitz's change in personality and the irritation on her scalp might have been the price she paid for influencing those around her.

How Sera wished for a fellow mage to discuss her theories with, but distrust made her keep her distance even from the helpful Lord Pendlebury.

Since her guest had a more relaxed air this morning,

Sera decided to venture a few questions. "Do you know what *die vettel* means?" The muttered phrase had been directed at Lady Zedlitz by Lady Haas, who claimed she couldn't remember saying it. That made Sera all the more curious about the unfamiliar words.

Inge wrinkled her brow and the toast paused six inches from her mouth. "It is a not so nice thing to say about a woman. *Hag* or *crone* would be the closest in English."

"Thank you. I overheard it the night of the ball and was curious." They already knew that Lady Zedlitz was generally disliked by her countrymen. But did the sentiment run any deeper for Lady Haas? Sera let conversation drift for a few minutes to the weather and Inge's plans for the day before returning to the topic. She didn't want Inge to think she was being interrogated over her sausage. "Do you know Lady Haas?"

Inge's fingers curled tighter around the cutlery she was using to slice the sausage. "We were friends once, but no longer. She married well. Lord Haas has several successful undertakings. Although he is very old."

Sera had been surprised when he'd entered the room to be questioned by Lieutenant Powers. He looked to be at least thirty years older than his wife, but it was not an uncommon situation. Some nobles chose to remarry if they lost their first wife in childbirth. Heirs had to be produced, after all; they couldn't be ordered from a shop, and that process required a spouse of a certain age.

"Was she well acquainted with him before they wed?" Sera asked.

Inge frowned. "No. When we were young, he was already an old man about town and I do not remember her ever mentioning him. But Lord Zedlitz would know more than I. He attended the ball where they announced their engagement. I believe it shocked those present."

As they finished breakfast, Sera pondered if the little she had discovered was worth passing to Lieutenant Powers. A woman with a much older husband was no indication of any involvement in Lady Zedlitz's death. No, she would dig a little deeper before deciding whether to mention it or not.

Sera adjourned to the parlour. She needed to call her friends together. Their assistance would be required to find the ensorcelled bracelet. Selecting a fresh sheet of paper, she wrote messages to Abigail and Hugh and then addressed them. She pondered where to send Hugh's missive. Would he be at his rooms or doing rounds? Rounds, possibly—the hour was still too early for him to be at court. With a sigh, she folded and sealed the paper. She could only try.

Handing the letters to Elliot, she waded through the mage correspondence. What few tasks they set her would be easily resolved. Apparently Lord Ormsby wanted her full attention on the upcoming magical display. Sera had thought little about her part past drawing her inspiration from Nyx. Finding a fresh sheet of paper, she began to scribble some ideas.

Later, as she sat watching the children play outside, from the corner of her eye she caught movement on the ensorcelled sheet of paper. A line of text marched across the page.

Father's man has returned from Oswestry with news.

Her heart skipped a beat. Clutching the page, Sera pushed the chair back with such haste it nearly toppled and she had to tug it back with a strand of magic.

"I'm going out to the Napiers', Elliot!" she called over her shoulder.

"Good lord, you can screech," the footman said from the doorway.

"Kitty has news of my parents. At long last I will have answers to some of my questions." Elliot held out her cloak and Sera shrugged it over her shoulders. Waving away her hat, she hurried out the house to seek a hired carriage.

In Mayfair, Sera burst into the parlour still wearing her cloak. A footman trailed behind her, waiting to catch it as she undid the clasp. She stopped before Kitty and declined to sit. Expectation zinged along her limbs and required movement, or she would burst.

"I came as soon as I saw your message. What of my parents?"

Kitty rose from her seat and set aside her book. "Father is in the library. Let us go talk to him."

The women linked hands as they crossed the wide foyer to Mr Napier's study. Kitty knocked on the door and waited for permission to enter.

He glanced up from his work and smiled at them. "Ah, I assume Sera has heard the news." He set aside the stack of papers and gestured to the chairs arrayed before the fire.

"Yes, I came as soon as I could." How convenient it would be if she could use her magic to transport her physical form from one place to another in an instant. But mages had worked on that problem for centuries and were no closer to finding a solution. Although they had theorised it should be possible to travel to and from fixed locations, rather like the gateways used to access the Fae realm. Sera thought it no real solution at all. People would still need to make their way to the transport locations or ports.

Kitty sat. Sera stood behind her friend, her hands clasping the back of the armchair.

Mr Napier took up a position beside the fireplace. "I am afraid the news is not what you were hoping. Nora, your mother, died some three years ago."

Disappointment plunged through her. The much-imagined reunion was no longer possible. "Oh," she whispered.

Sera made it to the sofa and dropped to the buttery soft leather. So many questions would remain unanswered. How unfair. Unless she found a reliable after-mage who could converse with the dead...but even then, souls often spoke in riddles and snatches that were hard to interpret.

"The news does not get any better. You must prepare yourself," Mr Napier continued in a soft tone.

How much worse could it get? Had her parents sold her at the local market like an unwanted piglet who was the runt of the litter?

Kitty's father rested his elbow on the mantel and concern pinched the corners of his eyes. "Your parents were not married when you were born. Winyard is your mother's maiden name. Your mother subsequently married a man who is not your father."

She let out a huff. The marks against her name multiplied. Beside *woman mage* would now be inscribed *bastard*.

"I struggle to grasp any memory of either my father or the man my mother married." Only vague memories drifted through her mind. A field. Sunshine on her face. Patting a soft lamb. Laughter.

Mr Napier smoothed his hand over the marble mantel, as though he imagined himself soothing the disruption in Sera's life his words created. "From what my man can gather, Mr Jones married your mother the week you were given to Lord Branvale."

The implication surged over Sera. Her mother didn't meet and marry the man within the span of a few days. They must have known each other for some time beforehand.

Had her mother's new husband insisted the child born out of wedlock be removed before he would marry her? Or had her mother shed any remnant of her old life before starting anew?

One thing, at least, was clear. "She didn't want me. I was a shameful secret to be brushed away."

TEN

Sera let the sadness flow through her, then pinched off the stream as another thought entered her mind. "Do I have any siblings?"

"Yes."

Sera gasped, speechless.

"Four half siblings ranging in age from twelve to five. From the discreet enquiries my man made, none are aware of your existence." Mr Napier kept a steady eye on Sera. Perhaps to judge when he had told her too much, so he might stop before she dissolved into tears?

But she would hear it all, no matter how it tore ribbons off her heart.

Kitty squeezed her hand. "They might not share the opinion of their father, Sera. Surely they would be delighted to know they have a half sister who is a powerful mage and holds the rank of duchess."

Or they might be horribly ashamed at being related to a bastard. Sera wasn't sure she could stomach the rejection of her half siblings. "I will think upon it, Kitty. Did Mr Jones say anything else about me?"

At this point, Mr Napier lowered his hand and laced his fingers together as he weighed some internal decision. "He does not believe the existence of a 'witch' has anything to do with him or his children."

Kitty snorted. "Well, at least they won't be turning up on your doorstep with their hands out. You do not need them, Sera. I am sorry you will never meet your mother, but do not forget that you have a family even if the same blood does not flow in our veins."

Sera reached over and took her friend's hand. "I could not conjure a better sister than the one you have been to me."

Mr Napier coughed into his hand. "There is the matter of your father."

Sera braced herself and leaned back on the sofa. "Let me guess. He wants nothing to do with his illegitimate offspring, either, and is relieved I do not carry his name."

"Actually, he would be delighted to meet you. Nora endeavoured to keep you from him when you were a child. He is a stone mason, now working not too far from London." His lips quirked in a smile.

"My father wishes to see me?" She sat forward, unsure she'd heard his words correctly.

"He does. He has been under the mistaken impression you wanted nothing to do with him. He sought to respect your decision by not making himself known to you." Mr Napier strode back to the desk and picked up a letter.

A million emotions flowed through Sera all at once. She didn't know whether to laugh, cry, or shout. "Truly?" she whispered.

"Truly. You have one parent who wishes to claim you. Speaking as a father, I have always considered you a daughter, but I am willing to share that honour with another. When my man told him you were seeking information about him, he wrote to you." He held out the letter, the page folded into a neat square.

Sera stared at the letter, sealed with a drop of red wax and a thumb print, her father's direction on the back. Then she leapt to her feet and wrapped her arms around Mr Napier's waist. "Thank you. I shall journey out to see him the day after tomorrow. I cannot wait longer than that."

Kitty's father laughed and placed a kiss on the top of Sera's head. "I will have my carriage take you there. It's a few hours' journey and I'd rather know you were comfortable for it."

"I will come with you," Kitty offered.

Sera smiled at her friend. "I would appreciate your support."

"Support? I'm going because I am dashed curious to meet him and cannot wait until the end of the day when you return with your tale!" Kitty grinned.

Sera hugged the letter to her chest. Her first contact with her father. She fought an instinct to rip it open and devour his words now. No, she would wait for the privacy of her house. When she had time to savour each line. Until then, the letter was tucked securely in a deep pocket of her gown.

"I have a question that you might be able to answer, Mr Napier," Sera asked.

"Oh? I shall endeavour to answer if I can."

"You mentioned that some people had unfortunate encounters with Lady Zedlitz during her last trip to England—some mishap with a cow. Do you remember any further details about that?" Surely the addition of a cow made any story more memorable.

He scratched his chin. "If memory serves, Lady Zedlitz wanted some beast, but was outbid by another noble. Then things turned mighty odd. Not long after, the man stripped himself naked and sat upon the king's throne with the beast standing beside him. No one could figure out how he had walked the cow through the palace without a comment from anyone."

An odd tale indeed. Had Lady Zedlitz influenced the man's behaviour? "Do you remember who it was?"

"No, unfortunately, apart from some minor Scottish knight. I think he had covered himself in blue paint as some form of protest. The scandal sheets were full of it at the time, if any copies are still to be found." Mr Napier returned to his desk.

They took their leave and as they left the study, Sera linked her arm through Kitty's and leaned closer. "I sent messages this morning to both Abigail and Hugh. There is something that requires your assistance and I thought to convene a meeting here to discuss it." While she had come to love her small and cozy home in Soho, the parlour wasn't large enough for too many visitors. Nor did she want Inge to overhear their conversation, however unlikely.

Kitty cocked her head and her eyes sparkled. "Something that involves murder?"

"Yes. I asked them to come here at one o'clock, if they were free." She glanced at the grandfather clock in the foyer, the stubby hour hand almost pointing to the one as the minute hand dragged itself past the eight.

"Abigail will arrive on the dot of one, if she is available. How punctual is...*Hugh?*" Kitty mimicked Sera's use of the surgeon's given name.

Sera considered their interactions. Hugh had appeared in either her parlour or at court of his own volition, with no summons necessary. Or she had sought him out. This was the first time she had reached out and requested his presence. She was about to tell her friend she didn't know when there was a rap on the door.

The butler appeared and strode forward to pull open the large door to reveal a familiar tall, broad shape.

"Ah. Eagerness makes him early," Kitty murmured into Sera's ear.

"Hugh. Thank you for sparing me your time," Sera said as she walked towards him.

Hugh glanced to the butler and crossed the threshold. He took Sera's hand and kissed her knuckles. "I always have time for you, Sera, and your message implied some urgency."

"Let us go into the parlour and wait for Abigail." Kitty gestured to the open door across from her father's study. She cast a knowing smile at Sera and then led the way.

Hugh kept hold of Sera's hand until the butler

coughed. Then he let her go like a schoolboy caught stealing a warm cookie from the kitchen.

"I think he is waiting for your hat and coat," Sera whispered when the surgeon appeared confused.

"Oh. Yes." With a bashful look, he slid off his hat and coat and handed them over.

While they waited for Abigail, Sera cast a protective spell around the parlour to ensure not a single word escaped. After some minutes of polite small talk, another knock came upon the front door. Sera and Kitty held their positions—Lady Abigail didn't approve of people rushing out to greet others in the entrance. They waited for the butler to announce her.

With their greetings out of the way, Kitty played hostess and requested tea. Then they all settled in a loose circle. Kitty sat in an armchair opposite Hugh. Lady Abigail, with ramrod straight spine, perched on a sofa next to Sera.

"This is all rather serious and secretive. What fun." Questions burned in Abigail's eyes.

Sera clasped her hands in her lap. "There is a matter that I cannot solve alone. It requires the assistance of all of you."

"To do with the murder of Lady Zedlitz." Kitty's gaze darted to Hugh and back again.

"Yes, but let me begin this story some years ago. When I first met Lord Branvale at the age of five, he placed a copper bracelet around my left wrist. He said it was a gift to welcome me into his home." The memory of that day remained as clear as crystal in her mind. The *click* as the bracelet sealed itself. The stab of pain that had driven into her small wrist and shot up her arm. It had stolen her breath and made tears burn in her eyes. She had cried out and Lord Branvale had taken her to task for being ungrateful.

"I remember it. A plain thing, but given you always wore it, I assumed it had sentimental value. Although I see you have discarded it on reaching your majority," Abigail said.

Sera rubbed her wrist. "No. You see, I *couldn't* remove it. The bracelet contained potent magic. It drew on my magic to suppress my ability."

Abigail gasped. Hugh's fingers curled into the leather arms of his chair. Kitty remained silent; Sera had already disclosed the effects of the bracelet to her.

"All those years, while the council mocked me as feeble and bemoaned the fact that my feminine body was a vessel for my line of power, it turned out the bracelet acted as a damper. That plain piece of jewellery was a most effective leash," Sera said.

Abigail leaned forward, her eyes wide. "The council did that to you, and your gift is truly greater than they claimed?"

"My magic flows through me now like a river that has washed away a dam," Sera replied. She couldn't answer the first part of Abigail's question. If the council had deliberately shackled her, she did not think Lord Ormsby would be silent on the subject. Until she knew who was involved, there were certain details she intended to hold close to her chest. Even if that meant being selective in what she told dear Abigail. Her grandfather, after all, was also a mage.

"How marvellous. I wondered, the night of my soirée. The images you conjured were glorious and far beyond the ability of any dim light such as the council claimed you to be." Abigail squeezed Sera's hands. "But how did you remove the cuff?"

"On the stroke of midnight when I turned eighteen and came into my full ability, I had enough residual magic to detect something wrong with the bracelet. The strands it used to bind my magic became visible. After some hours of effort, I managed to remove them all, and as I freed my physical form from the last thread, the bracelet fell open." It had taken her hours of sweat and white agony as, one by one, she removed the threads spun through her body and driven into her veins.

"Do you think my grandfather did that to you?" Worry dropped over Abigail's features and she wet her lips.

"He was still Speaker when I came to Branvale. But surely if it were a council edict, Lord Ormsby would have known. When I appeared to take my seat, he would have insisted I keep the damned thing clamped around my wrist." Sera dug her nails into her palms. No one would ever put a leash on her or her magic again.

The message she'd found on Branvale's ensorcelled paper implied another sought to deceive the council, and keep her true ability a secret from them. *There cannot be another Nereus.*

The frown deepened on Abigail's brow and she worried her lip. "I will discuss the matter with Grandfather the next time he emerges from his library and graces us with his presence. Seeking an audience with him is more difficult than approaching the king."

"How does this bracelet that shackled your magic relate to the death of Lady Zedlitz?" Kitty asked.

"The night I encountered Lady Zedlitz at the Edgecombe ball, we had a disagreement about who should curtsey to whom." Sera now knew that Lady Haas had muttered the unkind phrase as the margrave's mother swept through the Austrian party.

"You are a duchess—very few outrank you now," Abigail said, confident in the minutiae of etiquette.

Sera nodded to her friend for supporting her stance. "Lady Zedlitz grabbed my hand and insisted I curtsey to her. Against my will, my knees buckled. I sensed the spell forcing me to act in a way I did not want. When I looked down, I spied a cobweb of magic sneaking from under the bracelet and burrowing into my skin. It took little effort to remove it, but in that moment I realised what she wore. A bracelet similar to mine. Except hers acted on other people."

"It is possible she was murdered for the bracelet, if it has the power to influence others to act against their wishes," Hugh murmured.

"A charmed bracelet that can compel others to do your bidding." Kitty rose and paced to the fireplace, her hands taking flight as she spoke. "You could change the course of a nation. Take over Parliament. Force the king to abdicate and place yourself on the throne."

"Or pull strings from behind the scenes and become puppeteer of the country," Abigail mused. Then she shook her head and fixed Sera with a determined stare.

"It must be found if it was not among Lady Zedlitz's belongings. What help do you need from us?"

Sera had thought ahead how her friends might aid in the hunt. "Kitty and Abigail, you are placed in society to hear any rumours that might help us detect a victim of the bracelet. Keep your ears open to any whisper of someone acting out of character, or doing something others believe they wouldn't normally do."

"And what of me? How can I assist?" Hugh leaned forward in his chair, his elbows resting on his thighs.

She met his warm gaze and it cast a glow over all of her. "Lord Zedlitz said the bracelet changed his mother's character. Magic takes a toll and demands a payment. On me, it drew upon my magic to suppress my ability and left me physically weakened. I believe it hardened Lady Zedlitz's heart, and made her implacable and bitter. Physically, it might have been responsible for her hair loss and the lesions on her scalp. Whoever wears it now, their family may become concerned by such changes in them and think it has a medical origin. Lord Viner might be consulted, or you, since many at court are familiar with your service to the king. It is a slim possibility, but one we must be open to."

Hugh rubbed his clean-shaven chin. "Such a change in behaviour, if extreme enough, might be perceived as an emotional disorder. Such things are kept secret, especially in light of the changes affecting King George. Imagine if the court thought his disorder contagious. If a noble is using the bracelet, I agree there is a chance a concerned relative will seek a private word with my mentor, and by extension, me."

"Lieutenant Powers is using his skills to find the murderers. We will use ours to locate the bracelet." Sera hoped that among the five of them, they would discover who had stolen it—and Lady Zedlitz's life.

With tasks allocated, conversation turned to other matters.

"I am pleased to hear you are considering the council's candidates for your husband, Sera." Abigail beamed like a proud parent. "I have my own suggestions, of course, whom I think will be more suitable. I shall send their names to you, along with a brief description, when I return home."

"What? You cannot seriously be thinking of marriage?" Kitty uttered the words in a sharp tone and turned an equally sharp gaze upon Sera.

"Sera is one of the most eligible young women in England, if not Europe." Unvoiced pain simmered behind Hugh's eyes. "Quite apart from her beauty and intelligence, she is a duchess and a formidable mage. Men would fight bloody tournaments to win her hand."

"Well, if blood sports are involved, this might be a tolerable process to watch." Kitty perked up at the idea.

"There will be no tournaments," Sera said, even though she rather liked the concept. "Considering a thing does not mean doing the thing. But I will listen to the counsel of those who have my best interests at heart." Which was her polite way of saying the candidates the council pushed forward had no chance with her. Lord Ormsby wanted a solution that suited him, not Sera.

"There is much to consider in selecting one's partner in matrimony. Contracts to negotiate. I hope I am not too premature in saying I will have my own announcement soon." Abigail twisted a ring on her right hand. "Viscount Helensvale has spoken to my father."

Conflicting emotions arose in Sera at her friend's choice of future husband. Viscount Helensvale was the son of the Duke of Ketley, the man who had called her a witch and accused her of murder before the whole court. She could only hope the son didn't share his father's disposition or prejudices.

"Yours will be a spectacular wedding and you know I will provide whatever magical enhancements you want," Sera offered.

Strangely, the mood in the parlour became more sombre, not joyful, with talk of weddings, and soon Lady Abigail rose to her feet. "I must be on my way. I will seek my grandfather's counsel as soon as I can and tell you anything I learn."

In the foyer, Sera pulled Hugh to one side as Kitty and Abigail made their farewells. "I am to have my first dinner with Contessa Ricci in two weeks' time, once her potion is ready. She has agreed that you might attend, if you are available?"

His posture straightened and a question burned in his eyes. "You would have me accompany you?"

"Of course. You are my friend. I am not a married woman yet." The words caught in her throat. Marriage seemed horribly restrictive when a woman couldn't entertain a male friend. Although hers would never be a conventional marriage, should she ever walk that path.

Curiosity returned to his gaze. "Then I would be delighted to dine with you and the Contessa. I shall procure a carriage and collect you at the appropriate hour."

Her skin tingled in a reaction no other man provoked. While they would not be entirely alone, and the vampyre saw much with her preternatural eyes, it would be her first intimate evening with the surgeon. The coming days gave Sera much to look forward to. And at least this time she was not being weighed down by an accusation of murder.

Back in her home, Sera trod the stairs to her bedroom and shut the door. Sitting on the corner of the bed, she drew her father's letter from her pocket and slid her thumb under the seal. Unfolding it, she found only two scant lines, but the words made tears mist her eyes.

I HAVE THOUGHT of you every day. Know that you have always had a place in your father's heart.

ELEVEN

The next day, Sera had a busy morning inspecting and reinforcing the walls of King's Bench prison in Southwark. As she laboured to fix cracks in both stone and spells, she pondered what lesson Lord Ormsby was attempting to impart to her by this task. Perhaps she was supposed to contemplate how she would end up in such a drab grey place if she didn't do as she was told. The idea made her laugh out loud and she startled her guard. One didn't set the fox to guard the henhouse. Or allow a mage to learn the construction of prison walls if one wished to confine her at a later date.

She trudged back to her home in the early afternoon with joints sore from kneeling to examine foundation stones and hands covered with ingrained grime. Magic never seemed to get her skin as clean as a good scrub with hot water and soap. With the assistance of Vicky, they soon had a steaming tub ready before the window in her room. After a reviving bath, she dressed and headed downstairs. An insistent knock on the door made her pause as Elliot trotted along the hall to answer it.

"Keep your hair on," he muttered as the rapping grew louder.

His flinging open the door revealed the elegant form of Lord Zedlitz, hand raised to knock again. His eyes widened in surprise, as though he had not expected to find anyone at home.

"Lord Zedlitz, what a lovely surprise," Sera said as she descended the staircase.

He rushed across the threshold and practically threw his hat at Elliot. When she extended her hand, he caught it and kissed her knuckles.

"Lady Winyard, it is splendid to see you." His gaze shot around the tiny foyer as though he searched for something.

"Why don't you come through to my little parlour? Elliot, tea please, and any of that fabulous cake Rosie makes with the currants. If there is any left." Rosie had asked Sera to ensorcel the pantry to stop the footman raiding her supply of cakes and biscuits.

Leading the way, Sera gestured to the small seating arrangement in the parlour.

The margrave waited until she sat, then perched on the edge of the armchair. One hand curled and tensed on his knee. He swallowed, his Adam's apple bobbing above the linen of his cravat. "You are well?"

"Yes, thank you. Were you able to make suitable

arrangements for your mother?" The visit surprised her so soon after his mother's death. But grief affected people differently. Perhaps he preferred to be out combing the streets for her murderer rather than shut up in his room. Some people sought action over reflection.

His hand clenched tighter and he rapped it against his thigh. "Yes. Mr Miles was most helpful. *Mutter* has been...preserved and interred in a private mausoleum made available to us until we return to Austria." He stumbled over the word *preserved*, as though it left an unpleasant taste in his mouth.

"I am sorry your visit here has been marred by such a horrible event. But I assure you we are doing all we can to find those responsible and bring them to justice." *And find the bracelet*, she added to herself.

He nodded and they fell silent.

Elliot entered with a tea tray and placed it on the low table between them. The footman stared at them, shrugged, and left without uttering a word.

Sera poured tea and considered what to say that was appropriate when someone's mother had been murdered. She knew little of Lord Zedlitz and settled on a topic about his home that Kitty had mentioned to her. "I heard about a dish called *schnitzel* that comes from Austria. I confess I have never heard of it, but understand it is rather tasty."

He huffed. "It is a national dish of very thin veal that is dipped in egg, covered in a crumb, and then fried. Our schnitzel delights many an English noble-woman once she has nibbled upon it."

"Really? I would love the recipe for my cook. Unless it is some national secret?" If Sera couldn't travel outside England, at least she might have a culinary adventure and taste dishes from other countries at home.

"Inge could write it down. She is very clever and will know the full recipe." A smile lit his eyes as he spoke of the noblewoman.

"I shall ask when she returns." Sera slid the plate of cake towards him.

"She is not here?" His gaze darted around the room, as though checking she wasn't hiding behind the scant furnishings.

"No. Elliot said she has taken a walk." She sent a tendril of magic out to the location spell that attached to Inge when she left the house. Judging from the distance, the other woman was not too far away.

"Oh." The man looked positively crestfallen, and Sera wondered that his interest was far more than a lord enquiring after a former servant, or even an upset noblewoman.

Sera tried to find a lighter topic, and decided on something niggling in her mind. "Did you accompany your parents when they came to England last time?"

"Oh, yes. I was fifteen at the time, and my parents wanted to compare Oxford to our European universities. They also came here to procure the hairy Scottish cattle. Father wanted to crossbreed it with our stock to produce an animal that held its condition better in the winter months."

That fit with what Mr Napier had recalled of a

dispute over cattle that ended poorly for the noble involved. "Did your parents find the cattle they wanted?"

Lord Zedlitz rolled his eyes upward as he searched for the relevant memories. "Not at first. A noble won the beast at auction and *Mutter* was most displeased. *Vater* approached the man and they tried to repurchase the animal, a fine bull."

"Did he part with it for an additional cost?" How fascinating that breeding bulls were as prized as a magnificent stallion.

"No. He said the animal had to stay on British soil and not be sent to Europe. Then he laughed at my mother. I remember that quite distinctly, for it made her angry. She lunged at the man and grabbed his arm. *Vater* had to prise her fingers loose."

Sera sipped her tea and considered the story. His mother must have reached for the man's arm hoping to use the bracelet to force him to give her the beast. "And did he change his mind and offer the animal to your mother?"

Zedlitz frowned. "No. We acquired it at a cheaper price after the man was disgraced."

"Ah. The incident at the palace. Do you recall the details?" She set her cup down, and leaned forward.

The margrave's shoulders heaved as he laughed, before he continued the tale. "A few days later he was found sitting on the king's throne, naked and painted blue, while holding the bull's lead. I believe King George seized the man's property and banished him from court. The bull was going to be slaughtered for the insult to the presence chamber, but my mother purchased it before it could be butchered."

Her hand tightened on the cup. "Do you remember the man's name?"

Zedlitz tapped a finger against his teacup. "No, I am sorry. As a youth I found the details of the noble removing all his clothes and painting himself blue amusing, but did not learn his name."

Given what the man had done, Sera imagined many people would remember it, though Mr Napier had not when she asked him. While an amusing anecdote, she couldn't see how it could have any relevance to Lady Zedlitz's death. Perhaps Abigail would know about his disgrace and banishment.

"Is Inge well?" Zedlitz asked.

"I think she is comfortable here, and finding ways to occupy her time. She said it was nice to have nothing much to do after the long hours in your mother's service." The noblewoman's posture had stiffened when she spoke of her former employer. What had driven Lady Zedlitz to make the young woman a servant, rather than offering her home to a woman of a good family robbed of her parents?

The teacup in the margrave's hands rattled on its saucer. "My mother should never have done that to Inge." He seemed to snatch the words from Sera's thoughts.

A kernel of an idea sprouted. "You admire her."

His hand tensed, then he stretched out his fingers.

"Yes. Under the most trying circumstances, she has maintained her dignity."

"More than admire her, perhaps?" Now that the idea had taken root, it refused to be dislodged.

"Inge is gently bred and noble by birth. Our castle should have been a safe place for her until..." His voice trailed away and he sipped his tea.

"Until?" Sera prompted. Now that he had begun his tale, she wanted to know how it had unfolded. It seemed that like Cinderella, Inge had been cruelly treated by a sort of stepmother figure.

"Inge and I grew up together. There are not so very many nobles in our *Bezirke*—our district—and they were all invited to dances at the castle." He set down the cup and saucer to take a large bite of his slice of cake.

"Did you dance together?" Sera's hands moved of their own accord as her mind conjured a hilltop castle, and a magnificent ballroom where the couple twirled as snow fell outside the windows. The scene hovered above the teapot and faint notes of music floated from the ethereal castle.

His smile broadened at the enchanted scene. "Yes. Often."

Understanding crept over Sera. A romance had bloomed between the two young people. Sera wondered if the forthright Inge had not met with approval from Lady Zedlitz. "Why do you think your mother made Inge a maid?"

He let out a sigh and leaned back in the armchair.

The conjured castle faded away as Sera waited for him to speak. After several moments, she grew tired of waiting. "No one will overhear us in my home. Protective spells keep out prying eyes or ears."

Lord Zedlitz pressed a thumb and forefinger to the bridge of his nose. Then he lowered his hand and began. "*Mutter* did not like Inge, who is intelligent and outspoken. That is also why my mother insisted I could not talk to you at the ball. She sought a meek daughter-in-law who required less...control. My parents declared Inge unsuitable to be the future Lady Zedlitz and said I was to marry a wealthy noble from Vienna. We were not deterred and continued to see each other in secret. I think *Mutter* suspected. Not long after, fire struck the Wessler household. Inge had climbed out of her window to spend time with me and—thank God—was not in the house at the time." He turned his face away and drew a shuddering breath.

She would have perished, too. An uncharitable thought swirled through Sera—had Lady Zedlitz caused the fire? It would have been easy to touch a servant and tell them to spill hot coals over a wooden floor.

"When my mother suggested Inge join our household, I thought she had relented and meant to announce her as my fiancée while we planned the wedding. Instead, she pressed Inge into service. Whenever I tried to escape with Inge, I found I could not leave the castle and my feet stuck to the stones." His jaw clenched.

No doubt Lady Zedlitz had influenced their actions with the bracelet and ensured her son could never defy her. Like a fairy tale, the wicked stepmother had now been vanquished. She resided in a British mausoleum until her return journey to the Continent, and the couple could be together. But unlike fairy tales, laws had to be observed. Such as not murdering the obstacles in your path to a happily-ever-after.

Sera baited her trap in the vain hope he would confess. "Now you are free to wed as your heart desires."

"I will marry Inge, but the situation is complicated. Many in our delegation are against it and believe a margrave cannot marry a maid. If they report their suspicions to the emperor, he may command me to marry another. Then there are those who suspect I murdered *Mutter* to remove her from our path." He flashed a quick smile in her direction.

Sera bit her lip, since the exact same thought lurked in her mind. "What will you do, marry in secret?"

"I would marry her here, but Inge wishes to be wed in the church beside her parents' graves so they might, in a way, attend. And yet I cannot stay away from her. What am I to do, Lady Winyard? If I visit here on a regular basis, I fear people might talk and rumours will still fly to the emperor's ears." He spread his hands wide at the situation he found himself in.

There were a number of spells that would mask his appearance to allow for visits, but they would still need to explain his absences from the palace. Sera considered a number of different options.

The front door rattled as Inge returned from her walk. She burst into the parlour with a pink glow to her cheeks and excitement in her eyes. "Otto!" she exclaimed. Then she froze on spotting Sera.

Lord Zedlitz rose from his chair and rushed to Inge, taking her hands in his. "I believe Lady Winyard is an ally. She knows of my desire to marry you."

"Oh." The noblewoman turned an appraising gaze to Sera that reminded her of Kitty's keen, questioning look.

"I am sure that if you wished to wed in London in secret, it could be arranged." Sera imagined many couples knocked on church doors in the dead of night for a hurried ceremony. Once the two were married, the emperor could do nothing to stop them. Unless he threw them in prison, which wouldn't be a desired outcome.

Inge shook her head and pulled her hands away. "No. I will not do this under cover of darkness, as though our love is wrong. I will wed in our village, beside my parents, with our friends as witnesses."

"We will be in England for some months, my love. I cannot go that long without visiting you." His eyes widened in alarm and he glanced at Sera.

"I could cast an enchantment to disguise your appearance when you visit here, but we will still need to explain your frequent absences from court. People will talk." What they needed was a way for him to openly call on Sera and dampen any rumours before they started.

"Lady Winyard must be looking for a husband.

Why do we not put it about that you are courting her? Let our fellow nobles think that is the reason for your visits here." Inge said the words with a firmness that verged on a pronouncement.

Sera closed her eyes and rolled them behind her lids. Why was everyone so fixed on marrying her off? A refusal rushed up her throat, but Sera swallowed it down. As a ruse, the idea had merit. A temporary understanding would allow Lord Zedlitz to see his beloved, and it might also stop the Mage Council's pressuring her to select one of their candidates. Lady Abigail had introduced them for a reason, which meant she certainly thought the margrave a potential match. Entertaining him as a fake suitor would allow Sera time to consider her next move. It would also keep the Austrian couple close. If they had orchestrated the murder, they might inadvertently reveal the evidence Lieutenant Powers needed.

The more Sera mulled over the idea, the more she saw the potential for a little fun. The Mage Council would assume that if she married the margrave, he would settle in England. Imagine if she suggested how much she wanted to see the peaks of the Tyrol and live in a fairy-tale castle. Surely it would make them realise their mistake in insisting she marry.

Lord Zedlitz turned to her. "Please consider this, Lady Winyard. I would be indebted to you."

She couldn't stand in the path of true love. Her agreement would allow Inge and Lord Zedlitz's story to unfold right under her roof. How convenient. "I would be delighted to consider you as a fake suitor for my hand, Lord Zedlitz."

Inge clapped her hands together. "Then it is settled." A worry line ploughed across her brow. "You do understand, my lady, that we are engaged and Otto would never marry an Englishwoman, whether she were a mage or not."

Sera had no intention of putting herself at risk of being smothered in her bed if the other woman thought she had designs on her betrothed. "I completely understand. You will not be able to appear in public together, unfortunately, unless I accompany you. But you will be free to see each other under my roof." She had spoken the truth when she'd told the margrave that her home already had spells embedded in the walls and windows to keep out prying ears and eyes. That protection would extend to the couple.

Lord Zedlitz took Sera's hands. "Thank you for doing this. Perhaps I might be so bold as to suggest you call me Otto, on informal occasions at least, to lend weight to our plan?"

"And you must refer to me as Sera, as only my close friends do." Sera might have to include Abigail in their secret, otherwise her friend would have the wedding planned by the end of the week.

He shook her hand as though they concluded a business transaction. "If there is any service I can render you, you have only to ask."

The perfect opening for a question lurking in the back of her mind. "Do you remember the tale of how

Lord and Lady Haas came to be married? Inge said you were present at the ball where they announced their surprise engagement."

Otto made a noise in the back of his throat and cast his gaze to the ceiling in thought.

"Tea?" Sera asked Inge. She waved her hand and summoned an additional cup from the kitchen. It whooshed through the open door like a squat pigeon.

"Please." Inge took the chair opposite Sera.

"Ah! I remember," Otto said at last. "Her family suffered a sad fate, not unlike Inge's. Her parents are much impoverished now. A proud man who once commanded servants does manual labour to feed his wife and keep a roof over her head."

While curious about how the family could fall so far, Sera didn't see how the circumstances of Lady Haas's family in Austria had anything to do with the death of Lady Zedlitz in London. "Do you think she married Lord Haas to provide for her family?"

"It is possible. At the time, Liesel was much in love with Erik, a friend of mine. I thought they had an understanding between them. Lord Haas is thirty years her senior and I always wondered why she married him. We assumed she and Erik had some argument. He was quite heartbroken and has not married another." Otto took a plate from Inge, with another slice of cake upon it.

"Did your mother ever pass comment about the match?" Sera turned the situation around to examine it.

"I believe she found it amusing." He bit into the cake and made an appreciative noise.

An idea scratched at the base of Sera's skull. Had Lady Zedlitz used the bracelet to force the match? It warranted further investigation, and might provide a motive for Lady Haas after all. She needed to assemble her friends to discuss it.

TWELVE

The next day, Sera was to visit her father. Kitty collected her, a large basket on the seat opposite. "I had Cook pack us a picnic."

Delicious smells wafted from the basket and Sera's stomach grumbled, leaving her to wonder if she would last until midday. "On our return journey, I need to stop at a farm to examine a herd of cows. Apparently the farmer believes they are cursed and producing sour milk."

"Are you sure you are the best mage for the task?" Kitty managed to say as her shoulders shook with laughter.

"They will probably produce blood after I have touched them, as witches are known to do with cattle." Sera still waged a silent battle with Lord Ormsby. He continued to allocate her tasks carefully selected to either humiliate or pitch her directly against those who saw her as a crooked, wart-nosed witch.

Mr Napier had given the driver directions, and

after two hours the carriage turned onto a rough dirt track that opened into a meadow with fluffy sheep quietly grazing.

"I'll have to stop here, Miss Napier. Don't want to get us stuck," the driver said as the footman jumped down.

"Of course." Kitty climbed out after Sera.

Sera surveyed the building under construction—a stone church, by the looks of the pointed section at one end. The walls were unfinished, wooden scaffolding clinging to one side. Piles of stones sat in the grass and two men chipped at them with hammers and chisels. One looked up at their approach and set down his tools.

There was no need for introductions. Possessing a good height and dark brown hair, Sera recognised echoes of herself in her father—though of course his occupation added muscular bulk to his appearance that she would never possess. He wiped his hands down his trousers and then through tousled hair streaked with grey. His face might be weathered by time and the environment, but nothing could diminish the joy.

"My girl," he choked out, then his blue eyes filled with tears.

He held out his arms and Sera rushed to him. Her father's strong body shook as he cried and stroked her hair. Sera let her own tears free. She had found one parent and learned she was loved, even if she'd never known it until now.

After several quiet moments in each other's embrace, he held her at arm's length to study her features, and wiped her tears with a roughened hand.

Sera needed a walk after the long carriage ride. "Why don't you show me around this building while we talk?"

"I'll have luncheon ready by the time you return." Kitty, ever pragmatic, set about organising the meal they'd brought. The footman carried over blankets and cushions. He even drove the stand for a large umbrella into the ground to shade the ladies.

Sera linked arms with her father and they took a leisurely stroll around the base of the church while he told her stories of herself as a young child. "When Nora allowed you to come see me, you loved helping and getting your hands dirty."

She let out a laugh. "Nothing has changed there. I often have dirt under my nails."

"Your love of playing outside used to drive your mother to distraction. She was always trying to keep you clean, as though you were a vase on display on a table." He huffed a sad laugh. "It got harder and harder to spend any time with you. Nora always had some excuse or other to keep us apart."

"She wouldn't let you see me?" A mage had so few years with their parents. What a shame her time with her father had been so limited.

"You were a happy accident, and I would have married her if she'd have had me. Oh, how I loved her. A summer with a simple stone mason was one thing, but she didn't want to be shackled to me for life. Nora had her eyes set on bigger and brighter things. Jones is a merchant and rather well off, and he didn't like me around while they were courting." He flashed her an embarrassed smile and turned his gaze downward.

Given that Sera resisted all pressure to marry herself, she would never think differently of her mother for not rushing into matrimony. Women should be able to experience physical love in the same way that men were encouraged to sow their wild oats. As a mage, Sera had methods open to her to ensure she only conceived when she felt ready to welcome a child into her life. How would the lives of all women change if they could also decide on the right time to bear a child? No more would the working-class women give birth year after year until they had dozens of hungry mouths to feed or the poor women dropped dead from exhaustion. She made a note to discuss the matter with Hugh. Sera could brew a potion he might distribute discreetly.

"How did you discover I was a mage?" She knew little of the process, other than that an ensorcelled bowl in the mage tower lit up when a mage died. The blue mist rising from the liquid in the container revealed the location of the new mage, born in that moment to whom the deceased's powers had transferred.

He slowed and rested one hand on the stonework. "A mage arrived in town and asked about any newborns. Yours was the only recent birth. He looked right shocked to remove your swaddling and discover you were a girl. I heard him mutter there must have been some sort of mistake and he'd have to contact the council. While he used his magic to ask them what to do, I snatched you out of Nora's arms and legged it."

Sera stopped and stared at her father. "You *stole* me?"

He grinned. "Damned right. I'd heard the rumours, and no one was going to smother my girl. I was working on a gatekeeper's cottage at the time, not far from where we lived. I went there. I might not have any magic, but I knew ways to protect you."

"Ways?" A shiver raced over her skin, as though other eyes watched her. Glancing up, Sera stared at a hideous stone gargoyle leaning over the corner of the church.

His gaze shifted to the watching gargoyle with its claws curled around the stones. "Illegal ways, if you catch my meaning."

"Unnaturals," she breathed. Curiosity surged. What creatures might her father enlist to protect her? Was this the reason the Mage Council had let her live —because her father had rallied an otherworldly defence?

"They're just people, you know, like us." He swallowed and patted the side of the building as though it were a dog.

"I entirely agree. I do what I can to protect those of my acquaintance, and am trying to find a way to protect them all by proposing a new law." Or rather, Mr Napier worked to ensure Unnaturals had the same rights as all Englishmen. Drafting legislation and championing it through Parliament was a slow process and they were only at the very beginning. Her friend's father had warned it might take years, if not decades, before they saw any success.

Benjamin let out a slow sigh. "That would be grand, if you could do such a thing."

Sera continued their walk around the construction. The church would be a beautiful place when it was finished, with large, arched windows to flood the interior with light. "Having begun the tale of our escape, you must tell me what happened and who protected us. Since I was given over by my mother when I turned five, I assume you were not successful?"

He grinned. "You're alive, aren't you?"

In their stroll, they had circled back to where the carriage and horses waited. Kitty sat on the blanket under the umbrella, an open book in her hands.

Sera gestured to the meal waiting for them. "You must tell the story over luncheon. That will save me from repeating every word for my dearest friend Kitty."

Kitty set aside her book and her eyes sparkled with delight. "What tale is this?"

"Apparently my father stole me away after I was born—out from under the nose of the mage who came to find the new vessel containing my line of magic." She turned to him. "Kitty is also enlightened and a friend to Unnaturals, so you do not have to omit that crucial component." Sera filled a plate for her father, then plucked a small pie from a plate and bit into it.

Kitty picked up a metal container that kept their tea warm, and saved Sera from having to reheat the water. She poured a large mug for Benjamin. "I am all ears."

Her father took a sip of the drink and then ate half a pie before beginning. "My father was a stone mason, and his father before him. Some things are passed from father to son, like tools and the skills we use. My father passed along a secret in addition to those. About the Unnaturals he worked with."

Sera studied the stone church with its partially completed walls. There was only one creature that sprang to mind when she thought of such a construction method. "Gargoyles helped you."

Benjamin nodded and finished the pie. "They're quiet types. Don't say much, but they're as loyal and solid as rock. They're also resistant to magic. Something to do with being so dense."

Sera didn't know that, and tucked the information away. She tried to dredge up memories of the creatures from the recesses of her mind, but couldn't recollect ever reading much about them. Clearly, she must search for books about Unnaturals to grow her knowledge.

"I knew I couldn't run far with you, and the mage and his men were close on our heels. When we reached the cottage, Jakob and Nat stood guard over us. The mage threw magical cannonballs at the gargoyles, but they batted them away like they were balls of wool." Benjamin paused to finish off his pie and then selected another from the plate.

Sera closed her eyes and let the scene play out in her mind. Her father cradling her to his chest as the gargoyles, with their monstrous wings spread, kept the battling mage at bay.

"That went on for a while. I shouted that Nat and Jakob could keep it up for years and that he must either let you live and grow into a woman, or I was giving you to the gargoyles to spirit away where none of us would ever see you again." His voice choked up on the last words and he took a long drink from his tea.

Kitty refilled the empty mug and pressed more food upon him. "Well played, Mr Cohen. With stone guardians who are impervious to magic, Sera could not have had better protectors. It would also have robbed the council of a mage until Sera eventually died of natural causes. I can only imagine how displeased the king would have been with such an outcome."

Her father would never have seen her, either. It must have pained him to make such a declaration in order to keep her safe. "I assume he agreed to your demands?"

"Not at first. He had to talk to some other mage at the council again. He stood off in the dark, waving his arms and yelling like he was angry at the moon." He munched his way through another pie.

"Do you remember who the mage was?" Suspicion suggested a name, but she wanted to hear it from the man who had been present when her fate was decided.

He gestured with the mug of tea. "Oh, it was the one who took you in—Lord Branvale."

The air left Sera's lungs with a *whoosh*. Her former guardian would have ended her life, if not for the actions of her father? But who had he consulted before he struck the deal? Only the Speaker of the Mage Council could have made such a decision. At the time of her birth Lord Rowan had held that position. But if he had proposed letting her live, why then had he kept himself apart from her when he could have nurtured her gift? She had many questions for

Abigail's grandfather, if she managed to secure an interview with him.

"Well, I never," Kitty whispered.

"Nor I." Sera's mind spun. What would have happened to her that night, if not for her father's quick actions? "I assume you extracted some sort of promise?"

He set down the empty mug and surveyed the other savouries and sweets Kitty had laid out for them. "I wasn't handing you over until I knew you'd be safe. He said there were problems, as some of the other mages on the council objected. They said women weren't fit to be mages. I said how did he know, when none of you were allowed to live?"

"I am grateful for your efforts. Without them, I wouldn't be here today. I'm assuming he managed to get some agreement from the council in the end." Sera held her cup in two hands, warming her skin. Lost in thoughts of that long-ago night, she hardly touched her luncheon.

Her father nodded around a sandwich. He swallowed before continuing. "It took long into the night. Nat held you and sat on the top of the wall we were building, while Jakob curled his claws around the stone on a lower course. Some of the villagers appeared carrying torches. They assembled on the grass behind the mage and his men."

That would have been a novelty—lit torches held aloft in defence of the witch. Or would they have ignited her funeral pyre if Branvale had commanded his men to take her life?

"Dawn was creeping over the horizon before a voice

spoke from the shadows. It was another mage using a fox to talk. He said the council had reached a consensus and you would be spared. Then Nat spoke up and said there had to be a blood oath sworn before she would let you go. I'd not heard of such a thing. I'm grateful that she had," Benjamin said.

A blood oath was a powerful type of magic. A mage tied their life force to their promise. If they broke their word or reneged on the bargain, their life force would ebb away as the blood was wiped from wherever they had imprinted the oath.

"There was more yelling at the fox in the bushes after that. Lord Branvale didn't see why it had to be him. Then their voices dropped to whispers. When he returned, he sliced his palm and pressed his thumb into the blood. Then he made his mark on Nat's granite arm. He swore that as long as the mark endured, he would be held to his promise to do everything in his power to see you to adulthood. Or his life would be forfeit."

Branvale had made himself her ally and protector, yet treated her with cool disdain. As the only mage present that night, he had clearly been forced to tie himself to the deal struck. Resentment could fester for years and would have explained his attitude towards her. How sad they'd never had the chance to clear the air between them and make a fresh start.

"A blood oath sworn on a gargoyle. How I wish I could see such a thing." She'd read about such oaths in books, but hadn't heard a whisper of any mage making one.

"I couldn't do much for you as a father, but I can do

that." Her father grinned at her, then turned to the worker chipping stone in the shade. "Nat!" he bellowed.

The mason put down her chisel and hammer. Taller and broader even than Hugh, Sera hadn't identified the person as female. Then she chided herself—she shouldn't have made assumptions about gender based solely on occupation and size.

In her human form, Nat had a square face and a muscular build. Her dark hair had been cut short with an uneven hand. Yet there was a gentleness to her grey eyes and in the slight pull of a smile at her lips. She moved with a light grace that belied her size.

"Lady Winyard." She bowed to Sera. "I am Natalie Delacour, at your service. It is pleasing to see that you have grown from the squalling babe into a fine woman."

"Was I really a bothersome baby?" she asked her father. She had no tales of her childhood, unlike those Mr Napier told about a very young Kitty. She hung on every little thing she learned about her early years.

He huffed a soft laugh. "Not usually. You lasted very well, considering I stole you away without any clean clothes or milk to feed you with. You normally quieted right down if we set you somewhere you could watch the wind rustle in the leaves."

"The mage made more noise than you when he realised his magic was useless against us. Although your cries were of a higher pitch." A deep laugh came from Nat's broad chest.

Sera jumped to her feet and embraced the gargoyle. She encountered solid warmth and Nat smelled of damp earth after a summer rain. "Thank you for what you did. If I can ever repay you for your kindness, you have only to ask."

Nat returned the hug. "I prefer to stay out of magical matters, but you are Benjamin's daughter and that makes you family to us, too."

Letting her go, Nat pushed her shirtsleeve up higher. A reddish mark on her biceps resembled a birthmark. Then the gargoyle made a partial shift, turning her arm to granite. The thumbprint remained as clear as the day it had been marked, carved into her hide by the blood oath.

Sera touched it with a fingertip. At last she had some of the answers she sought. "He tied his life to mine and because of it, the council finally let a girl live."

Now she could concentrate on determining who had placed the bracelet on her wrist to dampen her power, and whether it had been crafted by the same hand as the one worn by Lady Zedlitz.

THIRTEEN

The council kept Sera busy over the next few days. She found herself on the outskirts of London stomping through pigsties and considering how to make their homes warmer to keep the pigs happy. Or she stood on the banks of the Thames to examine items thrown up by the action of the river that might have a magical residue attached to them.

On returning to her home one afternoon, Sera pulled off her hat and tugged the pins out of her hair. Then she scratched her scalp with both hands, working her nails into itchy spots. She had laboured all day out in the sun with the hat wedged on her head. No more, she decided. Let her skin be kissed by the sun, what did she care? Hats and parasols were inconvenient. All she needed was a lotion to spread on her skin so that she didn't burn. She would give that some thought and brew a sample to test its effectiveness against the heat of the day.

Elliot crossed his arms and clucked his tongue. "It was a waste making you a duchess when most days, you come home looking like a filthy street urchin."

Sera grinned at him, her long hair now tousled and hanging around her face. "I rather think I bring a breath of fresh air to the title."

"That's not fresh air I smell." Elliot scrunched up his face.

Sera batted at him. "You're just grumpy because I don't have another midnight job for you. Something will come along, just wait. Have you had any more sightings of my shy visitor?"

Some weeks ago, Elliot had spotted a man staring at the house. Twice he had returned, each time circling closer but never knocking on the door. Nor had he yet attempted to break in through the kitchen.

"No. But I've got eyes watching for him. The local children are also enlisted and keen to provide guard duty." He tapped the side of his nose, indicating one of his *birdies* would report in if the man returned.

It warmed Sera's insides that the community had rallied around to protect her and watch her watcher. If he returned, they would discover him and determine whether he was friend or foe.

Inside the parlour, Sera found Inge bent over a piece of sewing in her lap. The low table had been dragged closer to her and held her open sewing box. A length of blue thread tried to escape over one side. Skeins of green sat together in the top tray. Beside her, a crumpled drawing perched on the arm of the chair. She appeared to be following a design of entwined flowers.

"Good afternoon, Inge. That is gorgeous work. What will you turn it into?" Sera flopped on the settee and pondered pulling off her boots and stockings.

The other woman glanced up, her smile turned to a frown at Sera's dishevelled appearance. "It will be a reticule when I am finished. I like to design and sew. It keeps my mind and hands busy."

"Really?" An idea sparked in Sera's mind. "Do you draw and make larger things, like dresses?"

Inge's hazel eyes lit up. "Oh, yes. I love to draw gowns. Not the stiff, formal things you English wear, but soft, flowing ones that are conjured from dreams. Lady Zedlitz would not let me make such dresses, nor were they practical for my daily tasks." She smoothed a hand over her plain woollen skirt.

Sera and Inge might have something else in common—aside from Otto. "Would you be interested in a commission to make me a gown while I have the pleasure of your company here?"

Inge's hands stilled on the embroidery. "What sort of gown?"

"A fellow mage and I are putting on a performance for the grand dinner the king is hosting for the Austrian delegation. I am to play Nyx, the night goddess. Could you design and sew me a gown that looks like an evening sky? I will enhance it with my magic, but if I had a suitable gown to wear, it would drain less magic from me." Sera could conserve her energy for the other elements of her performance if she didn't have to maintain a glamour over her clothing.

Inge set aside the piece of embroidery and grabbed

her notebook from beside the sewing box. Her pencil hovered over the paper. "A night goddess deserves a Grecian-style robe, *ja?*"

"A simple dress, yes. One that flows almost like water." Sera thought panniers were a ridiculous fashion. Some women were forced to walk through doorways sideways as the silly things grew in width. They looked like theatre stages waiting for the curtains to rise. Thankfully their use was fading and mostly reserved for court and ceremonies these days. Or when a lady needed to conceal a lover beneath her skirts.

Inge's pencil made sweeping lines on the page and Sera had to resist the urge to lean over her shoulder. Instead, she removed her boots and stockings so she could wiggle her toes. A quick sniff of her dress confirmed Elliot's assertion that a bath was most definitely in order.

"Would something like this be suitable?" Inge turned the book towards her. With a few simple strokes, she had outlined a floaty gown that fell to the ground and then rippled into a train. The top of the gown bared the arms and collarbone, as it had only thin straps holding up the bodice.

Sera imagined the dress constructed of inky black silk and scattered with glittering stars. "Oh, yes."

"I will require fabric, thread, notions, and somewhere to work." On a fresh sheet of paper, Inge wrote a list of supplies.

"Would the table in the dining room meet your needs? As to the rest, I will have Elliot show you where they might be purchased." The only table larger was the one in the kitchen, and Inge couldn't work there while Rosie was preparing meals.

"Yes, that would be sufficient. I could start today if your footman is free to carry my supplies." Inge's eyes sparkled and Sera was glad to have found a task the other woman would enjoy.

First Inge took Sera's measurements and jotted them in her notebook. Next Sera summoned Elliot, and asked him to take Inge shopping. She discreetly handed him a pouch with some of her hard-earned coin to pay for the purchases. Sera had yet to establish accounts with such shops as Inge would visit.

With those two heading off along the street, and before she sank into a hot bath, Sera sat at her desk to send messages to her friends, once again requesting their assistance. One went to Woolwich, where she hoped it would reach Lieutenant Powers in time. Others were directed to Hugh's attic room and the grander address of Lady Abigail. Once again they would gather in the lush, and larger, parlour of Kitty's home. Sera would present two of her friends with their ensorcelled rings. Sera's own was shaped like a peacock feather, complete with tiny eye. Kitty's resembled kestrel plumage. For Abigail, she made the ring with filigree work that resembled delicate lace.

———⟡———

On arriving at the Mayfair house the next day, Sera found Hugh pacing in the foyer, waiting for her. He rushed to her side with such a worried look on his face that Sera wondered if something terrible had befallen Kitty overnight.

"Hugh, is something amiss? Is Kitty well?" Then Kitty's voice drifted from the parlour and reassured Sera that whatever gnawed at Hugh, it wasn't illness or accident in the Napier household.

His brow furrowed. "London is swirling with rumours that you will wed Lord Zedlitz and leave us for Austria."

Sera snorted under her breath. *Perfect. Their plan worked.*

"Is it true, then?" he asked with a raw edge to his voice. His hand hovered near her, but didn't touch her, as though she were behind a sheet of glass and unreachable.

She swallowed a lump in her throat. Perhaps her plan had worked too well. Never would she want to hurt the gentle surgeon's feelings. She took one of his large hands in both of hers. "It is a ruse to allow me a little space to breathe. The Mage Council is insistent that I marry, as is the king. By entertaining Otto, who has no intentions towards me, they believe I am taking their demands seriously."

His shoulders heaved in a sigh and he rubbed away the worry line in his forehead. "If not him, then I am sure some other lord will be honoured to win your hand and claim you as his wife."

Kitty's idea to hold a tournament bubbled up in

Sera's mind. As if any amount of sword waving, no matter how jewel encrusted, could win her heart. Although she could arrange devious tasks to sort out who might be tolerable to admit to her presence.

Then her gaze dropped to his hand. One that did not wield a sword, but scalpel and needle. "I do not wish to marry."

He placed his other hand over hers, a gesture that reminded her of the clasping of hands at a wedding ceremony. "Not at all? Is there no one who makes your pulse race a little faster? No one whom you could imagine as your companion, spending quiet nights before a fire?"

She studied the broad planes of his face and his expressive brown eyes. He possessed an alchemy that reacted with her blood. But she had not yet decided what that meant, nor would she be rushed into any declaration. She liked him, enjoyed his company, and wanted to kiss him again. None of that amounted to any urgency to wed.

"I am not ready to marry, Hugh. There is so much to experience first. I do not think a husband would approve of the adventures I wish to embark upon."

He leaned a little closer and lowered his voice to a conspiratorial whisper. "I don't know about that. I think the right man would be there at your side through any adventure, ready to haul you out of a spot of trouble. Should you require it, of course."

She had no doubt that he would be steadfast at her side. Should she request it. "I promise that when the day arrives that I am ready to seriously consider matrimony, you will be the first to know." She broke open the warm cocoon he had made of their hands to place hers flat against his heart.

He met her gaze with a serious one. "On that day, I could never hope to reach so high as to even ask such a question of you. But know you will aways have my loyalty...and my heart."

Her own heart beat faster at his words. "Oh, Hugh. I would choose you over any castle in Austria, any English title, any fortune. But I fear that neither king nor council would ever approve such a match, even if I were so inclined. I am a game piece to them, which they seek to use to their advantage, and I have little choice in how I am played."

He raised her hand and kissed her fingertips. "I refuse to believe you see yourself as a pawn now. You, Sera, are in control of this game. I see you moving like a knight, and jumping out of any tight spot in which they try to snare you."

She wriggled her eyebrows at him. "I do prefer the unexpected move. Kitty and I rather fancy setting up a household of our own and scandalising society. We could hold salons such as they do in France. Only people with fascinating minds will be allowed to attend."

A slow smile spread across his face. "In that case, I would be a frequent visitor to your home. I think Miss Napier has some regard for my ability to conduct a conversation."

Sera linked her arm through his. "Indeed she does. It is a rare thing for a man to win Kitty's approval, but there are a few others who would be welcome at our table, such as Lords Loburn and Fitzfey. Now, shall we turn our minds to murder and finding this missing bracelet?"

In the parlour, Kitty conversed with Lieutenant Powers. The army man bowed to Sera as she entered.

"Lady Abigail sends her apologies—she is detained by an audience with her grandfather, but hopes to have something to share afterward," Kitty said.

"A summons from Lord Rowan is a rare thing and of course takes precedence over any request of mine." Sera hoped that old Lord Rowan might have stumbled across such enchanted jewellery in either his long life as a mage or during his scholarly pursuits. Even better if Abigail could persuade him to meet with Sera. She had other questions he might be able to answer. Particularly surrounding the night Branvale had made his blood oath.

The butler appeared in the doorway with a laden tray. After carrying it to Kitty for her approval, he laid out the contents on a low table. The tea set was painted a brilliant blue, accented with silver and white. A cake stand held thick slices of cake, Sera's favourite marzipan fruit, and sandwiches.

Sera took the seat next to Kitty on the settee. Hugh and the lieutenant settled into armchairs.

"Shall we begin our investigative society meeting?" She spoke in a light tone infused with humour.

"An investigative society, eh? We need a code name —that one is a bit of a mouthful." Powers waggled his moustache.

If Kitty were capable of giggling (she claimed it was a silly affectation of some women) Sera suspected she would have at the moustache's antics.

"Winyard's Warriors?" Hugh suggested, his gaze resting on Sera.

She snorted. "Lord, no. Don't name us after me. I think in honour of my great friend here, we could call ourselves the Kestrels. They are intelligent hunting birds, often overlooked due to being commonplace and not as exotic or large as some falcons. But they are brilliant at flushing out their quarry."

"You know they are my favourite bird, so I am certainly in agreement. What say you gentlemen?" Kitty asked her visitors.

Powers nodded his agreement. "Such a hunter is fitting, in my opinion."

"Then it is unanimous." Hugh's gaze kept darting to the stand of cake and his stomach let out an almighty grumble.

Kitty picked up a plate and, using delicate silver tongs, selected a large piece of cake and a meaty sandwich, which she passed to Hugh. "I suspect you did not have breakfast this morning."

A blush flared over his cheeks. "I also missed luncheon. I had rounds this morning and then a difficult arm to set, though I am hopeful the patient will keep the limb. After we adjourn here, I will return to check on his progress."

"I will have the kitchen prepare a hearty meal for you, before you leave. We cannot have you fainting on us. You might crack the timbers when you fall." Kitty bestowed a smile upon the surgeon. He must be high in her regard for her to worry about feeding him.

"Thank you, Miss Napier. I never refuse the offer of a meal." Hugh held the plate in one hand, but declined to eat until the rest of them were served.

"Returning to our business, I've not heard of anyone acting out of character—well, no more than the usual stupid antics of the bucks," Kitty said as she poured tea and handed it to Sera.

"Nor has Lord Viner had any recent requests concerning behavioural changes." Hugh took a diminutive cup in his large hands. Since his thumb was unable to fit through the handle, he held it by the rim, then placed it on a table beside his chair so he could devour the cake and sandwich.

Sera stared at the contents of her cup, playing with the wisp of steam and turning it into a sprite that danced as it broke free. "In talking with Lord Zedlitz, he at first thought the change in his mother was temporary or related to her grief over losing her mother. It was only in hindsight that he saw how thoroughly the bracelet altered her. There was also the physical manifestation with the itchy scalp, but that might have taken years, and we do not have that amount of time to wait."

"I have studied the features of a hundred footmen and guards, and not found the one who matches the description given by Miss Wassler." Powers stroked his goatee as he spoke. "Two other servants of the Austrians remember a man in the corridor that morning. Their accounts are similar in terms of description, but one mentions the same scar Inge recalls on the man's chin, while the other says he had no scar."

"Could it be two men of similar appearance? We are, after all, looking for two culprits." Hugh suggested.

Powers gave a shrug. "I will not discount any possibility. Or it could be one man who waited to assist someone within the foreign party. Witnesses are often unreliable in their recollections."

Sera set down her cup, the tea untouched. "I have two pieces of information to impart. For some years, there has been longstanding affection between Lord Zedlitz and Inge Wassler. However, his mother did not approve of the match. With her using the bracelet to control his actions, the margrave could not act as he wanted and elope with Inge."

Lieutenant Powers's eyes lit up. "An obstacle that has now been removed from their path. Have they said anything of it to you?"

"I thought it rather convenient that they are now free to wed. But apparently some impediments still remain. Due to Inge's fall through the ranks of society to the role of maid, many of the Austrian nobles believe her to be beneath Lord Zedlitz. Apparently he should seek the emperor's approval to marry the woman he loves."

"If they celebrated their nuptials here, then surely there is nothing the emperor can do if he disapproves? Although I cannot imagine why he would disapprove of such a Christian act as raising Inge to her former position among the nobility." Kitty passed around a plate with slices of cake so fat she must have had them cut to accommodate the appetites of the men.

Her friend's thoughts echoed Sera's own. But Inge's wish to marry close to her parents' graveside added a poignant reason for not being wed in England.

"You seem to have made greater progress than we, Lady Winyard. Did your new guest have any other light to shed on the murder?" Lieutenant Powers declined the cake, perhaps for worry that crumbs would catch in his elaborate facial hair.

"The other tidbit concerns Lady Haas and her substantially older husband. Their engagement was a surprise to everyone, including Erik, the young man she was much in love with and whom everyone assumed she would wed. Lord Zedlitz commented that his mother found it rather amusing that she had married a man thirty years her senior. It might mean nothing, or she may have manipulated events for her own reasons... or enjoyment."

"I shall dig a little deeper on that topic while I continue to pursue our footman with the scar on his chin." The army man tapped his booted ankle.

They chatted for a while longer and discussed possible motives within the Austrian delegation. When Sera rose to leave, it wasn't thoughts of murder that echoed in her mind, but instead Hugh's words about how the right man would be beside her through any adventure.

Surely such a man would also possess the courage to kiss her?

FOURTEEN

The following day began with a conundrum. Sera received two urgent and competing summons from King George and Lord Ormsby. Both demanded her presence that morning. She weighed the correspondence in her hands. Given the conversation of the previous day with Hugh, it wasn't too difficult to discern the motive behind the summons.

"News of my impending marriage to an Austrian noble has travelled quickly," she murmured.

Lord Ormsby would have to wait—the king took priority. Besides, a demure denial of any engagement before the entire court would be more satisfying than answering to Lord Ormsby in the secluded chamber at the mage tower. Sera penned a quick response to the Speaker, offering her apologies and saying she was required urgently by the king.

Then she found Vicky in the kitchen and asked for her help upstairs. Sera selected a new gown of blue silk with white trim. The combination of the shade of blue and white accent made her think of nautical adventures. Like a voyage to Europe. Next they piled her hair high and teased a few curls loose on either side of her face. A straw hat with a blue and white ribbon completed her fresh look.

By the time Sera descended the stairs, Elliot had fetched a carriage and it waited out in the street. At court, more than the usual number of courtiers had crammed themselves into the presence chamber, their sheer numbers indicating they expected some sort of spectacle to unfold. Yet again, Sera became the provider of entertainment, even when it involved her private life.

One gentleman stepped into her pathway. "Lady Winyard." He bowed. Somewhere in his forties, with a sprinkling of silver among his dark locks, he had a fleshy form and a worrying red tinge to his complexion. "I am Kenwood. Forgive my presumption, but I could not wait to be formally introduced."

The name niggled at her before she remembered where she had seen it—on the list handed to her by Lord Pendlebury. The man before her was one of their approved suitors who hoped to secure her abilities for his own advantage.

When she stared at him without reply, he chose to continue. "I had hoped to have the opportunity to know you better. Would you consider accompanying me to the theatre tonight?"

"I am sorry, Lord Kenwood, but both the king and the Mage Council keep me busy during the day, and you would find me poor company in the evening. I have been known to fall asleep after supper." She glanced around the fleshy obstacle to find Hugh conversing with Lady Abigail. The surgeon's gaze kept drifting over towards Sera.

Lord Kenwood leaned closer and the aroma of fish wafted across Sera's face. He obviously favoured kippers for breakfast and didn't believe in brushing his teeth—both marks against him if he wished to compete for her hand. Instead of the fortunes and titles used by Abigail and the council, one of her criteria demanded a certain level of hygiene.

"A picnic, perhaps? Or a ride through Hyde Park? I'm sure you are allowed a little time with your suitors, since I am one of the candidates the council has proposed for your consideration. We cannot have one person monopolising all your time before a final decision is made."

The nerve of him, to press his suit and keep the king waiting, all so that the golden goose would not slip through his fingers!

Through sheer will, Sera managed to conjure a smile upon her lips. She preferred her fake suitor, Otto, and he should have as much of her time as he needed to visit with Inge. Otto made no demands on her, but entertaining another individual would keep the council guessing as to what she might do. A ride through the park might be tolerable and if not, it would be simple to manufacture a distraction to allow her to escape. The council couldn't object if she took an afternoon off to ride with one of their hand-picked stallions.

"A ride in your carriage through the park would be most refreshing. Tomorrow?" she suggested.

He beamed and she could practically see a miniature version of him rubbing his hands behind his eyes. No doubt counting how many golden eggs she would produce for him. Men soon overcame their objections to a working wife once they realised how much money it would add to their coffers.

"I doubt I will sleep tonight, such will be my anticipation. I shall collect you at two. Until then, Lady Winyard." He took possession of her hand and pressed a damp kiss to her skin.

Finding Abigail's gaze upon her, Sera resisted the urge to give Lord Kenwood a boil on his face for his impertinence. Now she understood how Kitty felt when the men in pursuit of her father's fortune drooled over her hand. Sera passed her right hand over her left and whispered a spell that brushed warm air over it to dry the spittle. She didn't want to wipe it on her gown and ruin the silk.

The crowd parted, and Sera made it to the king without any more suitors pressing their case. One prospective gentleman encountered the solid form of Hugh, who blocked his passage. She bit back a smile. The surgeon's devotion worried her—what if she never felt the same way about him? He gave his heart so utterly and easily, it would be cruel to let him believe she might one day return his obvious regard.

"Lady Winyard, what is this nonsense about your leaving England to go serve the Holy Roman Emperor?" King George roared. He half rose off the throne, his hands curled into fists around the ends of the arms.

The room fell silent, those assembled poised for the spectacle about to be unleashed by an angry monarch.

Sera had every intention of ensuring the observers were left disappointed. She curtseyed and schooled her face into an innocent expression. "I have no such plans, Your Majesty. Whoever whispered that in your ear is ill informed."

The king's face turned red and a vein throbbed in his temple. "All of London talks of how Lord Zedlitz courts you and that you will soon announce your engagement. Do you deny it?"

"Entertaining a suitor is a far cry from abandoning my country, Sire. I was born with an obligation to use my power in the service of England. I continue to do so." Silently, Sera thanked Mr Napier and Kitty for all the family meals they had shared over the years. The sometimes sharp dinner conversation had exposed her to the ways in which lawyers argued a case and armed her with the ability to answer a question without actually answering the question.

The king spluttered and struggled to draw breath. Queen Charlotte took his hand and murmured gentling words to him while Lord Pendlebury stepped forward and cast a calming spell over the monarch. After a few fraught seconds, the king drew a shuddering breath and slumped back on his throne.

The queen fixed Sera with a piercing look. "Speak plainly, Lady Winyard. I hold you responsible for the king's distress. Do you intend to marry Lord Zedlitz and leave our shores?"

"I can place my hand over my heart and swear that I have made no such decision, Your Majesty." Never would she deceive Queen Charlotte. The canny queen would see through her in an instant. Instead, she stuck as close to the truth as possible. "As instructed by both the king and the Mage Council, I am in the process of acquainting myself with the gentlemen put forward as prospective husbands. Lord Zedlitz is aware of my duties to this country. I am sure that if he were to be successful in his suit, our countries would negotiate some sort of arrangement that would satisfy both and allow us to split our time between Europe and England."

Sera kept her expression open and honest, her voice light and clear. Inside, she raged at the ridiculous situation she found herself in. What right had any of them to dictate how she lived her life or with whom? Let them think her a pawn, but if she made it across their board, she would make herself queen of her own fate. No one interfered in the marital arrangements of any of the other mages.

Or had they?

That crossed-out line beside Lord Branvale's name in the mage genealogy nagged at her memory. What if her peers on the council were more dutiful, and stayed within the strictures dictated by their monarch when selecting a wife? Except for one.

The king pressed a hand to his temple and appeared to recover his temper as the intense red of his face faded. "You are not to leave England under any circumstances. If this Zedlitz wishes to marry you, he can damned well move here and become English. The emperor is crowing that he is about to add another magical jewel to his crown, and I'll not have it!"

Sera curtseyed and retreated. She balanced on a knife edge to keep king and council believing she acquiesced, while giving Mr Napier time to drill into the fine print of the Mage Act. She would bide her time while she determined her next move.

Needing time to think without more men drooling over her hand, she avoided the main corridors of the palace and sought out the narrower and darker passages used by the servants. Casting a glamour over her clothing, her silk gown became a plain one of navy cotton, with a crisp apron over the top. Her ornate hairstyle became a simple, tight knot at her nape. To anyone she passed, she appeared to be another maid scurrying about on the orders of her lady. Out of curiosity, she wound her way to the area of the palace where the Austrian party had their rooms. Part of her hoped she might cross the path of the footman with the scar on his chin, at which point she could seize him for Lieutenant Powers.

As Sera wandered the narrow and dim hall, she passed a room with the door half open. In the windowless cell, a lantern burned low on a side table. A woman sat hunched over on her cot, shoulders heaving in silent sobs.

Sera rapped on the door with a soft hand. "I'm

sorry, but I could not help but notice your distress. Are you well?"

The woman glanced up and wiped her tears, but kept her face angled away from Sera. "Oh. Yes. Don't concern yourself about me."

"I am concerned for you and I cannot walk by someone who is obviously upset." Sera entered the room. A small and sparsely furnished chamber, one wall held another door. She assumed that beyond lay the larger room of the maid's mistress. If she had oriented herself correctly in the endless maze of corridors, the crying woman was a maid for one of the Austrian delegation. "I know some nobles can be right horrid. Or has some fellow broken your heart?"

The young maid drew a short breath and seemed to hold it for a moment, before letting it out. Her tears calmed and she turned to reveal a bright red swelling around her eye. The poor maid would have a shiny black eye by morning.

"Who did that to you?" Sera knelt before the girl and surveyed the damage. While she did not possess Hugh's medical knowledge, experience from below stairs with fighting footmen had taught her that most black eyes faded of their own accord after a number of days.

"It's not her fault. She's just ever so unhappy with him," the maid whispered.

Sera cast around the room. The ewer held water, so she poured some into the bowl and immersed a cloth. Wringing it out, she folded it into a square and gently laid it against the swollen eye.

The maid placed one hand over the cloth and whispered her thanks.

"Being unhappy is no excuse for hitting someone. Will you tell me the name of the person responsible, so others know who to avoid?" Sera could have a quiet word with Otto if someone in his party was abusing their staff.

The maid glanced at the closed door to the larger bedchamber. Her body tensed, perhaps listening to ascertain whether her mistress was beyond or not. Above the door perched a small brass bell, used to summon the servant in the smaller room.

"Lady Haas," the maid murmured.

There was a familiar name. When Sera sat on the cot, a tin flask tumbled from the folds of the girl's skirt and fell to the floor. Sera retrieved it and a quick sniff confirmed the contents were alcoholic. The girl might have sought something to numb the pain or ease her upset. It also made her more amenable to telling her mistress's secrets. "I know of her. She's married to the very old lord. Do you think that is what makes her so unhappy?"

The maid leaned closer to Sera. "Can you keep a secret?"

"Of course." A small white lie. Sera would tell her fellow Kestrels what she discovered, if it was relevant to their hunt for the murderer and the bracelet.

"She said she never wanted to marry him. But someone cast a spell over her, and gave her no choice in the matter. She said she was screaming on the inside when she wed him, but not a peep passed her lips." Having said her piece, the maid fell silent.

The confession dovetailed with what Sera had heard from Otto. Lady Haas had been in love with another when the unexpected union with Lord Haas had been announced. The additional information did indeed sound as though Lady Zedlitz had used her bracelet to compel the match for some horrible reason.

Mutter *found it amusing*, Otto had said.

Regardless of the unhappy arrangement, that didn't mean Lady Haas could go around hitting her maids. Did the loss of temper make her capable of more violent acts...like murder? "It cannot be easy to have a husband so much older."

The maid leaned back on the wall and stared at the bell. "She has a lover. He is one of the other nobles who came here to England. When she wants to be with him, she brings him to my room here and I must busy myself in her chamber, in case Lord Haas comes looking for her. She says that one day, she will find a way to escape her situation."

Find a way to escape? If Lady Haas had determined that Lady Zedlitz had forced her into the unhappy marriage, perhaps she had begun her quest for freedom with a spot of murder. Sera's theory hinged on a number of assumptions, but Lieutenant Powers could pursue those. How convenient if her lover should have a scar on his chin.

Although as she pondered the possibility of Lady Haas and her lover being responsible, it didn't quite fit. If he was among the party of Austrians, they would have recognised him standing in the corridor. Another accomplice, perhaps? Hugh said two had been involved in the murder, but could there have been three?

"Lord Haas is so very much older than Lady Haas. How is his health?" Sera approached another topic as delicately as she could. Lady Haas might still have murder on her mind, but with a different victim.

"He is hale and hearty. My mistress would divorce him, but it's not allowed and Lord Zedlitz…" The maid's voice trailed away and she sucked in her bottom lip.

"Did she seek Lord Zedlitz's support?" Sera wracked her brain, trying to think how Otto might have assisted in freeing Lady Haas from her situation. Nothing obvious leapt out at her beyond perhaps using him to approach the emperor or have a quiet chat with her husband.

The maid was silent. Sera suspected any further opportunity for conversation had slipped away if the other woman realised she had revealed too much.

"You should keep a cool cloth on the eye for a bit longer. It will help reduce the swelling," Sera said.

The girl nodded. "I will be fine. You should be on your way before your mistress wonders where you got to."

It took a moment for Sera to understand what the girl meant. Her glamour made her appear as another maid at the beck and call of a noblewoman, and she had dallied overlong. "Yes, I had better go see to her. I hope Lady Haas never does such a thing again."

Sera slipped from the room and pulled the door

closed behind her. Her mind swirled with possibilities. If Lady Haas had any involvement in the death of Otto's mother, she might intend to use the bracelet against her husband. She could compel him to grant her a license for divorce. Although that was frowned upon by many. There was one path easier, more socially acceptable, and far more financially rewarding than divorce: widowhood. Why divorce and lose everything when, if Lord Haas passed away, Lady Haas could control his estates or at least live off the income from them?

Had she disclosed her plan to Otto, and he had baulked at assisting?

FIFTEEN

Lady Abigail collected Sera in the Crawley family carriage for the meeting with Lord Rowan. She brushed a nervous hand over her skirts and kept playing with the hat pinned atop her head.

"You look lovely," Abigail murmured after Sera must have touched the hat for the one hundredth time.

"I'm nervous. Your grandfather has a formidable reputation." Meeting the elderly mage filled her with more dread than a summons from king or council. He had ruled the council for years before retiring to pursue his studies. Sera's only clue as to his opinion of her was that he had been instrumental in the vote that had allowed her to live. Would she find a man who regretted his decision, or one with an open mind, like Lord Pendlebury?

Lord Rowan lived on the other side of Mayfair from his daughter and granddaughter. His town house sat in a row of identical neighbours, apart from the glossy black of its front door. The exterior gave no hint that a powerful mage dwelt inside. The front door opened as Sera and Abigail were assisted down from the carriage. Sera stared up at the brick facade as they walked up the path.

"Good afternoon, Lady Abigail," the butler intoned as he held the door open.

A tingle of magic washed over Sera as she crossed the threshold. What sort of spell sealed the mage's home from the outside world? She teased apart the components as she waited with Abigail in the dim foyer. Silence was easiest to discern in the ensorcellment bound to the bricks—it felt metallic and reminded her of silver. She had cast a similar spell over her home to ensure no unwanted ears listened in on conversations under her roof.

Before she could isolate anything else about the spell, the butler coughed into his gloved hand.

"His Grace will see you now." He gestured to the double doors to one side of the foyer and led the way across the dark tiles. The butler hadn't left them and Sera assumed Lord Rowan had reached out with his magic to tell the butler he was ready for his visitors. Did he engage a trick similar to the one she used with Elliot, like making a bell ring by his head when he was needed? Or did he employ something more subtle? She added that to her list of questions, should he be in an indulgent mood.

The butler pushed the doors apart. "Lady Abigail and Lady Winyard, Your Grace." The highly polished toes of his shoes never crossed the threshold.

Sera entered the study at Abigail's side and gave a soft gasp. The room had no windows, every wall being taken up by floor-to-ceiling bookcases. Books of various sizes and thicknesses made haphazard stacks against the shelves. More tomes created hillocks and rough terrain across the floor. Sera was surprised that when the butler slid open the doors, books hadn't tumbled out as though from an overstuffed cupboard.

A sphere hung in the middle of the room and cast a soft yellow light from behind its paper shade etched with countries to resemble the globe. Sera peered at it, trying to discern whether magic made the light hang in place, or if an unseen wire attached the globe to the ceiling.

Lord Rowan sat behind a desk covered in papers and scrolls. He looked up as they approached, gazing at them through a small pair of gold spectacles clinging to the end of his nose. A blood-red velvet cap sat on his head and Sera suspected it covered his baldness, as no hair peeked from around his ears. His ability to grow hair seemed to have slid southward, for a long white beard covered the lower half of his face and fell to his chest.

"Ah. Abigail. You have bought the infamous Lady Winyard," he chuffed.

"Good day, Grandfather." Abigail navigated a path between towers of books and kissed a hairy cheek. "Seraphina has brought the bracelet I told you about."

"Thank you for agreeing to see me, Lord Rowan." Sera stopped before the desk and clasped her hands, unsure of how to proceed and willing to let Abigail show the way.

The old mage grunted and threw his pen towards its holder. The feather rippled as it floated to its final position. "Excellent. I am most curious about your little trinket and the tale Abigail related to me."

He pushed his chair away from the desk and waved his hand like a conductor. From a corner of the shadowy room came a rattle followed by a scrape. Two mismatched chairs dragged themselves over and halted to one side of the desk. Sera and Abigail seated themselves. The wooden back of the chair required a rigid, ladylike position; there would be no slouching or making oneself comfortable. No wonder Abigail had such admirable posture if she always sat in such a way around her family.

Sera reached into her reticule and extracted the cloth-wrapped bracelet. With a glance at her friend, she held it out to Lord Rowan. "I wore this from my very first day in Lord Branvale's care and until my very last day under his roof."

"And you believe it stifled your magic?" He peered at Sera, then took the object and undid the knot. When he pulled aside the cloth, the copper gleamed in the low light.

"Yes. As though I were a river with a dam blocking the flow of water," Sera said.

Lord Rowan held a hand over the bracelet. Though she believed she had rendered it harmless, a silver wisp still rose from the metal and reached for his palm. "Tricky little thing, isn't it?"

He pinched the end of the wisp, and pulled it free. The tendril wriggled and turned upon itself in his grasp, until one end stabbed into his skin. The old mage grunted and before the thread could burrow any farther, he whispered under his breath and tapped it. Instantly the strand turned solid. He pulled it free like a splinter and held it before his nose to examine it.

"I was hoping you might know who crafted the piece." If Sera could find the creator of this bracelet, she might learn more about the other one.

Lord Rowan muttered under his breath and a thumb-sized vial flew from a shelf and presented itself before him. He dropped the sliver inside and thumped the stopper in. "No mage living made this thing."

Disappointment plunged through Sera. *Blast.* Such was the problem with magical objects—they could outlive their creators. "Do you think it is very old?"

Using the cloth, Lord Rowan picked up the bracelet in one hand. With a snap of his fingers, a magnifying glass appeared in his other hand and he examined the carving of the tree. "Hard to tell with Fae work. It could be a hundred years old, or a thousand." Having peered at the outside of the wide cuff, he turned his attention to the inside.

"*Fae?*" Sera had never considered *that*.

Abigail sat in silence, her hands clasped in her lap.

"Yes. This wasn't made by any English mage. Fae do like their ensorcelled jewellery—this has their runes hidden among the leaves of the tree." Lord Rowan rotated the cuff as he examined every part of it.

"I never noticed any runes." The clue had been on

her wrist the whole time. Not that she was overly familiar with Fae runes. Lord Branvale had given her only a broad overview of the history between their realm and of the Fae and how they preferred to stay out of human affairs.

"Here, let me show you." He put the bracelet down and then waved his hands in the air, where an image of the tree appeared. As he drew his hands apart, the tree grew in size until it stood four feet in height. "Now, concentrate on a single leaf."

Sera peered at the canopy of leaves and chose one that hovered closest to her. She mentally traced the outline of the leaf, sinuate like that of an oak. Next she followed the lines of the veins. As she stared, the lines re-formed and created a rune.

"Oh! I see it now. What do they say?" She blinked and refocused on the whole. So many leaves. Did each bear a single rune?

"It would take some time to transcribe and translate the spell. Most likely they contain the enchantment. Hiding the incantation within the tree of life makes it stronger and would allow it to endure for centuries." He tapped another leaf to magnify it and a different rune appeared.

A bracelet from another realm. Her curiosity itched to step through their doorway one day. "All those years I wore it and I never discerned anything magical about it. I believed myself to be weak and ineffective. If only I had known." She could have confronted Lord Branvale about it and had it removed. Then a shiver ran down her spine. No. That might have been a mistake—to alert the council to the full extent of her power while she was still under their control.

Lord Rowan drew his hands together and the tree shrank to the size of a small topiary perched on the corner of his desk. "Fae magic is different. It does not emit the faint signature of the hand that crafted it like our magic does. It is especially hard to identify if you have not encountered their touch before."

Sera pondered the ramifications. Had Branvale visited the Fae realm and procured the bracelet, or purchased it in the human world? Did that mean Lady Zedlitz's bracelet likewise had Fae origins?

"There is another bracelet, Grandfather, that Lady Winyard encountered recently," Abigail said.

"Another one? That dampens magic like this thing?" His bushy white eyebrows shot up.

Sera paused, contemplating how much to tell Lord Rowan. But she trusted Abigail, and the whole reason for her visit was to learn if the old mage knew anything that would help her in their search for answers. "Similar, yes. But its spell worked not on the wearer, but on whomever the owner touched. It could compel a person to do whatever the wearer commanded. Even a mage."

Lord Rowan wrapped Sera's bracelet in the cloth. "A dangerous item, then. Do you possess that one, too?"

"No. Sadly, it was removed from the body of the person who last owned it and I have not yet hunted it down." Did the murderer have it secured around their wrist, forcing those around them to do their bidding? Or did it rest in a hidden spot, unused?

"Does the council know of these?" He pushed the wrapped cuff across the desk towards her.

Sera tucked it into her reticule before answering. Lord Rowan had been Speaker when she went to live with Lord Branvale. If he had been involved in the secret to suppress her power, he was playing his cards close to his chest.

"I have not told the council what I know of these bracelets. I thought to study them first and learn all I could." First up would be finding all the hidden Fae runes on her bracelet.

Lord Rowan huffed a low laugh and leaned back in his chair. "Let us keep it that way for now. No need to spark a treasure hunt that will send whoever possesses the thing into hiding. But if you find it, do bring it to me. Such a dangerous item needs to be stored securely. Do you suspect Ormsby acquired yours and ordered Branvale to snap it around your wrist?"

Her instinct said no. Whatever web she was caught in, Branvale and the council were on opposite sides. Of that she was certain. "I don't know, but I wish to learn the answer to that question. The council deemed me an inferior woman and the bracelet made it easier for them to continue in that belief."

He grunted and stared at the ceiling, which seemed as far above them as if they sat outside under a starless sky. "When we discovered old Dewlap's power had been transferred to a girl, the council was understandably upset. None of them could imagine a woman being admitted to mage tower."

"This is not as simple as letting a woman into a

gentleman's club. The objections of some run far deeper than that. I think Lord Ormsby is afraid of me." Sera leaned forward as she studied Lord Rowan. Did he share their beliefs? But no, he must support her right to be as free as he himself was, for he had allowed her to live.

Silence drifted over them. The globe above spun and golden dust motes danced away from it.

"You may be correct there," he said at length. "A woman has never sat at our council table. Your presence among us gives life to many a possibility, but stirs up old fears for others."

They were afraid of their own shadows. If no woman mage had ever lived to adulthood before, what on earth were they frightened of? There had to be more to their prejudices, surely.

"Who started the horrific practice of infanticide in England if power was born in a girl? Women mages live, work, and study in Europe. Why not here?" Questions, anger, and frustration collided under her skin. Sparks flared along the backs of her hands and raced to her fingertips.

Lord Rowan picked up a scroll, where a single spark was burning a hole in one corner. "Take a few deep breaths, Lady Winyard, lest you set fire to my precious books."

Abigail reached out and wrapped a hand around her forearm. "Temper, Seraphina. Grandfather is trying to help you."

She stood and circled a towering stack of books. With each step, she remembered Hugh's warm grasp on her wrist and his gentling words in her ear. *Don't give them fodder for their delusions.*

Why was a woman labelled hysterical for acting defensively when a man would be called strong or heroic? That was something else about society that needed to change. She completed another circuit of the bookish mountain before returning to her seat.

"I apologise, Lord Rowan. I often find myself with an excess of magic and no outlet for it." She clasped her hands in her lap so that if she threw off any more sparks, they would alight on her own skirts.

He narrowed his gaze at her in the same manner he'd used to inspect the bracelet. "Have you tested your limits?"

"No. But I know I am more powerful than the council believes me to be." The forthcoming entertainment with Lord Tomlin was the perfect opportunity to show them the true extent of her power. The time had come for her to launch an attack and let the council make defensive manoeuvres for once.

"Indeed. You have grown into something rather extraordinary. Exactly why I believed the time had come to let a woman mage flourish in England. And the dusty old yard around mage tower was in desperate need of a shade tree." He tented his fingers and huffed a satisfied laugh, as though he had orchestrated a great joke at the other mages' expense.

Sera glanced at Abigail, who beamed like a proud mother. Hope surged through her chest at finding her friend and her grandfather supporters of her cause. "After Lord Branvale saw I was a girl, my father told me he stole me away and demanded a promise from the Mage Council that I would be allowed to live. Thank you for championing my right to exist."

"I saw your birth as the dawning of a new age. One where we could leave behind such antiquated prejudices. It was fortuitous that your father had a gargoyle present that night. The idea of losing Dewlap's line for decades in a gargoyle nest helped change their minds and the vote was passed." He held out his hand and a scroll wriggled free of a pile to settle itself in front of him. Lord Rowan peered at the text and muttered under his breath.

Abigail rose and kissed his cheek. Silently, she gestured to the door. Sera took that to mean the interview was over before she could ask about the erased entry in the genealogy next to Branvale's name. But she had learned a few valuable tidbits. The bracelet was Fae and Lord Rowan might yet prove to be her ally.

The butler slid open the doors as they approached and escorted them across the foyer. Once they were settled in the carriage, Sera broached another persistent topic on her mind. "Do you recall some fifteen years ago, when Lady Zedlitz visited England and there was some scandal involving a naked noble and a Scottish steer?"

Abigail's eyes widened, then she covered her mouth as she laughed. "Oh, yes. Why, everybody talked of nothing else for at least two weeks, until a bigger scandal overtook it."

Sera took a moment to digest that. What could outdo someone painting himself blue and sitting in the king's chair with an oversized cow in the presence chamber? "A bigger scandal?"

Abigail nodded. "An unmarried noblewoman who gave birth to a furry babe at a ball. Ruined her reputation in a rather dramatic fashion. An expensive rug never recovered from that night. Everyone thought she had grown overfond of sweetmeats and never imagined an Unnatural lover to be responsible."

A thousand more questions crammed into Sera's brain and she had trouble dismissing them. Another day, she promised herself. "Coming back to the blue nobleman—do you recall his name?"

It might be nothing. But when someone brushed up against Lady Zedlitz and then did something unexpected afterward, she suspected the woman had used the bracelet to exert her influence.

"Oh, my, that is testing my memory. His family was banished and ruined." She tapped a finger against her wrist as she sought to bring forth the information. "Ah! Sir Athol Gollach. A baronet. Had some holdings in Scotland, I believe, and retreated to the misty hills there afterward, never to be seen again. Why do you ask?"

"Lord Zedlitz mentioned it happening after some dispute between his mother and Sir Athol over the bull. She seems to have left a trail of ruined lives in her wake. I wonder if the baronet also fell afoul of the bracelet."

"While it is impolite to speak ill of the dead, she did not appear to be a particularly amiable person." Abigail sat up straighter and glanced out the window, as though she feared someone might have overheard her.

For Lady Abigail, that was as close as she got to criticising another noble. But Sera agreed. Every story she heard was one of heartache. Why did Lady Zedlitz not use the bracelet to make the world a better place? "Otto said she was not always like that. She used to have a light heart and sang often. The bracelet changed her. I think the magic had a reciprocal effect. Every horrid thing she did was visited back upon her and altered her personality."

"Otto?" Abigail arched one finely shaped brow.

"It is part of our ruse, nothing more." The carriage came to a gentle halt outside the Crawley home.

"Good. I have a fine specimen I wish to throw in your path. Lord Thornton is quite a catch, but rather shy when it comes to finding a bride. He would be an excellent choice for you. I shall arrange a meeting for the two of you, away from prying eyes." Abigail patted her hand as the door swung open and the footman lowered the steps. Once her friend had alighted, the vehicle would take Sera back to her modest home.

"Thank you, Abigail," Sera murmured. When the door closed, she let out a sigh and leaned back against the velvet cushions. She needed to talk to Kitty. Their plan to find someone to fill the void in her father's life so they could set up house together was becoming more urgent by the day.

If her plan for the display worked, the council would not bother her for much longer.

Sixteen

Sera only vaguely registered the brisk movement past the window as she read correspondence at her desk. A sharp rap upon the door followed not long afterward. Elliot pounded up the stairs from the kitchen, but apparently not quickly enough for their visitor. The rapping grew in intensity. Sera set aside her papers, curious as to the urgency of the matter.

Once Elliot opened the door, a strident voice carried through the foyer. "Take my bag upstairs, and don't dilly-dally. Where is your uniform? You look like a vagabond."

Sera rose to her feet and crossed to the parlour door. A short, stout woman stood in the foyer and appeared to be attacking Elliot with a leather bag. He still clung to the open front door and was using it to fend the woman off.

"Who are you?" Sera waved her hand and removed the bag from the woman's hand, depositing it once more on the front doorstep.

The woman patted her straw hat, checking its placement, then brushed a hand over her skirts. Straightening her spine and reaching barely to Sera's chest, she announced, "I am Mrs Dalrymple, your new housekeeper."

"You appear to have the wrong address, Mrs Dalrymple. I have no need of a housekeeper, nor have I engaged one." An itch took up residence in the base of Sera's skull. She didn't like where this conversation was heading and the itch presaged a horrible realisation.

"I have been employed by the Mage Council at the request of King George." Mrs Dalrymple peered around Sera at the small but perfectly functional parlour. "I am tasked to run your household and to provide advice to you, my lady. Since you are in want of a steadying and experienced hand on the wheel as you navigate these waters."

For a brief moment Sera pondered which was worse—the sailing analogy or king and council trying another tactic to interfere with her life. She decided to continue with the nautical theme.

"There is no room in my port for you to moor. You are neither necessary nor wanted." With one hand, Sera invited her to use the still open door.

A confused look crossed Mrs Dalrymple's face. Then she set her shoulders and marched towards the parlour. "Given the unruly appearance of the individual answering your door, you seem in desperate need of my advice, my lady. Besides, my wages have been paid in advance for some three months."

"Consider them enough to fund a holiday. Perhaps

you could sail to a tropical island?" Sera inhaled deeply and, on the exhale, swept her hands from side to side.

Water bubbled up under the housekeeper's feet and tangled with her skirts. "Oh, my!" she cried as the tide surged and knocked her off her feet. She fell in the hallway ocean with a splash, then the water carried her out the door and deposited her on the pavement like something tossed up on a beach. Water cascaded along the path and soaked into the cobbles.

"Don't forget your bag," Elliot called as he strode out and dropped it beside her.

"It will be most unfortunate if I have to report this incident to the Mage Council, Lady Winyard." Seemingly undaunted, Mrs Dalrymple climbed to her feet and shook out her skirts, which had remained dry throughout the impromptu swamping. Sera wasn't an utter monster—her intent had not been to drench the woman.

"I shall save you some time, Mrs Dalrymple. I am headed there now, and will discuss this matter with them." As soon as Elliot's feet crossed the threshold, Sera pointed to the door and it slammed itself shut. "Do not admit her again."

To ensure the dour woman didn't gain access to the house, Sera cast a quick exclusive spell and sent it to attach itself to the housekeeper. No matter how hard the council's employee tried, she would encounter an invisible wall on Sera's threshold that she could not cross until the spell was removed.

"I'll fetch a carriage, then." Elliot reached for the door handle.

"I'm too angry to wait. I shall find one for myself." Her hands clenched into fists and her skin tingled with excess magic. She slowed her breathing to reduce the risk of unwanted sparks.

"You need to calm down and look in the mirror first. Have Vicky help you while I go. It won't take long." He gestured to the maid, who had climbed the stairs from the kitchen to investigate the noise.

Sera glanced in the mirror. Her loose hair did give her a rather angry appearance. Better to not resemble an unhinged wild woman while trying to make her point to the council. She shook her hands and let the magic flick to the floor, and changed the worn timbers to a pretty tiled mosaic of white and yellow flowers on a sunny blue background.

"Very well," she said to Vicky when she appeared. "Let us see what we can do in a hurry."

Less than twenty minutes later, a tidier Sera sat in a carriage on her way to mage tower. The carriage decanted her at the tower gate and Sera strode across the packed earth to the tower. As had become her custom, she stroked the leaves of the growing oak.

"Grow strong, my friend," she murmured.

In the circular body of the tower, she asked one of the retainers carrying a tray, "Where would I find Lord Ormsby?"

"In the Speaker's study, milady." He gestured with his head up the stairs.

Sera held her skirts out of her way as she trotted up the stairs to the next level. The Speaker had a study above the council chamber. Everyone else either found a corner in the library when they wanted a quiet space to themselves, or used one of the rooms in the basement.

She stopped outside the solid oak door and took a moment to calm herself. Only when her emotions were tightly reined in did she rap on the door.

"Enter," came the command.

Pushing inside, she found a quiet oasis. A mullioned window that reached from floor to high ceiling allowed light to enter the room, but here on the north side of the tower, no sunlight harmed the books that lined two walls. The carpets, drapes, and rugs were in soft hues of caramel and darkest orange, bronze, and copper. The effect was peaceful and welcoming.

Unlike the look on Lord Ormsby's face.

"What can I assist you with, Lady Winyard?" His hand paused over the page spread out before him, the quill wavering as it waited. He sat behind a desk of dark walnut that could have served as a bed, such was its breadth and length. The carved legs resembled some sort of sea serpent with a twisted body that held aloft the desktop.

"I had a rather confused visitor today. A Mrs Dalrymple. The poor woman held the mistaken belief she was my housekeeper." She congratulated herself on keeping her tone light and incredulous, as though she shared an amusing anecdote with the Speaker.

He placed the quill back in its silver holder, but the feather continued to wave. Either he had a breeze circulating around him or the pen had an enchantment over it. "She is not confused. The king has agreed to pay her wages for three months. After that, it will be deducted from your stipend."

Oh, double insult! Not only would they force the woman upon her, but they expected Sera to pay for the privilege.

"This is where there is some matter of confusion. I have no need for a housekeeper, nor is there room. As I am sure you have observed, my home is rather modest. There are no spare rooms."

"Miss Wassler can share until she returns to Austria. I am sure Mrs Dalrymple will not object for a few weeks." Lord Ormsby remained seated and did not offer a chair to Sera.

She walked to the window and gazed out at the surrounding countryside. The Speaker's study was situated high enough to see over the wall and to the new buildings being constructed. "I shall of course thank the king for his generosity, but I have no need of a house-keeper. My cook and maid manage exceedingly well for my small household."

Lord Ormsby made a noise that sounded like a cross between a snort and a bark. "Let me be plain. Mrs Dalrymple is to provide a steadying hand."

"Yes, she did mention that before she swept out the door." Sera clasped her hands together and dug her nails into her palms while reminding herself to stay calm.

"She is not a guardian, as you have made it plain you do not require one. The king provides you with an older woman who is more experienced in the world, and who can offer her advice on a daily basis." Then Lord Ormsby pulled his lips back to reveal his teeth.

Sera noticed one tooth had the rot and wondered if Hugh could pull it for the Speaker before the gum festered. Then she realised Lord Ormsby was trying to...smile.

How horrifying.

"Lady Abigail Crawley offers me counsel, should I require it." Sera thought ahead to a solution, one that would allow king and council to think they had won a small victory against her.

"We of course encourage your friendship with Lord Rowan's granddaughter. Her influence on you is clear. But she herself seeks the guidance of her father. We are concerned that you have no such figure to guide you." He maintained the grimace and Sera found anger replaced by amusement at the effort it cost him.

"You think I need someone much older than myself to guide me?" As Mr Napier had taught her, Sera picked away at the words, searching for the loophole.

"Naturally. Someone you could consider an aunt or other feminine relative to provide advice." He nodded, as though pleased she was seeing reason.

"And more experienced in the world?"

"Yes." The grimace widened. He had another brown tooth farther back in his mouth. "Someone who is less inclined to be impressed by magical outbursts when they occur."

She ignored his reference to her temper, because while they spoke she had thought of the perfect candidate, one to whom they could not possibly object.

"Imagine if you could find me one who is impervious to magic," she suggested.

Lord Ormsby spread his hands and chuffed in laughter. "Mrs Dalrymple is the closest we could find to such a person."

Sera smiled and approached the desk. "I have a solution. I shall select my own housekeeper who meets all these criteria."

"Oh?" He drew his brows drew together, only now sensing a possible trap.

"Mrs Natalie Delacour. She is an old family friend of my father's and a rather solid and dependable type. She has already offered her many years of wisdom should I require it. I shall ask her to fill the role of aunt for me." Sera rapped her knuckles on the desk once to emphasis the suitability of her suggestion.

Nat met all their criteria. Older—by centuries. Experienced in the world—having trod its soil for over five hundred years. And resistant to magic—as Lord Branvale had discovered when he tried to snatch the baby Seraphina from the gargoyle's arms.

The grimace fell away and confusion flashed across Lord Ormsby's round features. "I don't know that name, but I shall agree to her placement if you will agree to be guided by her."

"Indeed. I am glad we have found a solution that is satisfactory to us both. I only hope that Mrs Delacour can be prevailed upon to take up residence with me." That was the only tricky bit, but if Sera stressed that she needed help against the council—again—the gargoyle might settle on her rooftop for a few weeks.

"Once you confirm she will take up the position, I shall inform the king that Mrs Dalrymple is not required. You will, of course, have to pay Mrs Delacour from your own accounts." He picked up the quill again and it wriggled in his fingers.

"Of course, Lord Ormsby. She is currently visiting with my father. I shall send a message to her as soon as I return home. Thank you for your time." Sera took her leave, biting her lip to stop her laughter at the confused yet satisfied look on Lord Ormsby's face.

She took the spiral stairs down to the hidden library. There she wandered the shelves, hunting for any books about the Fae. She wished to learn about their mages and the type of magic they cast. At length she found a section with a few slender books on the topic. Choosing two at random to begin, she carried them to a reading table.

One book was a history of the Fae court and the divisions between the Seelie and Unseelie factions. "It sounds like human politics with Whigs and Tories," she murmured.

The Seelie regarded humans kindly and would help when called upon. The Unseelie had a dim view of humans and could be malicious in their actions. For some centuries, the Fae realm had been ruled by a Seelie queen, the grandmother of Arwyn Fitzfey. She forbade the Unseelie folk to harm humans or meddle in their affairs. But rather like English politics, the faction out of power sought to grow their support base so they could challenge authority.

The book contained little about their mages, saying only that they served the Crown and their people in a way similar to how Sera and her fellow mages were employed in England. She wondered about the etiquette of visiting the Fae. Did one just walk through one of the gateways, or did she need the permission of the Faerie queen? Lord Rowan would know—she would write to him and ask.

She plucked a sheet of paper from a stack in the middle of the table. Then she dipped a pen into the ink pot and made notes. The books could not be removed from the library, but she could make as many notes as she pleased. After an hour or two and with her own sketched-out history of the Fae court, a hired carriage took her home. Once she uncovered all the runes on her bracelet, she would return to the library to translate the spell.

Her first task once home was to write to her father and request Nat's assistance. With the letter in his hand, Elliot promised to find the quickest way to deliver it.

"What a day," Sera murmured. Then her mage correspondence box rattled. Pulling forth the papers, she found detailed notes from Lord Tomlin about the entertainment. He had even been so bold as to suggest small spells she might cast...

... WITHIN YOUR RANGE. *Fireflies, to flit around in a pretty pattern. A white owl, that could glide above.*

· · ·

SHE SNORTED and tossed the papers on the desk. Her mood couldn't tolerate his patronising words. What she needed was time with Rosie and a fresh batch of cookies.

THE NEXT DAY, in a much better mood, Sera stalked back and forth in front of the fireplace. While the sun shone high in the sky outside, inside resided in deepest night. Stars drifted across the ceiling. An owl with wide eyes sat atop the bookcase, furry bats clung to the underside of the wall sconce, and a small pair of tawny nightjars perched on the mantel.

"What on earth are you doing?" Elliot asked on walking into the room with a tray tucked under his arm. "Are you in mourning for someone?"

"I am figuring out my part of the entertainment for the grand banquet. I am representing Nyx, goddess of night. I want to cloak myself in creatures of darkness, as I refuse to play along with the insipid part Lord Tomlin has assigned me. But bats just don't seem very awe-inspiring." She waved a hand towards the small creatures wrapped in their wings.

"That's because they look like rats with wings. Owls are better, but they are a rather sweet, which I'm guessing isn't the look you're after. Nightjars are an improvement, but only if you have a goat as well." Elliot referenced the legend of nightjars sucking the blood from goats.

"Nothing seems appropriate." She waved a hand and the creatures dissolved into stardust.

"Try crows." He placed the used tea things on the tray.

Yes, they might work, with their glossy black feathers and piercing stare. Crows were rather small, though. "Ravens would be better—they are much bigger."

Elliot *tsked* under his breath. "Ravens might be showy, but crows are the carriers of souls."

Carriers of souls, yes—she had forgotten that old legend. Upon a person's death, a crow carried the soul to the afterlife. Sera crafted a spell and sent it singing through her veins. A half dozen crows appeared and circled above them.

"There should be only three." Elliot swiped a hand through one and it dissolved like mist.

"Three? Don't be silly. I need to fill a ballroom." She would struggle to conjure anything impressive-looking under the cover of night as it was.

Lord Tomlin planned to practically blind the guests with his golden chariot carrying the sun. Sera dropped to the settee and chewed her lip as her footman batted at the phantom crows and dispersed them. The council expected her to play along with Lord Tomlin's plan for the evening. But she intended to play by her own rules, not those imposed on her.

"Sometimes fewer of something has more impact

than dozens." Elliot left three birds. One perched on the sconce, another on the mantel, and the third on the armchair opposite Sera.

If she couldn't dazzle her audience, perhaps she could instill a little fear instead. Closing her eyes, she imagined the desired effect. Words flowed through her mind and Sera whispered them softly, before releasing the magic from her hands.

The crow across from her let out a squawk and took flight. As it brushed over Elliot, it drew a shadow from him. A smoky grey form now dangled from the crow's claws, as though it clutched an empty suit of clothes. Phantom Elliot's face elongated in a rasping moan.

"That is...disturbing. It's not really my soul...is it?" He patted his chest as though he expected to find a hollow where the spectral crow had pulled free his soul.

Sera walked from crow to crow, fine-tuning her creation. "No. A brief contact with the crow allows it to trail a shadow image of whoever it touched, and it will moan in their voice. I am hoping it will send a shiver down the spines of the guests."

"I should think it will bloody well terrify them." Elliot picked up the tray and edged out of the room.

"Excellent. They will be certain to remember my part of the entertainment, then. I can alter the spell so that each crow will take a soul and circle the room with it. Perhaps I can conjure a void for them to disappear through and only the crow reappears before claiming another." More ideas bubbled up in her mind. Her version of Nyx would embrace her association with the night and shadow realm where souls journeyed after death. It would be a memorable evening for everyone involved.

Especially Lord Tomlin.

SEVENTEEN

With an outline for her magical display decided, Sera's mood greatly improved. Her father's response to her letter the next day said that Nat had agreed to lend her presence at Sera's home to stymie the council's plans. However, the gargoyle disliked London and would only stay a short while. Which for a gargoyle could mean a decade.

"Excellent!" she said to an empty room.

She took up her pen to tell Lord Ormsby before the Speaker found out the selected woman was a gargoyle. One who had already stood up to a mage to protect Sera and who had vowed to do so again if required. Once that letter sat in the mage box, she pressed the relevant signal on the top to send the message to his wooden container.

Next Sera penned a carefully worded message to Kitty, suggesting a quiet dinner party. They might invite Lady Plimmerton so that her father could converse with someone his own age. Having planted that seed, and hoping it would grow into a romance, she considered her tasks for the day. The Mage Council had allocated her more agricultural tasks on the outskirts of London. While she hated delaying such work, knowing the men had probably already been ignored for months or years, she had a more pressing engagement.

Sera sent a reply saying it would have to be delayed until the next day, as she was meeting with one of the council's fine recommendations for a husband—Lord Kenwood. She liberally gilded the truth, saying how much she wanted to settle on a candidate and needed to give each of them her full attention in appreciation for the effort the council had put into their selection.

Two hours of her morning were spent with Inge. Sera stood on a footstool in the converted dining room, now a marvellous sewing room, with fabric draped over chairs. Inge pinned a dreamy black silk around Sera. Boning sewn into the bodice allowed the dress to shape Sera's body and offer support, without the need of wide shoulder straps. A thin silver cord would wind over her shoulders and cross below her bust.

Inge had purchased a few samples of glittering beads that would be sewn on the gown to represent stars. They pinned them on and compared the different sizes and cuts before deciding on which ones would be used.

"The gown is beautiful—thank you, Inge. What a shame to lose you to Austria when I could have commissioned an entire wardrobe." Sera stroked the silk. What she would give to wear such loose gowns every day and no busk or stays.

"I have your measurements. So long as they remain the same, I can make gowns for you from Austria. Although once I wed Otto, as margravine I will have other duties to fill my time." She spoke around a mouthful of pins.

"Perhaps if you had time, you could draw designs I could have made up here?" Sketching was a pastime permitted a noblewoman, was it not?

"I would enjoy that. I shall buy more paper on my next walk." Inge rose to her feet and stabbed the pins into a miniature blue velvet cushion.

After a light luncheon, Sera chose her sweet pea embroidered gown for the afternoon's outing. She matched it with a jacket in a light green silk that complemented the climbing flowers. Vicky fussed with her hair, pinning it up high and perching a saucer-shaped straw hat on an angle. A green silk ribbon decorated the brim and secured a posy of fabric sweet peas, then it tumbled down one side.

Sera plucked a parasol from where it leaned against the dresser and descended the stairs in slow steps.

"What's got you so glum? You look like you are off to your execution." Elliot leaned on the newel post.

"A potential suitor is taking me for a jaunt in Hyde Park." She swished the parasol through the air. If she wasn't allowed to use magic, the little umbrella would serve as a weapon to deliver a smack to Lord Kenwood if events did not go well.

The footman placed one hand to his chest. "Oh, no.

How horrible for you. A rich noble is trying to win your hand."

Sera narrowed her gaze and snatched her gloves from the side table. "They are only interested in how my magical abilities can make them even richer. I only agreed to the outing with Lord Kenwood to keep the Mage Council happy in a belief I am considering their candidates."

"Ah, another fake suitor. It's so hard to keep track of them all. By the way, has the surgeon kissed you yet?" Elliot opened the front door.

"No. He has not." Why did Elliot have to remind her of Hugh? She would much prefer to stroll the park in his company.

"Tick tock," Elliot murmured as she stepped outside.

Sera pushed Hugh to one side in her mind as she approached the open carriage with four perfectly matched grey horses waiting in the street. Lord Kenwood, in a ridiculously tall hat, stood next to it. He kept one hand resting on the open door in case the locals weren't sure who owned the thing.

"Lady Winyard, you look delightful." He swept the hat off in a bow.

"You cut a striking figure yourself, Lord Kenwood," she murmured as he handed her up. He wore a bright blue silk jacket with embroidery that flashed in the sunlight.

"I should hope so. I pay my tailor an absurd amount of money to keep me in the pink of fashion. My wife would, of course, have access to the very best dressmakers in England." He sat next to her and gestured for the driver to move off.

"I have never been a follower of fashion." Sera plucked at her pretty but modest gown. Fancy dresses would be ruined out in the fields and sewers. She would rather follow Marie Antoinette's example and adopt simpler attire outdoors, such as the French queen did in her farmyard. Inge might be able to sketch a few before she returned to her homeland.

"I'm sure you could learn how to be fashionable, with the right maid to select your dresses and an adviser to whisper in your ear." He grinned and revealed misshapen teeth, which rather spoiled his fine appearance.

Sera wondered how much the council had told him of her. His words sailed close to the events of the previous day. Fortunately, she had rejected the council's choice of housekeeper to spy on her. With Nat, Kitty, and Abigail, she had women she trusted if she ever needed to seek advice about society or life. The last thing she wanted was a husband interfering in her life and dictating what she could and couldn't do...or wear. She imagined herself like a doll, dressed up and made to perform by others.

"Do you spend much time in London?" she asked as the driver guided the horses and carriage through the streets towards the green expanse of the park.

"I am here for the Season and may stay longer depending on what entertainment it offers. Winter I spend at my estate in Sussex." He leaned both hands on a walking cane with a round silver top.

"How marvellous. I long to care for the gardens of an estate." She tried to find common ground.

"My father paid handsomely to have ours landscaped by that Capability Brown chap, but I suppose we could find an acre or two for you to grow roses or whatever pretty flowers catch your fancy." He winked at his potential generosity.

An acre or two to nurture as she wished seemed grand to her. Gardening would also get her out of the house and away from any annoying husband or staff.

"Do you attend Parliament?" A husband with a seat, and preferably some influence in the House, would greatly assist Sera's endeavours to change not just the Mage Act, but to bring to fruition legislation to finally recognise Unnaturals as productive members of society.

"Not if I can help it!" He laughed. "It doesn't matter if you're a Tory or Whig, they all make long and boring speeches that send one to sleep. I only attend and vote when compelled to do so."

"But do you not wish to use your privileged position to benefit your fellow Englishmen and this country?" What was the point of giving peers a seat in the House of Lords when they would rather be sporting over the fields or between the sheets? Kitty would be a force to reckon with if *she* were allowed a place in the country's governance.

A frown drew across his brow. "Why would I do anything for them?" He gestured to the ordinary people going about their day around them.

"Should you not see to the needs of those less fortunate than yourself? Especially when you have a position that could be used to better their lives." Many poorer people struggled to earn sufficient to feed and clothe their families. If he could not lend a hand to his fellow man, Sera couldn't imagine herself ever marrying Lord Kenwood. Kitty would cut him down at their first meeting and refuse to ever dine with him again.

"If they want to improve their lives, they shouldn't be so lazy." He spoke with a sharp tone that whisked away the retort bubbling over Sera's tongue.

He might learn to change his views over time, but that seemed like a lot of hard work. How much more agreeable life would be if she could select a companion who already held beliefs similar to her own. Nonetheless, she resolved to enjoy the outing. There was a slim chance Lord Kenwood might yet say or do something to redeem himself.

The carriage turned onto the wide avenue of Hyde Park and the gravelled drive that ran beside Rotten Row. Some people gathered by the rail to better see those on display. Nobles in fine open carriages drove slowly in front of them as more vehicles fell in behind. Riders trotted on the other side of the trees. No one galloped—that wouldn't give them sufficient time to be appreciated. Sera caught glimpses of women sidesaddle in smart habits, feathers curling from their hats. Strolling people called out to those they knew on the worn paths.

Sera flicked open her parasol. Holding on to the carved end stopped her from fidgeting and imagining spells to cast if Lord Kenwood bored her. They travelled along in the dappled light cast by the numerous trees in the park. While part of Sera admitted it was a pleasant way to spend an hour or two, another part of her saw only the artifice of it all. The horses were prepared by legions of unseen grooms, both to ensure the shine to their coats and to undertake the training so the noble wasn't unseated in front of his peers. They were all players upon a stage, performing their expected parts and delivering lines scripted by society. How dull.

She imagined much more adventurous evenings. How she longed to attend a music hall, or a working-class tavern, and immerse herself in the lives of common Londoners. She could better serve their needs if she understood the problems they faced every day.

There came a point when she realised her companion had said something and awaited a response.

She smiled and twirled the parasol. "I'm so sorry, Lord Kenwood. I was admiring that fine chestnut over there and didn't hear your question."

His moustache twitched. "I said, I have a town-house in Mayfair and the estate in Sussex. Should you wish a small cottage for...magical purposes, something could be arranged. I don't want to upset my mother or aunts, who are more old-fashioned in their beliefs about witches and such. My estate does possess a folly among the trees that could be converted for your use."

Old-fashioned in their beliefs. It seemed even in the country, taunts of *witch* might follow her every move. If his mother disapproved of the very essence of Sera, how could she face such a woman over the dinner table every night? The idea alone seemed exhausting. Even if it did come with the chance to garden on a modest scale. Her mind flitted to rolling hills and flat pastures waiting for her to cast a different kind of magic.

He nodded. "Your house will not be needed. Since the Crown will not take it back and increase your stipend, it can be rented out."

Sera's dream of avenues of soaring trees and curving rivers experienced an earthquake as his words shook her fantasy world into a shambles. "What do you mean, the Crown won't take my house back? How do you know that?"

He huffed. "I enquired, of course, since your income will come to me after we wed."

"To you?" She wiped a hand through the air to disperse the last of her daydream. They hadn't even completed one circuit around the park together and already he had calculated her net worth.

"Such is the way of things. Ordinarily your family would provide your husband with a dowry, but in this unusual case, the Crown will pay over the annual income for your services...to me." He spoke in a slow and measured way that, had Sera been a cat, would have ruffled her fur the wrong way.

Gripping the parasol handle tighter, she considered turning it into a sabre and running him through. She'd have to push hard, in case the silver embroidery covering his jacket acted as a sort of chain mail. "My income is my own to manage. I do not need a husband to oversee my affairs. I am quite capable of paying my accounts and investing any surplus as I see fit."

Lord Kenwood laughed so loud he startled two

horses riding past. The lady snatched at her reins as her mount danced sideways and she glared at them. Her companion pushed his horse closer on her off side to settle the worried equine.

"Come, Lady Winyard, you cannot be insensible of your position?" Kenwood chuckled and moved his walking cane back and forth between his hands.

"My position?" Anger flared inside her and magic pooled in her fingertips.

He smiled, but it sat upon his lips only and never reached his eyes. "May I speak plainly, since it is clear this will be a business transaction?"

"Please do." The parasol handle heated in her grip and Sera drew a breath to calm herself before she set fire to the smooth wood.

He gestured at her with his cane. "While your features have a certain appeal, you possess neither great beauty nor great fortune. You have been elevated to a rank far beyond the circumstances of your birth. If not for an accident that slipped magic into your body, we would never have met. You are as far beneath me as any scullery maid would be. Your stipend from the Crown is vital if you are to find a husband—no man of breeding will take you without it. You are also expected to use your abilities to the benefit and entertainment of myself and my family."

Rage poured hot through her body. His words created such an inferno she didn't know where to start putting out the flames. No man would take her? She didn't even *want* a man. And what was this talk of *my* family? Not *our* family. He saw her as a tool to wield. A plain and common one at that.

There were many ways she could retaliate. As much as she wanted to strike out at Lord Kenwood and slice him in two with a flaming sword, that would guarantee her imprisonment in the Repository of Forgotten Things—assuming it didn't result in a quick execution. She wasn't so foolish as to risk her own life. A pig's tail, perhaps? But that didn't seem like a grand enough reaction. Since they were in Hyde Park to be observed, she wanted something that would be *seen*.

"You're not going to cry, are you? I thought it better to be clear about what is expected of you." He huffed and turned to watch a woman in a scarlet habit ride past.

"No. I am not one for tears. Thank you, Lord Kenwood, for being open and frank." That was one name she could cross off the council's list.

Sera contemplated turning his horses into giant slugs, but that was unfair to the horses, who had no part in the ignorance of their owner. Another idea came to her. With a tight smile on her face, she placed one hand on the side of the carriage and whispered in an arcane tongue. Magic flowed through the timbers to the axles and then out to the wheels.

A loud *thud!* sounded and the carriage lurched to such a sudden stop that Lord Kenwood was flung off the plush seat to his knees. The horses neighed in alarm and danced in the harness. The driver called out reassurances to them and jumped down to find out what had stopped the carriage.

"What the devil did we hit?" Lord Kenwood called.

"Your ignorance."

With a flick of her wrist, Sera opened the half door and lowered the steps. With her parasol over one shoulder, she descended to the ground. The carriage had hit nothing, apart from dirt. Sera had simply sunk them all into the ground. The vehicle now sat atop four half circles protruding from the otherwise undisturbed gravel of the drive.

"I have no need of you, Lord Kenwood. It's such a lovely day, I believe I shall walk from here."

The driver stared at the carriage and scratched his chin. People gathered at the rail and pointed to the sunken carriage with the crest upon the doors that identified its owner. Conversation and a smattering of laughter rose around them as Sera ducked under the rail.

"You spiteful woman! I'll make sure no noble will ever touch you!" Lord Kenwood shouted after her.

Sera laughed into a gloved hand. Perfect. That suited her rather well.

As she proceeded along the path, more people rushed to see what had happened and to laugh at the unfortunate lord. It would take Lord Kenwood some time to move his carriage. Either a mage, new wheels, or a shovel would be required.

Sera's delight in wreaking havoc was tempered somewhat when she imagined what Abigail and the Mage Council would say when they heard. Her ruse would be difficult to maintain if all her suitors withdrew their offers. At least she still had Otto, and there might be men without titles who would brave her wrath. One tall, broad gentleman in particular appeared in her mind's eye.

"Lady Winyard?" a familiar voice with a European accent summoned her from her thoughts.

"Otto!" Sera called on seeing him. He was strolling with a few of his fellow Austrian nobles and broke away from his group to join her.

"Are you in the park alone?" He offered his arm.

"Not anymore." She took his elbow and they continued along the path.

"Whatever is everyone staring at?" He glanced over his shoulder at the growing crowd.

"Lord Kenwood has met an obstacle he cannot surmount," she murmured, and gave him the sunny smile of a woman happy to be courted.

Eighteen

The rest of Otto's group trailed behind them as they chatted. Sera drew a deep breath and her previous anger dissipated into the ground. The park was a lovely place, but how she wished she could remove her shoes and stockings and run across the grass in bare feet. Part of her longed to join the children playing with boats in the pond. But if she hitched up her skirts and waded through the water to animate little captains on the vessels, no one would regard her as a serious mage.

"How go your negotiations?" She knew a little of trade negotiations due to discussions at the Napier table, but thought it an area she should learn more about. The manner in which nations approached such contracts might have parallels in drafting legislation.

"They progress at a slow pace. Every tiny change must be reported to Vienna. We await a response from His Holiness about accepting a half-percent reduction in one tariff for a half-percent increase in another." He pulled her to one side as a group of children ran along the path bowling a hoop.

As Sera turned to watch their fun, a sudden burst of outrage from nearby caught her attention. A man with a cap pulled low over his brow pushed through a group of chatting women. How rude, she thought as the women glared after him, his hurried pace at odds with the relaxed strolling of people enjoying the late summer's day. Wearing a dark brown woollen coat, he must be over warm. Given his haste, perhaps he was late for work and was taking a shortcut through the park.

As he approached, one hand slid under his coat and drew forth a metallic object. Sunlight glinted along its length. Her brain registered the shape of the thing in his hand as he stretched his arm out towards her. Instinctively, Sera swung her parasol in front of herself and Otto.

"What—?" Otto exclaimed as Sera pulled him to a halt and simultaneously discharged her magic along the parasol handle and into the fabric. The delicate umbrella shook in her hands as it bloomed in size and solidified to become a shield. In the next instant, a projectile slammed into it and a *bang!* startled horses and people alike.

Otto exclaimed in German and wrapped an arm around her. People shouted and pointed. Some ran away from the noise. Women screamed and grabbed their children before dashing for the cover of enormous tree trunks. One horse reared, while others danced on the spot. Sera peered around the shield and tried to find the man in all the commotion, but he had turned tail and fled.

One of the more youthful members of Otto's party leapt the barrier rail to dash down the path in pursuit.

"Blast! Can anyone see him?" she called as she lowered the enlarged parasol, but kept it ready to fling up if another attack occurred. She could use her magic to freeze the assailant's feet to the ground and stop his escape, but she needed to know where he was first.

"Are you hurt, Lady Winyard?" Otto asked.

The other members of his group clustered around them. The men scanned the panicked pedestrians, the women huddled together clutching their parasols.

"I am quite unharmed, thank you." Sera lowered her parasol. It shrank in size and soon returned to its original proportions. Turning the handle, she examined a tiny tear in the fabric that had severed a few fibres, but hadn't been large enough to allow whatever had hit it to penetrate. "We must ask if anyone who was close by can describe him." She gestured to the group of women the marksman had pushed aside.

Otto spoke in German to one of his associates and waved him towards the women. Sera assumed the young man to be some sort of secretary or artist, as he drew a sheet of paper and pencil from a pocket of his jacket.

"Someone shot at you. I cannot believe anyone would attempt such a thing against a mage." Otto spat the words with such anger that a nearby group of young bucks scurried away.

Sera closed the parasol that had protected her from

more than sunlight. It didn't take much effort for her to imagine someone wishing her harm. An assassin's shot was a most effective way to remove a troublesome mage and allow their power to be reborn in another vessel. What worried her was who might have organised such an attack. Had Lord Ormsby sought to cure his constant headache? Or perhaps it was the Duke of Ketley, who had once tried to have her arrested for Lord Branvale's murder? Lord Kenwood might even have sent a man after her for what she'd done to his carriage.

Her problem was that her list of possible enemies was too long.

A thought occurred to Sera as the people around them overcame their shock and either resumed their walks, or formed groups to gossip about what just happened while casting glances in her direction. They'd probably expected her to produce a thunderbolt and strike down the marksman. "Let us see if we can find the ball. I might be able to use it to locate the hand that last touched it."

"Come, everyone. Let us search the grass," Otto said to his companions.

"But try not to touch it if you find it, please. Pick it up with a handkerchief." Sera bent over and used the tip of her parasol to brush aside the grass.

It didn't take long to find the spent lead ball—a ray of sunlight caught the side and gave away its position not far from where they stood. Otto knelt down and wrapped it in a pale blue handkerchief and held it out to Sera.

"Thank you, Otto," she murmured as she knotted the fabric and dropped it into her reticule.

The Austrian noble who had given chase returned, carrying the brown overcoat the would-be assassin had worn. "I found this abandoned behind some trees."

"Part of his disguise, perhaps," Otto said. He took the coat and turned out the pockets. Then he inspected the lining for any clue as to who it belonged to. He poked a finger through a hole in the elbow. "It is poorly constructed and worn. It must have belonged to a commoner, but there is nothing to give us any idea as to whom."

The other man waved his sheet of paper in the air. "They saw very little, Lord Zedlitz. Describing mostly his clothing and build. One woman said he had a scar on his chin."

"A scar on his chin?" Sera leapt on the small detail.

"Yes, Lady Winyard." He bowed and offered up the page with his scribbled notes.

The noble had recorded what details people could recollect, from the colour of his cap and coat to vague descriptions of size. Incredibly, accounts varied wildly. One person said he had worn a blue coat, when obviously it was brown. One said he was tall and broad, another of barely average height.

She folded the sheet and tucked it into her reticule with the spent ball. "I need to find Lieutenant Powers."

Given the comment about an old injury to the man's face, there was a chance that Sera had not been the intended target at all, but her companion.

"Our carriages await up ahead. We can convey you

to wherever you need to go." Otto pointed to where three carriages were lined up in the shade. The horses all stood with their heads bowed and they appeared to be enjoying a snooze.

"The palace first. The lieutenant has been scrutinising all the household staff and he might be there." Sera set a determined pace across the park to the vehicles. She climbed into one with Otto and two others. The rest of the party dispersed between the remaining carriages.

Ideas swirled through her mind as they travelled to the palace. Had the assassin aimed for her or Otto? Could it have been the same man who waited in the hall outside Lady Zedlitz's room, and if so, why would he strike at Otto? They had assumed the murder to be motivated by the bracelet. Now she wondered if they had missed a vital clue that linked mother and son in such a way that someone wanted both of them dead. A feud over property or the late Lord Zedlitz's will might have sparked such rage.

They found Lieutenant Powers in the courtyard, finishing an inspection of guards. He bowed on seeing her. "Lady Winyard, always a pleasure. I've been staring at chins all day, but none of these have a scar such as we seek. I think I have chased the wrong rabbit down its burrow."

Sera heaved a sigh of relief at not being obliged to track the cavalry officer down. There a simpler way to communicate with those in her inner circle—the Kestrels. So far she had only provided Kitty and Abigail with an ensorcelled ring that connected them to her.

But she would brew more mage silver for the lieutenant and Hugh.

"Lieutenant, I am glad to have found you. Our man with a scar is not among these household staff members, because he has been busy in Hyde Park this afternoon."

"Oh?" Light sparkled in Lieutenant Powers's eyes.

"He took a shot at Lord Zedlitz and myself." Sera gestured to the margrave at her side.

The opulent moustache shot up a full inch. "An attempt on your life in broad daylight? The gall of the man! Are you both unharmed?"

"Yes, but we do not know for sure which of us was the would-be assassin's target." Two deep frown lines pulled at Otto's brows.

"I was able to deflect the shot, which we found in the grass. I am going to try to locate the last hand to touch it. We also have the fellow's overcoat, but my magic cannot work with it, as it has passed through too many hands during its life. Those who saw him cannot agree on his description, but one woman did notice the odd scar on his chin." She tapped below her lip. "That detail leads me to believe that Lord Zedlitz was the intended victim, not I."

Lieutenant Powers made a noise in the back of his throat and his eyes became unfocused as he pondered events. "How innovative you are to use yourselves as bait on our line to lure this man out into the open. But can you be certain this assassin was aiming for Lord Zedlitz? We might be pursuing two different murderous parties."

She snorted a quick laugh. "I am sure there are

many individuals who would wish the shot meant for me. But it is simply too coincidental for the man in the park to have the same distinguishing feature as the footman seen in the hall outside Lady Zedlitz's room. I believe it was merely chance that I happened to be with Lord Zedlitz when the man took aim and fired."

Otto took her gloved hand and kissed her knuckles. "And I am grateful that you were, Lady Winyard. Your shield saved my life."

Odd. The gallant gesture from the margrave did not make her flesh tingle as it did when Hugh took her hand. "I am only sorry I could not freeze the man to the spot." She was untested in such dangerous situations, where one needed to respond in an instant with magic. Her mind played the moment over and over, and each time she imagined taking a different course of action and changing the outcome.

"If you had taken the few seconds required to freeze the man's feet, he would still have fired and you would not have had a shield in place. We might have captured him, but it would have been at the expense of Lord Zedlitz's life—or your own." Lieutenant Powers seemed to read her thoughts and his words reassured her that when tested, she had chosen the best way to use her magic.

She flashed him a grateful smile. Her instincts in this case had saved a life. Yet she still mourned not being able to save Jake Hogan on that rooftop. Although it was a sad fact that death had awaited him no matter how he'd left the building.

Pushing aside such maudlin thoughts, she concentrated on the matter at hand. "I fear our assassins are not yet finished with their task."

"You think I am at risk?" Otto's spine stiffened. "What of Inge?"

"I will send word to Elliot, but Inge is protected by my magic while she is under my roof. I am more concerned for you, Lord Zedlitz." Sera laid a hand on Otto's arm. Not only had he removed himself from their suspect list, he had provided an additional clue. Why was someone targeting both him and his mother?

"I will inform the rest of our party of what has happened. I think it might be prudent to excuse myself from the negotiations and return to Austria. It seems I am not welcome on these shores and I wish to return *Mutter* to our home." Otto bowed and gestured to one of his men, who presented the overcoat to the lieutenant.

"You are a marvel, Lady Winyard. You have gathered more clues in one afternoon than I have in several days. You should add *investigator* to your title." Powers winked and watched the group disappear into the palace.

"We also need another conversation with Lady Haas," she said. "I met her maid the other day, crying in her room. She let slip that Lady Haas is most unhappy in her marriage and, I believe, may have appealed to Lord Zedlitz to help her in some way." She could only speculate as to what the maid's slip of the tongue had meant.

The lieutenant *tsk*ed, as though his thoughts were a horse to be urged along. "You think we are pursuing the wrong motive? That perhaps there is something else that Lord Zedlitz has in common with his mother?"

From the start, Sera had believed the murder to be motivated by the bracelet. But what if Lady Zedlitz's death and the missing bracelet were only loosely connected? Otto or Inge might have seized the opportunity to pocket it before raising the alarm. If that were the case, she imagined them using it to smooth their path to matrimony.

The murder became like broken glass in her mind, each fracture a possible motive. Which way ought she to turn?

"What of a common enemy, or someone wishing to end a family line?" Her need to find the bracelet and understand the one she'd once worn had blinded her to other possibilities. They needed a fresh perspective and to dig deeper into the Zedlitz family's past.

"But why now, and here?" The lieutenant stroked his pointed goatee.

That was the bit that bothered her. If someone in the Austrian party had fatal designs on the Zedlitz family, why wait until they'd reached England? "The timing is odd," she agreed. "If someone meant harm to the family, there would be easier ways to do such things. Such as in a remote castle during winter, as Lord Zedlitz once observed."

"I will question Lady Haas. But however unhappy her marriage, I cannot see how murdering Lady Zedlitz or the margrave would remedy her situation." The men the lieutenant had inspected had dispersed while they were talking, and they now stood alone to one side of the expansive courtyard.

"Unless we return to the bracelet as a motive, and Lady Haas intended to use it to force her husband to divorce her." But such a motive didn't sit right with Sera. Even if her religion allowed a divorce, Lady Haas would lose all the trappings of her position. She would not only be ostracised, but penniless to boot.

"Another possibility is an old wound that has festered and become worse with the passage of time," Powers murmured.

Sera had questioned her friends about one such event from long ago. "You think it could be related to what happened here on their last visit to England?"

He raised one eyebrow. "I think your words were that the previous visit left people still pained to this day."

Certainly one family in particular bore deep and enduring wounds. "Sir Athol and his bull. Lady Abigail said the family was ruined afterwards. They might believe that if they possessed the bracelet, they could restore their fortunes. But they were banished from court fifteen years ago and have never returned." Such a motive didn't explain why they would seek Otto's death, too. Unless the man really had aimed for Sera and their attacker's scar was no more than a coincidence. Hugh, with his knowledge of the lower classes, would know if such scars were common among thugs and assassins.

Perhaps those who sought to harm her had employed an assassin who juggled a busy schedule.

NINETEEN

As Sera and Powers strolled the wide hallways towards the suite of the Austrian delegation, Hugh rushed towards them and took Sera's hand. "Sera, are you harmed? The court has been informed of the assassination attempt." He drew her close, keeping hold of her hands as he scrutinised her for holes.

"I am perfectly well, as is Lord Zedlitz. I suspect I was not the intended target. At least, not this time." His touch spread warmth along her arm and a part of her settled at having him near. She hadn't realised how the events of the afternoon had rattled her nerves until, like a cat whose fur stood on end, his soothing hands restored calm.

"I am relieved you do not require my professional assistance," he murmured, his attention returning to her face, having found no evidence of blood or injury.

"I think we can safely remove Lord Zedlitz from

our short list of suspects." Lieutenant Powers huffed a quiet laugh.

"Are we still searching for someone using the bracelet?" Hugh tucked her hand into the crook of his elbow as they continued along the hall.

"Yes. We will also speak to Lady Haas about a personal matter and try to find a baron who had an unfortunate encounter with Lady Zedlitz fifteen years ago," Sera said.

Hugh angled his body to deflect a cluster of courtiers rushing towards them. "An old grudge?"

"Possibly. If your family had been ruined by someone, what lengths would you go to in order to restore them?" The lieutenant posed the question.

"But first, Lady Haas. Then we must find Sir Athol." Sera wondered if Lady Haas's maid would be in attendance, and if so, would she recognise Sera as the person who had sat with her and asked too many questions while she nursed her black eye?

The lieutenant rapped on the door to the private drawing room that connected the bedchambers of Lord and Lady Haas. It was opened by the maid, now with an impressive greenish-black shiny eye.

"I say, who did that to you?" Hugh pushed the door wide and attempted to examine the girl. She turned her face away and tried to shrink into the woodwork.

"Leave the maid alone. Clumsy thing walked into a door. What do you want?" Lord Haas leaned forward in his chair, but did not move from his spot by the fire.

Lady Haas sat opposite him. In her hands was a

hoop containing a piece of embroidery. She stabbed at it with a needle threaded with yellow silk.

The lieutenant bowed to the couple. "Lady Winyard needs to speak with Lady Haas."

"She didn't walk into a door—someone struck her," Hugh murmured to Sera as the maid closed the door and scurried through another to her mistress's chamber.

"Have you found the murderer yet? None of us are safe on English soil until you catch the madman." Lord Haas slammed his book shut.

"We are pursuing several possible suspects," Powers said.

Lord Haas grunted. "Talk to her if you must, but my wife is ignorant about the matter."

Sera glanced at her companions to make sure they stayed put, then turned to Lady Haas. "I should prefer we speak in private."

Lady Haas sighed and tossed the embroidery on the settee. "Why?"

"There are delicate matters best discussed one lady to another, without the men overhearing." Sera had little sympathy for the woman after discovering she had struck her maid. But neither would she announce that they knew about her lover in front of Lord Haas, and further suspected she plotted either to divorce or murder him. Any awkwardness could be avoided if he already knew about the lover, but his impending death by foul means might be a bit of a surprise. "Perhaps the gentlemen could discuss your maid's unfortunate accident while we are in the other room?" Sera suggested.

Lady Haas narrowed her gaze and pursed her lips.

Sera smiled and whispered ensorcelled words that she knew exactly what Lady Haas had done.

The other woman's eyes widened as the words vibrated inside her ear. "I shall only be a few minutes," she said to her husband, then gestured for Sera to follow her to the adjoining bedchamber. The maid sat on a chair mending a chemise draped over her knee.

As soon as the door closed, Lady Haas turned to Sera and crossed her arms. "What is it you think I am guilty of?"

"I'll not detain you long. I need the name of your lover." Sera glanced at the maid, who hadn't given any indication of recognising her.

The other woman's cheeks puffed in and out, the denial coating her tongue.

"Don't bother to deny it. I am aware he is a member of your party. I only need to know whom. Or I can ask every man who travelled here with you if he is the one sleeping with you, if you prefer?" She turned back to the closed door.

"Erik Gerber. He accompanies his father," Lady Haas hissed, trying to keep her voice from reaching the other room. "But you do not understand our situation."

Indeed, there were some things Sera didn't understand. Like striking someone, no matter your frustration or unhappiness. But there was one aspect of the sad tale she feared she understood too well. "Did you have any choice in marrying Lord Haas?"

Liesel Haas drew a long breath and stood taller. "No. I was going to wed Erik until that horrible day. I screamed inside my head, yelling *no!* over and over, but words that were not my own kept coming from my mouth."

As Sera suspected, Lady Zedlitz had forced the match for some reason. What a horrid woman. So many lives had been ruined because of her actions. But those actions had returned to roost, perhaps, and resulted in her death.

Sera stepped closer and wrapped them in a silence spell so that even the maid would not overhear their conversation. "I believe Lady Zedlitz used magic to compel you. Think back to the night of your engagement. Can you think of any reason why she would force you to take a husband thirty years your senior? Did you have any disagreements that night?" If Sera had provoked the woman's anger the night of the ball, what mischief might she have tried to wreak on a mage? It didn't bear thinking of. While Sera could repel the magical strands of the bracelet when used directly against her, Lady Zedlitz could have forced any number of people to strike against Sera.

Lady Haas stared at the painted ceiling with its hunting scene and hounds drinking from a river. "I did not let Lady Zedlitz join our game of cards. I—I—" Her voice trailed off.

"What is it?" There was one piece of information Sera sought, but there might still be a clue in understanding the old encounter with Lady Zedlitz.

Her attention darted around the room and she wet her lips. "I told her that only young people could join our fun. That she needed to sit with the other old people, and gestured to where Lord Haas sat by the fire playing chess with someone who was ninety."

Ah. One cruel remark had resulted in a much greater cruelty. "Does your husband know of your lover?"

"No. He is rather possessive of his things. But I thought I might be able to negotiate an agreement with him." She dropped to a green paisley chaise and pressed one hand to her forehead.

"Divorce?" Sera perched beside her.

Lady Haas laughed. "Divorce is something you English people do. It is not our way. Nor do I wish to lose my position by doing such a thing."

Sera tried to make sense of the little the maid had revealed to tailor her questions. She had mentioned Lord Zedlitz's name, but what role did he play? "You sought Lord Zedlitz's help."

The hand dropped and cool hazel eyes regarded Sera. "Yes. I wanted Lord Haas to provide me with my own household and an income so that I might live a separate life. Lord Zedlitz is well respected and I asked him to approach Lord Haas to arrange it."

"Somewhere your lover could visit without meeting Lord Haas in the hall." What the other woman wanted was not an uncommon situation. Noble couples often lived apart with their own households. Usually the wife was left on some rural estate while the husband spent his income on entertainments in town. Although with a husband as old as Lord Haas, perhaps Lady Haas wanted to reverse those roles and live in a city while he retreated to the countryside and the company of his dogs. "I assume he has not agreed to such an arrangement?"

Lady Haas wore a gown with shortened sleeves trimmed with lace at the elbow, and while her wrists were wrapped in bracelets, none was the engraved copper cuff. If she wore the item taken from Lady Zedlitz, Lord Haas would have agreed to anything.

"No. He requires an heir. His only son died in a hunting accident last year, and his two daughters cannot inherit." Lady Haas reached for the glass on the table beside the chaise and traced a fingertip around the rim. "I will not provide a replacement until he signs our agreement."

A faintly acrid aroma that reminded Sera of burnt toast drifted from the glass. The smell triggered a memory of a particular potion she had brewed for a few of Lord Branvale's women clients. If taken the day after intimate relations, it kept a woman from conceiving. "Is Lord Zedlitz negotiating your terms with Lord Haas?"

Lady Haas huffed and her hand stilled. "He claims he is too busy with the treaty talks. When he is not at that table, he is dining at yours. A duty to his fellow countryman should come before dallying with an Englishwoman."

The more Sera talked to Lady Haas, the less she thought the magic bracelet was hidden somewhere in the room. Not if the other woman had any inkling of its abilities. Nor did it make sense she would send an assassin to shoot Otto simply because he hadn't extracted what she wanted from her husband.

"I shall be sure to mention it to him the next time he

calls upon me. I leave you to your embroidery, Lady Haas." Sera walked through the bedchamber door and returned to the small parlour.

Hugh appeared to be inspecting Lord Haas's knee. "I believe it is rheumatism, Lord Haas. Walking will help, as will a diet rich in fatty fish, vegetables, and nuts." The surgeon refastened the knee buckles of his lordship's breeches and stood.

Lord Haas waved a hand. "My doctor said a leech would help, that my humours are out of balance."

"Medicine has come a long way since our reliance on leeches, my lord. Try an extra fish dish each week, and a gentle stroll each day." Hugh rolled his eyes but he kept his tone conversational.

Taking their leave, they walked some distance along the corridor until they found a window seat away from the bustle of courtiers and footmen. Sera sat with the weak sunlight behind her, the men on either side. The lieutenant had an expectant look and balanced on his toes.

"Erik Gerber is her lover," Sera said.

"Huh. I recall him—a fresh-faced young man with light blond hair." Powers leaned on the wall by the window seat. "But he does not have a scar. As we already suspected, the lover is not the missing footman. But do you think Lady Haas would wish to harm either Lady Zedlitz or her son?"

Sera shook her head. "Lady Haas seeks a separate household in exchange for providing her husband the required heir. She asked Lord Zedlitz to negotiate the agreement. I do not believe she possesses the bracelet, nor does it make sense for her to attempt to murder Lord Zedlitz when she asked him for help."

"A remote possibility, then. I will have a chat with Gerber, anyway." With arms crossed, he tapped the nails of one hand against his scarlet sleeve.

"Where does that leave us trying to find either murderers or bracelet?" Hugh asked.

"I will see what the recovered shot has to tell me. We need to find the last known address of Sir Athol and try to trace him forward through the years." Abigail thought the family had retreated to Scotland, but they might have returned to London without alerting the court to their presence.

The lieutenant pushed off the wall. "I will hunt down Gerber. Will the Kestrels report at Miss Napier's home?"

"Shall we say tomorrow at one?" When Sera returned to her home, she would alert Kitty that once again they needed her parlour.

"Until then." Powers bowed to Sera and clapped Hugh on the shoulder. Then he strode away.

"I wish I could do something to assist." Hugh held out his hand to her.

"I need to find a spell to reveal who last touched the shot. Perhaps you could help me find the necessary ingredients?" Sera took Hugh's hand to rise and they strolled back through the palace.

"If it would help, I have access to the Physic Garden in Chelsea," the surgeon offered.

"Oh, yes please. I would love to stroll its paths and cut the herbs I need." Sera had never seen the medicinal garden. The dried plants she needed were procured from apothecaries, but she much preferred to select her own. Often a fresh leaf or flower had more intense power.

Hugh escorted Sera through the palace.

As they neared the main entrance, Lady Abigail approached from the other direction and waved to Sera. "Lady Winyard, might I steal you away from Mr Miles?"

"Of course, Lady Abigail," Hugh said. "I will call upon you tomorrow morning, Lady Winyard, and take you to the garden."

Sera watched Hugh's tall form navigate the swarm of courtiers and nobles assembled outside the presence chamber. Then her arm was wrenched sideways.

"How could you do such a thing to Lord Kenwood?" Abigail hauled her into a shadowy corner. "The queen has been informed that you caused considerable damage to his property. You must apologise."

"I will do no such thing. He insulted me and said I was as far beneath him as a scullery maid. You keep reminding me that I am a duchess now. Would you have let such a slur pass?" Sera loved her friend, but had no intention of making amends for burying Lord Kenwood's carriage wheels.

"Did he, indeed? Well, he omitted that part when telling his tale to the queen." Abigail let out a sigh. "I suppose I cannot blame you. He should be grateful you didn't give him cloven feet."

Cloven feet would have been too easy to disguise. "I

was considering a pig's curled tail so he couldn't sit down."

Silence dropped between them. Then Abigail let out a laugh. She hastily covered her mouth with one hand and glanced around to ensure no one else caught her moment of levity.

"I am sorry he turned out to be abominable. But really, Sera, you must control your temper. Word spreads, and no one will want a wife who lashes out in such a way. Already two other nobles on the list presented to you by the council have withdrawn their suits. Fortunately, I know of a noble who is—I promise —a true gentleman. He is rather shy and rarely in society, so if we are lucky, he might not hear what you did to Lord Kenwood for some time. I thought to invite him to a quiet dinner where you are also in attendance."

Apparently hexing gentlemen wouldn't stop the match-making. She could suffer through one dinner to make Abigail happy and to continue her ruse for the council. "Very well. Who is this one?"

"Viscount Thornton. He is well read and rather scholarly. But I thought you might appreciate that. His estate is not as wealthy as some, but he is, in my opinion, a good man." Abigail winked, which Sera took as some indication he was the preferred candidate.

"I shall leave you to make arrangements. Now I must go to the mage library. We think we are close to the person who might have murdered Lady Zedlitz. Are you free tomorrow to discuss matters at Kitty's home?"

"I heard this madman fired a shot at Lord Zedlitz.

But do you think it was meant for you?" Worry shone in her friend's eyes.

Sera dismissed the concerns. The attempt did make her think of the fragility of life. Clearly she needed to learn defensive spells, because the next time she might indeed be the intended target, and have no parasol to hand. "I think what happened today is related to Lady Zedlitz's death. I am going to try and find the man who loaded the pistol. There is something you could do to help, though. Could you find out whether Sir Athol ever returned to London?" Abigail had a network of ears among the cream of society and would hear if the disgraced baron had slunk back.

"Of course. I will make discreet enquiries. Until tomorrow, then. I wish you luck in your search." Abigail kissed Sera's cheek and rejoined her group.

"Another suitor," Sera murmured. What would she have to do to this one, to make them all run scared?

TWENTY

Sera spent the next few hours in the mage library, searching for a spell or potion that would meet her requirements. She had managed to scatter a number of dusty old tomes over the reading desk before she spied something that sounded like it would work.

"A spell to reveal an unseen hand," she murmured to an empty room. Those who had been shuffling among the shelves when she arrived had left some time ago.

She copied the potion and spell onto a fresh sheet of paper and rolled it up before tucking it inside her reticule. When she emerged from the tower, twilight had claimed London. A shabby carriage waited for her, the driver snoozing in his seat and even the horse standing with lowered head. The horse's head jerked upward as she approached, the equine alert to his environment.

The movement of the reins woke the driver, who

jumped down to open the door for her. "Where to, milady?"

"Soho." She climbed inside and dropped onto the seat. Then her stomach rumbled, reminding her of how long it had been since luncheon. The events of the day had left her exhausted. How she longed for a hearty meal, the comfort of her found family, and the prospect of stretching out under a blanket.

At home, as she descended from the carriage, her front door opened and Elliot emerged with a lantern to light her way, full dark having by now fallen over the city. A figure detached itself from the shadows and revealed itself to be Bernadette, her neighbour.

"Bernadette, how lovely to see you." Sera offered a tired smile.

"And you, milady. I spied you returning and wanted to speak with you, if I might?" She held out a hand to halt Sera's progress.

"Of course." Curiosity relieved a little of Sera's tiredness.

Elliot stepped back to the front door to give the women a measure of privacy.

Bernadette cast a glance at her home, where a yellow glow played over the inside of the drawn curtain. "It's about that man who's been seen in the street staring at your house."

"Oh? Has he been spotted again?" She raised an eyebrow at Elliot. He also kept his eyes open for the mysterious watcher.

"The children saw him, surrounded him, and

pelted him with questions." A quick smile flashed over Bernadette's face.

Conflicting emotions surged through Sera. Pride at how the children leapt to her defence and their resourcefulness, but also fear for their safety. "How brave of them. But please caution them to think of their safety first. If these people who watch my home are not friendly, I would never forgive myself if one of them were harmed."

Bernadette swallowed and a tiny frown pulled at her brow. "I will tell them that is a direct order from you. They pay little heed to their mothers. The gent told them that he watched you for a friend, but he did not say who."

"His friend or mine?" Sera considered the answer. "Thank you, Bernadette."

The woman nodded and disappeared into the shadows once more as she returned to her home.

"Inge has gone to her room. Said she didn't feel safe sitting in the parlour after the attack on Lord Zedlitz," Elliot said as he closed the front door.

"Lord Zedlitz doesn't feel safe, either, and is seeking permission from the emperor to return to Austria before the treaty is finalised." She shrugged off her cloak and handed it to Elliot before stripping off her gloves.

"Everyone is talking about how you sank that noble's wheels in the ground. I reckon he must have deserved it." The footman's shoulders quivered in silent laughter as he hung up her cloak and hat.

"He did. Let us see if others will learn not to insult

me." She worried at her lip. The council would cast her actions in a different light and no doubt see them as further evidence of her hysterical feminine nature. If they pushed the matter, she would lay a complaint at court for the grievous insult Lord Kenwood had dealt her. If she were a man, she would have taken off her glove, slapped his face, and demanded satisfaction. If a champion were to step forward to avenge the insult, Kitty might yet see a tournament among Sera's suitors.

As she considered the idea, the certainty formed inside her that Hugh would leap to her defence. An image appeared in her mind of the surgeon naked to the waist and teaching Lord Kenwood a well-deserved lesson through bare-knuckle boxing. A sigh escaped her as she contemplated Hugh's broad chest stripped of a shirt.

"What are you sighing about?" Elliot asked as he followed her down to the kitchen.

"Just considering how my list of suitors grows smaller." Any choice she might have to make one day would be so much simpler if Hugh had been born noble.

"You either need to figure out how to be quiet and demure, or find a man who will put up with you as you are." Elliot pulled out a chair and sat down.

Sera snorted. She could no more change who she was than a star in the sky could turn into a turnip. Besides, it suited her plan if, one by one, the council's suitors developed cold feet. Perhaps once no noble in England would have her, they would leave her free to choose her own life's companion.

THE NEXT MORNING, Hugh appeared at an early hour to accompany her to the Chelsea Physic Garden. Dew still clung to the plants as they strolled the paths and birds called from the trees above. When she spied a plant needed for her spell or that would be useful for other things she might brew, Hugh snipped off the leaves or flowers and placed them in her basket.

"Thank you for asking me to accompany you. I know very little about plants and defer to the apothecary to craft the potions my patients need for their illnesses," he said as he snipped bright purple verbena flowers.

"You have some knowledge of plants, for you grow a fine potato," she teased. The plants in his attic room were very healthy, although an odd choice of decoration. "Besides, I enjoy your company."

"And I yours." He took her hand and tucked it into the crook of his elbow.

Sera leaned closer, enjoying the shelter his large form offered against a light breeze. She could have cast a blocking spell around them to stop the wind, but then she would have no excuse to be close to him. She delighted in Nature's own magic that stirred into life between them.

"I am concerned, though, that I cannot return the

depth of feeling you hold for me." It gnawed at her, that their relationship rested on so uneven a keel. She did not want Hugh putting his romantic life on hold waiting for her. Although when she considered him with another, it made her stomach roll.

They reached a spot where an iron bench sat surrounded by lavender and sheltered by a bay tree. Hugh seated himself and drew her down beside him. "I ask for nothing you are not ready to give. A man can admire a woman and be her friend, without expecting anything in return."

Sera snorted. "Then you are a very rare type of man."

There was one problem with being solely Hugh's friend—his touch summoned a reaction that demanded more from him than friendship. "The issue with merely being friends is that I rather liked kissing you, and even more shocking, I'm not opposed to doing it again."

He turned to her with a gleam in his eyes. "Ah. So if I took such a liberty, you wouldn't turn me into a toad?"

"If it were you, no. Which does not solve our quandary about the nature of our relationship." She wanted to be clear on what was developing between them, and to give herself time to decide whether she wanted to pursue anything deeper.

"Perhaps we need to create a new type of friendship to define what exists between us. One with additional benefits besides companionship. Like kissing." He draped his arm along the back of the seat.

"Yes, I like that idea. We are more than friends," she

murmured. Of her small circle, he alone would be allowed certain liberties.

Hugh stroked her cheek and rested his bent fingers against her chin. "I would like to avail myself of such an arrangement now, if you agree." He moved closer until his breath brushed over her closed eyelids.

When she murmured her consent, he closed the distance between them to kiss her gently. His hand slid from her chin to cup her face. Sera turned towards him and parted her lips, allowing him to deepen the kiss. She wrapped her arms around his neck, his solid body grounding her even as her emotions flew upward.

Yes, she liked kissing him very much. Theirs would be a friendship with certain benefits until she was ready for more.

After a few minutes of pleasure in his arms that set loose an army of butterflies in her stomach, he pulled back to rest his forehead against hers. "Shall we find everything on your list, before you so bewitch me I am unable to use the scissors?"

Sera breathed in the moment. *What list?*

As her pulse calmed, she remembered their purpose in the garden. "I suppose we should not linger all day with a murderer on the loose in London. I cannot perform the spell until we find a ginkgo biloba. I require both its leaves and a scraping of its bark."

For some reason, she couldn't stop smiling. As soon as she returned home, she had to tell Elliot that not only had she kissed Hugh, but that he had initiated the kiss. Sera would win their bet with only one day to spare.

She might have cheated a little, but it still counted as a win.

Hugh accompanied her home, with a promise to collect her that afternoon for their meeting at Kitty's. Sera had asked both Abigail and Kitty to see if they could find any information about Sir Athol and his current whereabouts.

"You look happy," Elliot said as Sera thrust her jacket at him in the entrance.

"Hugh kissed me! You lose." She grinned. She had won far more than the bet. A kiss from the surgeon was quite the prize.

His eyebrows rose. "Did he? So is he courting you now?"

"No, he is not a suitor. He is my friend, but he is allowed certain additional benefits." Sera intended to enjoy the new arrangement and couldn't wait to tell Kitty.

"Friends with benefits? I'll have to remember that one." A sly smile crossed his handsome face.

In the small study she used as a workroom, Sera cut and weighed the leaves, bark, and flowers needed for her spell. Then she ground them to a pulp with mortar and pestle. Next she whispered the spell over the mush as she added a few drops of oil to bind everything together. A white mist rose from the bowl and tickled her nose with a faint lemony tang. Fetching the handkerchief with the lead ball tied inside, she carefully undid the knot and shook the piece of metal into the mortar.

With care, she coated the ball in the thick and

fragrant concoction. Now it had to sit for at least three hours before being used. That gave her time to head to the outskirts of London to complete her task for the council. She'd be back in time for the meeting of the Kestrels and to use the ensorcelled ball to find the hand that had loaded the pistol.

To save time, she would ride. Thanks to Lady Abigail, Sera had been taught how to ride sidesaddle. But she still required a horse.

"Elliot!" she called along the hall, wondering where he might be.

The footman appeared from the parlour, shaking his head. "You're a bloody mage—no need to screech all the time. What do you want?"

"I have to go help a farmer with some sheep. Can you go to the local mews and hire me a suitable horse?" For once her dark green riding habit would actually go near a horse.

By the time Vicky had helped her change into the habit and piled up her hair under her hat, Elliot stood in the road holding the reins of a plain brown horse with black stockings. A group of little girls surrounded him and patted the horse's nose. On seeing her leave the house, Elliot handed the reins to the tallest of the girls.

"Let's get you up there." Elliot had no experience giving ladies a leg up, but apparently a groom at the mews had given him a quick lesson. The process still elicited giggles from the watching children.

Sera had to use a dash of magic to assist the upward motion provided by Elliot to settle herself in the sidesaddle. Once her skirts were arranged, the girl passed up the reins. With a wave to her audience, Sera turned the horse and headed northwest.

The necessarily controlled walk along the London roads gave her time to remember her riding lessons, so by the time the swirl of other horses, carriages, and pedestrians thinned, Sera was ready for a faster pace. She nudged the horse with her left heel, and it broke into a steady and comfortable canter.

Over the preceding weeks, Sera had noticed a theme in the missions allocated to her by the Mage Council. They were usually horticultural, agricultural, or related to drains. The first two didn't bother her in the slightest; she much preferred her trips outside the city, where she could dig her fingers into the dirt. Drains, while they did much to improve the quality of Londoners' lives, did embed a certain stench in her hair and clothing that even magic couldn't mask.

Her destination was somewhere on the edge of Paddington. Slowing the horse to a walk, Sera muttered a guiding spell and as she whispered the last word, a red arrow shot from her lips and zigged across the road. It flew towards a house with a thatched roof across the fields and burst into a red-tinged cloud that hovered over the premises.

She guided the horse through the meadow, the equine snatching mouthfuls of long grass as they passed. At the property, chickens scratched in the dirt and ignored a dog chasing a child around a tree. From the shrieks, Sera hoped the child was having fun. A cart laden with hay waited for it to be forked into the loft of a barn. Two men and a woman were nearby, and stopped their assorted tasks as she approached.

Suspicious eyes watched as she performed an ungainly dismount from the horse and tied its reins to a low-hanging branch. She approached the man leaning on the side of the cart. "Good morning. I am Lady Winyard. The Mage Council sent me to assist with some issue involving sheep."

Eyebrows rose. Would they grab their pitchforks to repel the witch?

"If you're really that lady mage, prove it. Do something magical." The old woman wriggled her fingers.

Sera rather thought that was the whole point of their requesting help from the Mage Council—that they had an issue requiring magical assistance. But it appeared she would have to audition for the role. There were innumerable things she could do to prove her magical ability, like fish swimming through the air, but she'd pick a useful demonstration. "What task could I help with right now?"

"We're about to unload the hay. If you could get it up there we'd be right grateful." The taller man gestured from cart to the door in the loft.

That seemed easy enough—hay couldn't be too heavy. Sera rubbed her hands together, then she mimed picking up a tied sheaf of hay and moving it to the loft. The bundle of hay flew through the air and neatly popped through the open door before flopping on the loft floor. In a few short minutes she had the entire cart emptied and the hay stored in the loft.

"Blimey. You're right handy to have around," the woman said.

"I do try to be useful," Sera said. Unlike her male counterparts, who preferred showy and pointless displays of their power. "Now, what is this issue with the sheep?"

Twenty-One

"Pardon us for doubting you, milady. I thought someone might have been playing a prank on us. I'm Adam Cole and I could use your magic with my ewes, if you don't mind." He gestured to a nearby field, where a number of the fluffy creatures grazed.

"What exactly is the problem with them?" Sera accompanied him to a set of timber yards. She shielded her eyes with her hand and squinted at the creatures. From her limited experience, the animals looked happy and healthy.

"The problem isn't them so much, milady, as it is the old ram. We think he's getting past it, if you know what I mean, and needs replacing. But it would help to know if any of these girls are in lamb or not. We'll bring them into the yard for you." He gestured to his companions and whistled to his dogs.

In a display that seemed magical to Sera, Mr Cole's dogs followed a series of whistles to round up the sheep and soon had them all trotting into the enclosure. One by one, Sera laid a hand on a ewe's fluffy side and let her magic feel for the faint trace of a foetal heartbeat. The old woman kept a tally of those in lamb by marking a plank of wood with a piece of chalk.

"Knew the old bugger was getting past it, but Mr Cole there wouldn't listen to me." She spat into the dirt after the last ewe bounced back into the field to rejoin her companions. There were far more barren ewes than pregnant ones. A dire situation for a farmer who relied on the spring lambing both to renew his flock and to have animals to take to market.

"Yes, yes, Sally. You were right all along. We still have time to try this lot again with a young ram." The farmer gestured to the flock as he closed the wooden gate.

Sally shook her head then winked at Sera. "He gets attached, he does. Thinks that if the ram is past it, then so is he." She chortled in laughter.

Mr Cole ignored Sally's jest. "Thank you, milady. You've been right helpful."

Sera rubbed her hands together, her skin softened from the lanolin in the fleece. Before she left, she thought to ask if they could in return help her with something. Kitty had sent her a quick dispatch to advise that Sir Athol had once farmed somewhere in the area.

"Do you by chance remember a family who used to live around here—Sir Athol Gollach? I hear he used to breed those Scottish cows with the shaggy coats and big horns."

"I remember him and his family. Had a farm up the

road a ways." Sally gestured to the north. "I used to help in the kitchens on account of my sister being their cook. Good man he was. Right odd what happened. They said he was upset about how the English treat the Scots, but it never made no difference to us where he was born or that he sounded a bit funny."

"I believe blue paint is rich in Celtic symbolism and he was discovered while holding a beast from the High-lands," Sera murmured. Doubt surged through her. Were they pursuing the wrong line of enquiry? The paint and choice of beast had to have been a protest against the English occupation.

"Wasn't right, though, was it? To sit his naked arse on the king's throne. I'd be right unhappy if I found a bare bum where I wanted to sit." Mr Cole leaned one elbow on the fence.

"Do you know where he went after that?" Were the rumours true that the family had retreated to Scotland after their shame and banishment?

Sally screwed up her face, resembling a dried apple left too long out in the sun. "Back to Scotland with his tail between his legs. My sister wrote that he died a few years back."

"Oh." Bother. If Sir Athol was dead, he couldn't be involved in Lady Zedlitz's murder unless he'd returned as a malevolent spirit.

Mr Cole wiped the sweat from his brow with the red kerchief tied around his neck. "Gregory would be the baron now, then."

"Poor lad has the title, but nothing to go with it."

Sally gave a ewe that had returned to the yard a tap on the nose as it tried to nibble her skirt through the fence.

"I remember his boys. Couple of young scamps they were. Always galloping across my crops on the big old draught horse Sir Athol had, clutching sticks like they were knights from olden times off to a joust," Mr Cole said.

Sally cackled. "Gregory and James were always off on some adventure together. Oh, how little James looked up to his big brother. Gregory used to lose patience sometimes with the way he followed him around like a puppy."

Sera smiled at the tale, imagining the two lads running through the long grass. A rural setting had much to offer children, with its open spaces, rivers, and trees.

Mr Cole rubbed the ears of the dog sitting at his feet. "I remember one time Gregory was running away from him when he tripped over a sleeping bull. Poor lad cut his chin open on a sharp stone. I heard James's scream for help from where I watched my flock."

"Wait. What?" The words collided in Sera's brain.

"He caught his foot on the animal's leg and went face first into a rock." Sally continued the tale. "Had blood all over his face and the doctor had a terrible time trying to stitch it up because he squirmed the whole time. He was left with quite the scar. We told him ladies would find it dashing."

A chill washed through Sera as Inge's words during her first interview tumbled through her mind. "He didn't trip over a *stair*, but a *steer*!" It had been Gregory in the corridor that morning.

"There's no stairs here, milady, or do you mean up to the loft?" Confused, Mr Cole pointed to the barn.

"I must get back to London. Could you give me a leg up, please, Mr Cole?" Sera untied her mount and flicked the reins over his neck.

Mr Cole was less adept than Elliot, or perhaps he didn't want to grab a mage's leg too firmly. Between the farmer and her magic, Sera again managed to land in the saddle. Putting heel to the horse, she cantered back to London.

Sera rode straight for her home and, with a lack of dignity that would have horrified Abigail, managed to dismount, but somehow left her skirt caught over the saddle's pommel.

"Just as well you're wearing a petticoat and not flashing your legs at everyone," Elliot said as he took the horse's reins while Sera freed her wool skirts.

"Hang on to him. I am running out of time and need to get to Kitty's house. The horse will be faster than a carriage." Picking up her skirts, Sera ran up the path and through the house. In her study, she used a spoon to scoop the lead shot out of the mortar and drop it into a vial. Popping a cork into the top, she eased the vessel into the top of her bodice. A quick glance at the clock in the parlour showed the meeting of the Kestrels was not far off.

"Here we go again," Elliot muttered as he boosted her back up on her resigned-looking mount to the amusement of those in the street.

Sera navigated the bustle of London streets to Kitty's home. A footman rushed along the path and took the horse's reins, while another helped her to dismount with the grace required in Mayfair.

"Could you see that he is returned to the mews in Soho?" Sera asked the man holding the reins.

"Yes, milady." He led the horse away around the side of the house as Sera headed inside.

"Miss Napier is in the parlour, Lady Winyard," the butler said as she breezed into the foyer.

Turning to the right, Sera strode across the tiled floor.

"You look a mess," her friend announced as Sera entered the room.

"I have been out to a farm in Paddington and back. Sir Athol has two sons and I believe the elder, the current Baron Gollach, is the man we seek. Do you have a map of London and a length of thread?" Sera pulled off her hat and dug her fingers into her hair to find stray pins. Then she tossed hat and pins on the sideboard.

"I will find one." Kitty fetched the map from her father's study and unrolled it on the low table. Then she opened her sewing basket and snipped a piece of blue thread from a skein. "Abigail sent her apologies—apparently she has a previous appointment she could not cancel. I suspect it is with that viscount who is courting her rather seriously."

"Ah. Duke Ketley's son. She is hopeful that an official engagement is not far away." Sera knelt on the floor before the map.

"I understand those negotiations are as delicate and nuanced as those between England and Austria over the trade contract," Kitty said.

Sera removed the vial from her stays and took a saucer from the tea tray. A whispered spell urged the shot to wriggle free of the vial and deposit itself on the saucer. Then she wiped away the sticky mash from around it with a piece of cloth.

Hugh and Lieutenant Powers arrived as Sera tied the thread around the piece of metal.

"Usually we remove shot, not stitch it back in," Hugh said, watching Sera manipulate the strand of silk.

Sera flashed him a smile before returning to concentrate on tying a knot in the thread. "This is going to locate who loaded the pistol. Although I know the identity of our footman with the scar on his chin, who is no footman at all. He is Sir Gregory Gollach, son of the late Sir Athol, the man who argued with Lady Zedlitz over a bull. Ironically, the new baron acquired his scar when as a lad he tripped over a *steer*."

"Our lives can be riddled with strange coincidences. But this explains why I could not find him among the staff. He must have stolen a uniform and everyone simply assumed he was a footman." Lieutenant Powers took the seat opposite Kitty, but he leaned forward to survey the map.

"Apparently Sir Athol died some years ago and left two sons. James is the younger. After Sir Athol's disgrace and banishment, the family was ruined. Gregory inherited the title of baron but nothing else." A waft of magic pulled the strand tight around the shot and Sera was ready for the next part.

"Two brothers with murder on their minds. Why, though?" Powers mused.

"That is a question we can ask once you find them," Kitty said. She directed the footman with the refreshment tray, once again laden with enough to feed Hugh, to the sideboard.

Hugh eyed the tray and hesitated only a moment before crouching next to Sera. She held the thread with its bait over the map and murmured the spell, asking the lump to seek out the one who had touched it last. Or second to last, as it would home in on the impression left when she'd coated it in the oily mush.

The thread swung back and forth before pointing to the area west of Charing Cross. Sera lowered her hand as it moved more to the left. Then it snatched the end from her fingertips and plonked itself on a street not far from Covent Garden.

"It's not an exact address, but it certainly narrows our search to a few buildings." Sera stared at the lump of metal, which wriggled a smidge to the right, then settled again.

"We have names and the description from Inge. Coupled with what you have just achieved, Lady Winyard, I am confident we shall find the pair before nightfall," Powers said.

In the small amount of time it took to organise the next step, the men devoured the selection of pastries and sandwiches, Sera sipped a cup of tea, and Kitty issued orders. She called for a carriage and a maid. Sera frowned at that request.

"You look an absolute fright. Even I have standards," her friend said.

In a few short minutes, the maid wrestled Sera's hair into a semblance of order and secured her hat once more. Then they climbed into the carriage and headed for one of the older parts of London.

"These men are dangerous," Lieutenant Powers murmured as the carriage lurched into motion.

"I have no intention of doing anything foolish, like throwing myself at them and wrapping my arms around their knees to stop them. It is simple mathematics—four of us can search faster than three." Kitty glared at the lieutenant as though she dared him to order her to remain in the carriage once they reached their destination.

Being a wise individual, he said no more on that topic. "Perhaps you could accompany me on one side of the road, while Hugh and Lady Winyard take the other?"

"There is the possibility that one of them is wearing the bracelet," Sera cautioned them. "Whatever you do, don't let them touch you. The compulsion needs physical contact to work. The mage silver ring Kitty wears will afford her some protection." Trying to apprehend someone who could force you to do things with a touch was a fraught enterprise. The wearer could set the Kestrels against one another, or create a defensive mob. And heaven forbid one should gain control of Sera herself.

"Can you reverse such a compulsion?" Hugh asked.

"I don't know. Possibly. When Lady Zedlitz used it on me, removing the thread of magic also removed the command she forced into my mind and body." Sera considered defensive spells as the carriage moved through the streets. Ideally, some way to stop the thread from burrowing into the skin would be best, like a repellent. The problem was that she needed the bracelet to understand how it worked in order to craft the best defence.

Fae magic. How she itched to learn more about them and the power they drew upon.

The carriage lurched to a stop and the Napier man opened the door and set down the steps. On the side of the road, they broke into pairs and Sera and Hugh crossed the road to begin at the building on the corner. Hugh knocked on doors and asked for Sir Gregory or his brother, James. Sera stopped pedestrians and asked the same questions. Across the road, Powers and Kitty undertook the same task.

Lips were pursed and heads shaken, but no one knew the brothers. By the time they reached the third building, disappointment flowed through Sera. What if her spell hadn't worked? Or the man who had loaded the pistol was someone other than the brothers? They could have borrowed or stolen it already loaded. So many tiny details could be wrong that meant they were searching in the wrong place. Or the person might have been to Covent Garden and then moved on to somewhere else between the time she'd cast the spell and when they'd arrived in the area.

"At least one of them is here," Hugh said as they paused for a moment. "Trust in yourself."

She reached out and squeezed his hand, grateful for his unwavering support. What would it be like to live a life with such a man at her side? Imagine the things she could do, knowing he believed in her and would join her on any adventure.

With a lighter heart, Sera was considering the next house...when an ear-splitting scream made her spin and stare at a pretty townhouse across the road.

TWENTY-TWO

Sera hesitated only a moment before picking up her skirts and running out into the traffic. She dodged between horses, Hugh right beside her. Kitty and Lieutenant Powers came running down the steps of one house and joined them as they stood outside the property in question.

People gathered on the pavement and stared up, as the scream warbled and was then cut off abruptly. As they considered what to do, a lower-pitched wail drifted out to the street.

Lieutenant Powers held out an arm to bar the way before Sera and Kitty stormed the front stairs. "We do not know if the scream is related to the man we seek."

"Regardless, someone is in distress." Kitty pushed his arm down.

"Very well, but at least let me go first. In the cavalry, we do consider ourselves chivalrous." His moustache wriggled as his lips pulled upward in a brief smile.

Kitty gestured for him to lead the way. "I wouldn't want to stand in the way of a cavalry charge."

The lieutenant rapped on the door as another shriek came from behind it, followed by shouts, and a loud thud. He waited only a few seconds before grabbing the handle and opening it himself. The entrance and hall beyond were a scene of chaos.

A young man covered in blood was held up against the wall by an older gentleman with grey hair. The young man sobbed, "She asked me to do it and I could not refuse."

"We need a surgeon. Hurry!" A woman with wild eyes shrieked and pulled at her hair.

Hugh pushed himself forward. "I am a surgeon. My name is Hugh Miles. What has happened?"

The woman's cries came to a hiccupping stop and she grabbed Hugh's sleeve to pull him farther into the house. "He cut off her arm. You must save her life."

Kitty pushed Sera forward. "Help Hugh. The lieutenant and I will get to the bottom of this."

"I will need hot water, towels, and some bowls. I have only a field kit in my pocket and may need other supplies," Hugh called back as the woman pulled him towards a closed door.

Inside was a genteel parlour turned into the gruesome scene of a crime. Blood splattered in an arc across the pale green wallpaper. A young woman lay on a chaise and appeared to be unconscious. A maid pressed a blanket around the woman's right arm.

"I don't know what to do, sir, but have been trying to stop the bleeding." The maid cast red-rimmed eyes to

Hugh, but her voice had a calm edge missing from that of the older woman.

Hugh took one look and gestured to Sera. "I need the scarf from around your hat."

She obeyed immediately, pulling the length of silk free. Hugh placed it around the woman's upper arm and tied a tight knot. Then he peered under the blanket and revealed a bloody stump, a piece of white bone jutting out.

"I will need to even this up before I can stitch it shut. Go to the kitchen and ask your chef for his sharpest vegetable knife and a meat cleaver. Then heat the blades in the fire and bring them here without touching them." He glanced around the room. "We need to move her to a table."

The older woman continued to sob and bite her knuckles. Sera assumed her to be the mother, given her fine clothing and the heart-shaped face similar to that of the unconscious woman.

"The dining room is across the hall, sir. I'll get straight to the kitchen for the knives." The maid took off at a trot, holding her skirts in one hand.

"As least she is unconscious," Hugh murmured as he slipped his arms under the woman's limp form and picked her up.

Sera turned to follow, but two things arrested her progress. Firstly, the woman's hand and forearm lying in a pool of blood on a rug. Secondly, a glint of copper. The two sides of the Fae cuff had pulled back from the delicate wrist.

Finding a handkerchief in her pocket, Sera used

one end to pick up the bracelet. As it turned in the light, tiny diamond chips twinkled from the engraved vines.

"Found you," Sera said to it. "I only wish the circumstances had been different." Then she wrapped it in the cloth and shoved it into her pocket before hurrying after Hugh.

He had laid the woman on the dining room table. A footman moved all the chairs away and stacked them by the walls. The surgeon shrugged off his jacket and rolled up his sleeves as a maid entered carrying a pitcher with steam curling from the top. Another footman came in with stacked bowls in his hands and towels draped over his forearms.

From his jacket pocket, Hugh retrieved a leather roll. Untying the strip holding it shut, he unrolled it to reveal a sort of sewing kit. Except in this one, a scalpel nestled alongside the thread and needles.

"What can I do to help?" Sera asked.

"Anything I ask of you to save this woman's life. If she rouses, are you able to lull her back to sleep with your magic?" He removed the small blade from his kit.

"Yes." Sera had never tried such a thing, but this was not the time to doubt herself.

He sliced the sleeves of the woman's gown and they stripped her to her chemise. Sera assisted Hugh, handing him whatever he requested. The woman's parents tried to enter the impromptu surgery, but the lieutenant held them back. Snatches of Kitty's orders to staff and family alike drifted into the dining room, and a sense of calm returned to the household under her command.

Hugh worked in silence, only making short requests of Sera. The clock marked the passage of time. After an hour, the surgeon was nearly done. Sera marvelled as Hugh made tiny, neat stitches over a flap of skin. Then he bound the wound with a bandage and stood back. He nodded. "Now we must hope it does not become infected, but she will survive the injury."

He washed his hands in a clean bowl of warm water while Sera opened the door. Her parents stood outside in the hall, but there was no sign of the young man.

"Charlotte!" the woman cried and she rushed to embrace the unconscious woman.

"Thank you, Mr Miles. We are grateful you were in the street. I am Mr Mosley and as you may have gathered, this is our daughter, Charlotte." Mr Mosley extended a hand to Hugh and the two men shook.

"She may be moved to a bedroom and should regain consciousness soon. Lady Winyard kept her asleep so she would not feel anything, but she will be in some discomfort when she awakens. Perhaps an apothecary will have something to ease her pain." Hugh returned to the table and washed his needle and scalpel before returning them to the leather roll.

"She wore the bracelet," Sera whispered to him.

Hugh sucked in a breath. "Shall we see what tale the young man has to tell?"

Mr Mosley fetched a solidly built footman to carry Charlotte upstairs.

"I will check on her before we leave," Hugh said as the servant lifted her with care.

Kitty met them in the hall, her eyes wide. "Charlotte's suitor is James Gollach. Powers is holding him in the study."

They had found the hand that had loaded the pistol. James must have given it to his brother, Gregory.

In the study, Lieutenant Powers sat in a chair by the window.

The young man paced the short length of the book-lined wall. James's eyes were rimmed with red, his light brown hair dishevelled as though he had tugged at it with sweaty hands. He wore no jacket and his shirtsleeves were rolled to the elbow. Brownish stains were dotted across his waistcoat. He rushed towards them, his hands outstretched. "How is Charlotte? They will not tell me anything. Me! Her fiancé."

"As long as the wound does not become infected, she will live," Hugh said.

James gave a relieved sob. "I did not mean it. You must tell them that. I would never hurt her."

"I think we can safely assume the wedding will be called off." Kitty seated herself in the chair vacated by Lieutenant Powers.

"Charlotte's parents have rather strong opinions of Mr Gollach. He will be lucky if he escapes charges." Powers leaned against a bookshelf and kept a wary eye on his prisoner.

"He won't escape charges. He's the one we seek," Sera said.

"I only wanted to give Charlotte something pretty." James pulled at his hair and resumed his pacing.

"An object you took from a woman you murdered."

Sera struggled to find sympathy for the man and whatever fate awaited him.

His feet froze to the rug and his entire form stilled. Then a shuddering sigh ran through him and he turned to meet her gaze. "You don't understand," he whispered, and licked dry lips.

Sera clenched her jaw. Understand? He had killed one woman and maimed another! She could save the city the expense of a trial by pulling the air from the man's lungs right now.

"No, we don't. Let us put aside the matter of *how* you came to acquire the bracelet for now. Why don't you tell us what happened here? How did you come to remove half Charlotte's arm?"

James swallowed several times and wiped his eyes with the heels of his hands. "The bracelet is such a pretty thing, with its tiny diamonds. I wanted to shower Charlotte in jewels, as I had promised her I would do once our family name and fortune were restored."

Sera wondered how he thought that would happen after he'd killed Lady Zedlitz. Had they planned to use the bracelet to force the king to overturn his long-ago decree?

"You gave her the bracelet today?" she asked.

James nodded. "Her parents would not admit me. I tried to see her at the Edgecombe ball, but I was removed."

Sera glanced at Kitty, his words sparking the memory of the man being escorted out by the footmen.

The young man continued with his tale. "They were supposed to be out today. Charlotte sent me a note that she would be alone. I showed her the bracelet and she thought it pretty enough to try on. She held out her right hand, and I snapped it into place around her delicate wrist."

An old muscle memory slithered down Sera's arm. The cuff Branvale had placed on her had burned as soon as he closed it. Five-year-old Sera had cried to have it removed. "Did Charlotte say anything about it then? That it was too tight, or overly warm?"

He shook his head. "No. She admired it for a little while and wished for a bracelet made only of much larger diamonds. I promised her such a thing once our lands were returned to us, and my brother recovered our fortune."

"What happened next, Mr Gollach?" Hugh prompted.

"We talked of the wedding. It is to be next spring. Her father insisted on a very long engagement, as I must prove to him I have sufficient funds for us to live on first. Charlotte said she wanted to have hummingbirds flying around the church. I thought that rather fanciful. And expensive." He paced as he spoke, the fingers of one hand pressing the bridge of his nose. At times, he paused and stared at the closed door.

The Kestrels remained silent, waiting for him to resume the story.

"Charlotte was most insistent. Then an odd thing happened. I could not imagine denying her. In fact, my sole purpose became ensuring there would be hummingbirds enough to delight her. I would have rushed from the house there and then to start capturing them, if she had not stopped me." He shook his head, unable to believe his own tale.

Sera pondered the sudden change of heart. "Why did you change your mind, can you remember? Did she touch you at all?"

James crossed his arms and stared at the floor. "Yes. Charlotte pressed a hand to my chest, and said how much she wanted hummingbirds, if only I would agree. I was going to scoff, but my mind was changed as quickly as the wind changes course during a storm."

"She touched his chest, and that was all the opportunity the bracelet needed to compel him," Sera murmured to Hugh.

"Charlotte said there was something sharp under the bracelet that scratched at her, and she had a headache developing. She asked me to take the piece off. Well, try as I might, I could not find the catch to release it. My beloved became more agitated, demanding I take it off however I could. Then we heard her parents returning, and I became obsessed with freeing her body of the bracelet before they discovered me alone with her. I pulled and twisted it on her hand until she cried out in pain and her skin tore. Still some compulsion drove me to find a way. That was when— when— I spied the sword hanging over the fireplace in the parlour." Sweat beaded on his forehead and he swiped at it with his sleeve.

Sera didn't need to hear the rest of the tale, its horrible conclusion evident in the upstairs bedroom.

Hugh bent his head close to Sera's. "Is that how it felt with the one you wore?"

"Yes. It burned through my veins when first activated. I believe the magic within the bracelet needs to connect with its host to work." She let out a sigh. The poor woman had lost her hand, but who knew what might have happened if she had unwittingly influenced all around her. What if she had told someone to shut up —would they have cut out their own tongue?

"The bracelet is cursed," Lieutenant Powers said.

"The bracelet? No." James frowned. "That is not what Father said. He was quite clear that Lady Zed—" He cut himself off.

"That Lady Zedlitz cursed him?" Sera finished the sentence for the unlucky suitor. "In a way she did, through the bracelet. It is ensorcelled. The wearer can compel anyone to do anything with a single touch. That is why you became obsessed with removing it from Charlotte."

Mr Gollach's eyes widened. Then he clasped his head in his hands and, with his back to the wall, slid to the ground. "No," he whispered. "What have I done? Father said the compulsion roared through his veins to take the beast into the presence chamber and try as he might, he was powerless to stop himself. He said he sobbed as he removed his clothes, unable to keep them on."

I screamed inside my head, yelling no! *over and over, but words that were not my own kept coming from my mouth.* Lady Haas had suffered a similar compulsion, her life likewise ruined.

Only one question remained in Sera's mind. Had Mr Gollach held down his victim's feet that fateful morning, or the pillow? "We know you were in Lady Zedlitz's bedchamber at the palace, and I am sure the authorities are on their way. You may as well tell us the whole of it. What exactly did your father say about Lady Zedlitz?"

"That she had cursed us because he won the bull she wanted. That it would only be once she no longer breathed that the curse would be released and our family fortune restored." He spoke with his head bowed, his arms resting on bent knees. "On his deathbed, Father made us promise that we would do whatever we could to restore the family name and the lands the king seized from him."

"Were you both dressed as footmen?" Powers asked.

"Yes. It was easy to steal the uniforms. Then we spent a couple of days roaming the palace to discover where the Austrians were staying and which was her room. Then all we had to do was wait until she was asleep and her maid out of the room." James leaned his head back against the wall.

Sera watched a tear roll down the man's face. He didn't seem the sort to press a pillow to another person's face. But you could look away while holding a woman's feet—that seemed less personal. "You held her ankles while your brother took up the pillow."

He glanced up. "Gregory tossed me the bracelet and said Charlotte might like it."

"You took a woman's life for nothing," Kitty said.

"Not for nothing! She ruined us. After Father was banished, no one would do business with him. He died in squalor. We promised to avenge him and restore our family to its previous position. Charlotte's father only agreed to our engagement on the condition I show him sufficient means to support her within two years. My time was running out." When he looked up, a glint shone in his eyes, but whether from tears or defiance, Sera could not tell.

Sera tried to find a small measure of sympathy for him. "Lady Zedlitz used people for her own amusement, with no regard for the consequences. Yours were not the only lives ruined by her. English law, however, takes a dim view of murder."

"And attempted murder. Why did your brother try to kill Lord Zedlitz?" Lieutenant Powers reminded them that the brothers had almost continued their murderous vendetta.

"Because her death wasn't enough. We were still excluded from court and all good society. The curse was supposed to reverse when she died. Gregory thought—thought that—we needed to remove her entire line." He struggled over the words, perhaps only now realising the magnitude of their terrible actions.

Powers pushed off the bookshelf and stood over the young man. "Where is Sir Gregory now?"

"He said if a single shot wasn't enough, he'd try something larger to ensure he blew the curse away."

Sera's blood seemed to freeze in her veins.

Powers hauled the young man to his feet and pressed him to the wall. "What is he planning?"

"The banquet for the Austrian delegation is tomorrow night." Kitty rose from her chair.

Sera had forgotten it in the rush of the day's events.

The palace would be busy with the preparations, and with his stolen uniform, Gregory could slip in unnoticed.

"He was going to procure a keg of gunpowder and set it near where Lord Zedlitz will be. To make sure the job was done." James slumped in the lieutenant's grip.

Lieutenant Powers shook him. "Damn fools. You would kill or injure dozens."

Dread flowed through Sera. A keg of gunpowder might look similar to a cask of wine, but would have a far more devastating effect on the gathered nobles. To say nothing of Their Majesties. "The palace will be swarming with servants, preparing for the evening. How does he intend to light the fuse?"

"During your performance. He said no one will notice him." The murderer's accomplice scrubbed his hands over his face.

Sera blew out a short huff. "Lord Tomlin, as Apollo, intends to shower the room with sparks from a spinning sun. No one will notice one more spark flaring into life on a fuse."

"Well, Sera, you had intended to make the evening memorable," Kitty quipped.

TWENTY-THREE

"What part were you to play in this?" Lieutenant Powers gazed at the distraught man without emotion.

"I was to fetch the horses and have them waiting near the gate for when he comes out. Gregory said he'd slip in when they unloaded the wine and brandy at midday." Now that James had been captured and realised he had no future with Charlotte, the life seemed to drain from him like a scarecrow whose straw is pulled out by hungry birds.

The magistrate sent his men, and James Gollach was loaded into a black windowless carriage to convey him to prison. Hugh checked on his patient and assured the worried parents he would return the next day, but early indications were promising. Then they returned to Kitty's waiting carriage. James had provided the address of the rooms the brothers had used. They travelled first to the shabby rooms, only to find them apparently abandoned. The neighbours had not seen the older brother all day.

"We need to find him, obviously, before he enacts his horrible plan," Kitty said as she rapped on the roof for the driver to move off once more.

Powers drummed his short nails on his knee. "At least we know where he will be tomorrow and that he will be carrying a keg. His scar will be hard to disguise."

"Unless an aftermage changes his features," Kitty said.

"Can they do that?" Hugh turned to Sera.

Sera had heard of those with a trace of mage blood who had some skill in altering someone's appearance with a type of glamour. It didn't last long, but Sir Gregory only needed a few hours at most. "A rare few can, but such services would be expensive. Let us hope that is beyond their means. But talking of altering features gives me an idea of how we might trap him."

The lieutenant leaned forward in his seat. "Any additional bait to our hook would be handy. What do you propose, my lady?"

Sera thought to use to their advantage the obsession the men had, believing that Lady Zedlitz had cursed the family. "What if Gregory discovered that Lady Zedlitz was not, in fact, deceased?"

Powers stroked his luxuriant moustache. "A brilliant idea—we lure him out into the open and trust he makes a rash move."

Sera outlined her idea, which required Hugh, Lieutenant Powers, and Lord Zedlitz to play roles. With nothing more they could do that night, the friends parted company. The lieutenant hurried to the palace to inform the king and to ensure the guards were alert to any facial scars of those entering the grounds.

The next day, after confirming the approximate time the wine merchant would make his delivery, they assembled in the shade cast by the high wall. The cobbled courtyard buzzed with activity. Servants rushed back and forth to prepare the banquet room for the grand evening. Chaises were carried past, along with low tables and cushions of bright pink, rich blue, and sea green.

Sera placed one hand on top of Lieutenant Powers's bare head and whispered the spell. When she wiped her hand down his face, his features altered in her palm's wake. James Gollach now stood before them.

"So this is the man who murdered my mother." Otto peered closely at the magical transformation.

Sera placed one hand on Otto's forearm and the other upon the surgeon's beefy arm. "Picture your mother, Otto, and imagine you are introducing her to me," she murmured.

The features of James were fresh in her memory, but the encounter with Otto's mother had faded with the passage of time—and the indelible image of the woman in death would not help. Since Mother Nature didn't allow mages to meddles in people's minds without their permission, Sera needed Otto to push a thought or image towards her that she could capture. Using his memories, she performed a similar spell on Hugh. This time when she removed her hand, Lady Zedlitz stood before them. Otto made a startled noise.

With their faces changed, the magic filtered down to their forms and clothing until two replicas stood beside Sera.

"I cannot disguise your voices, so avoid speaking," she said.

The fake James rubbed his fingers along an unadorned upper lip. "I will wait by the main gate and signal if I see him enter the courtyard. Most of this rests with you, my friend." He slapped Lady Zedlitz on the shoulder.

Sera waited with Hugh and Otto, the three of them scanning the bustle of faces for that of Gregory. Time ticked by and it seemed each second scratched along her skin. The array of furniture and table decorations being moved into the palace for the banquet amazed her and part of her surged with excitement for what lay ahead—her magical battle with Lord Tomlin.

The clock struck the hour and people called out to make way for a team of heavy horses with feathered legs pulling a loaded wagon. The driver pulled them to a halt in the middle of the busy yard. Men swarmed the cart, untying the ropes and grabbing at the casks of wine. One man on top of the stack yelled out orders and waved his arms at a particular doorway where he wanted them taken.

"Where is he?" Sera whispered.

The part of the murderous plot they didn't know was whether Gregory had hidden his gunpowder among those barrels being unloaded, or if he would carry his in with him and join the procession.

"There is Powers." Hugh raised Lady Zedlitz's arm

and gestured to the young man who stared at the shadow hiding them.

"Where is the other one, though? There are a dozen men working here," Otto said.

Men marched to and from the cart like busy ants. Each followed the other as they carried out their task. The barrels on the wide cart diminished with almost magical haste.

"We don't have to find him. He will make himself known to us. If you will go first, my lord?" Hugh's deep voice came from Lady Zedlitz's stout form.

Otto hesitated for a moment, then cut a path through the busy courtyard as though he were on his own mission. Hugh waited until the other man neared the heavy horses, then he bustled after the margrave.

"Otto! Otto!" Hugh shrieked in a high-pitched tone. "I am tired of hiding in my room. I wish to attend the party!"

Lord Zedlitz halted as staff parted around him and then fled from the imposing force of his mother bearing down on them. He pinched the bridge of his nose. "You should not be here, *Mutter*. You must go back inside at once. You are not well."

"I am *bored*. I will not stay there a moment longer." Hugh placed his hands on his hips and glared at his companion.

Someone in a group of servants dropped a platter. Porcelain shattered as it hit the cobbles. "You oaf!" a voice called out.

That has to be Gregory! Sera cupped her hands together. She had failed once, being too slow with a freezing spell, but not again. Opening her palms, she blew on them and sent a gust of polar air across the courtyard. A rug of ice a yard wide unwound itself and raced over the cobbles to slide under the workers.

Men cried out and fell on the slippery surface. That knocked them into others. Casks were dropped and split open, spilling brandy onto the ground. One of the men managed to stumble off the ribbon of ice and the wooden keg in his hands escaped his grasp. But instead of cracking open on the ground, it rolled to a stop intact. The man's foot shot out and kicked it, and a black substance poured from the open hole in the top to mingle with the alcohol.

"Blast." Sera had meant to freeze feet to ground, but in trying to conserve her use of magic, instead she'd created a narrow skating rink that added to the chaos. Where was Gregory?

The man closest to the intact keg drew a brass cylinder from his pocket, his gaze intent on the disguised surgeon. Sera scanned his face, heavy with grime, almost as though he'd tried to draw on a beard with soot. To disguise his scar!

Gregory's thumb flicked open the top of the thing in his hand.

"It's a tinderbox. The gunpowder! Otto!" She stepped from the shadows, but before she could throw another spell, James rushed his brother with the purpose and speed of a dog after a ball.

Both men hit the ground with an audible grunt and the combination of brandy and ice carried them a few feet along the cobbles. Lady Zedlitz leapt on top of

Gregory as the lieutenant had him pinned by the knees. The fake woman drew back her arm, and struck.

The workers cheered and quickly surrounded the thrashing bodies. Footmen and workers formed a ring, some called out bets, and they egged on the combatants.

"Oh, honestly." Sera couldn't see past the yelling throng to immobilise Gregory, nor did she want to risk another generalised spell and possibly give him an advantage.

"Blimey, look at her go! Pummel him, missus!" someone screamed.

Sera took that to mean Hugh appeared to be winning in the impromptu ring. She squeezed between the bodies and stood on her toes, trying to see the melee.

By the time she broke through, Gregory struggled in the grip of the enchanted Hugh and Powers. He possessed more fight than his brother. "Why are you helping her, James? She must perish so the king will return our lands. Finish it, lad. Now!"

Sera clapped her hands and the spell fell away. Lieutenant Powers and Hugh held the man. Gregory's confused gaze went from the man he thought was his brother to the imposing surgeon who had replaced Lady Zedlitz.

"There was no curse on your family, only a compulsion laid upon your father against his will," Sera said.

"No! Her line must perish." Gregory continued to tug his arms free, but to no avail.

Guards rushed forward and broke up the workers, sending them back to their tasks. Powers took charge of his prisoner, who was given into the custody of two burly guardsmen.

"Thank you for your assistance, Lady Winyard. I shall see to it that this man joins his brother in gaol," Powers said.

Gregory squirmed in the guards' grip. "She cursed us and stole all we had," he yelled as the men led him away.

Otto stared after the man who had murdered his mother and twice attempted to kill him. He shook his head. "My mother must account for her actions before God, as will he. Let English justice be done." Then he spun on his heel and retreated inside.

With that matter finally resolved, Sera now had another battle to contemplate. Vicky and Inge waited in Lady Zedlitz's former bedchamber inside the palace to help her into her gown. "I have to make myself ready for this evening."

Hugh took her hand and drew her close. "I cannot attend, but have secured a spot by the door where I can watch. I look forward to seeing Nyx defeat Apollo." Then he leaned down and kissed her, which elicited a cheer from the workers around them.

Preparations took the rest of the afternoon, as Sera gave her magic time to replenish itself from the spells she'd cast that day. A bath with lavender revived her senses. Inge fussed over the gown she had designed while Vicky brushed out Sera's hair. Tonight it would tumble free down her back.

Wrapping a grey cloak around her shoulders, Sera kissed Inge's cheek in thanks, and hurried along the halls to the banquet room. She waited in the shadows by an archway, watching the guests. The long banqueting table had been removed, and instead there were smaller tables arranged around the room, along with divans, *chaises longues*, and enormous cushions scattered on the floor. Mist swirled around the ceiling of the room and mountaintops shimmered on the walls.

King George and Queen Charlotte reclined on two white silk–draped chaises set on an angle to each other so that their heads met but their toes pointed away. Crowns of gilded laurel leaves rested atop their heads and they each had a servant standing behind them to wave a man-sized ostrich-feather fan.

Other members of the Mage Council were arrayed among the attendees. They would cast events inside to those outside. Sera and Tomlin would become ghostly titans, battling on the Thames for those Londoners crammed along the riverbank to watch.

A master of ceremonies, in a toga draped over his normal livery, strode to the centre of the room. He carried a long, golden staff that he rapped on the parquet floor three times. "Your Majesties, ladies and gentlemen, tonight we dine among the gods on Mount Olympus!"

Brief applause erupted and he waited for it to settle down.

"Hark, here comes Apollo, the golden son of our beloved ruler, Zeus." He bowed to the king, who represented Zeus, and retreated to the side of the room.

Lord Tomlin entered the room in a blaze of light that made people gasp and avert their faces. He outshone the sun but, perhaps realising it didn't pay to blind one's audience, dimmed his radiance so they could all see him. He stood in a white and gold chariot pulled by a glistening white unicorn. He was clothed in brilliant white and shimmering gold. The golden laurels in his hair left a trail of fiery sparks as he moved.

Halting the unicorn, Lord Tomlin left his chariot and, with the swipe of his hand, it shimmered and dissolved into a glittering mist. With each step he took across the parquet floor, swaying yellow wheat appeared bearing fat seed heads. Copper sparrows chatted happily while they flocked around his head.

Fool, Sera thought. His entire outfit was a conjured glamour. He would drain his magic simply keeping up his appearance.

Tomlin paced between the tables and divans as a glittering form among the nobles. Wheat sprang up in his wake like a carpet rolled out over the floor. He strode in a spiral until he reached the middle of the room. There he crafted an orb of pure gold that cast a yellow glow. With a clap of his hands, the orb rose to hover close to the ceiling and bathe the room in light and warmth.

Next he rolled his hands together and released a flock of phoenixes that frolicked and played in the air above the nobles. Delighted gasps and murmurs of conversation followed their progress. Light, whimsical music could be heard without benefit of musicians. The phoenixes performed an aerial ballet to the music, then roosted atop the sun.

Apollo bowed to his enraptured audience.

The master of ceremonies waded through the wheat. "Thank you, Apollo, for sharing your radiance with us. But who is that in the shadows? Why, it is Nyx, goddess of the night."

He gestured with his arm to the archway where Sera hid. She unfastened her cloak, let it fall to the ground, and added the barest touch of magic to enhance her appearance. The silver stars sewn by Inge were given an extra luminosity. Vicky had added a black dye to her hair when they washed it and her locks were a velvety curtain tumbling around her face and down her back.

Sera emerged from the shadows trailing darkness behind her.

The gasps of those present had a shocked edge to them as the wheat conjured by Lord Tomlin disappeared under the hem of her gown of shadow, to be replaced by smooth, dark slate. A dark mist rose from her sweeping train and spread twilight over the room. People gasped and murmured as the lights dimmed to tiny firefly dots. Around and around she spiralled, wiping away the lush crop with her blanket of night. Behind her, three crows took flight and circled the room, their caws mocking the startled diners. Ebony feathers gleamed as they absorbed the small amount of light.

A crow flew down and touched a diner, pulling from the startled noble a gossamer-thin image of the person. It emitted an eerie moan as the crow flapped its wings and ascended, taking the soul with it. Another crow dove at a guest and its touch freed another wispy image, its cry creating a mournful music. Shouts of alarm went up from the nobles. Men batted the crows away with napkins.

Her crows dangled captive souls from their claws as they circled above the phoenixes frozen on the orb. As one, they released the spirits and they floated down like sheets in a breeze. The phoenixes cried out and seemed to melt into the sun at their feet as the souls blanketed them.

When Sera reached the middle of the room and stood opposite Lord Tomlin, she whispered over her hands and crafted a net. Then she threw it high. The net snared the sun and enclosed it, like a mourning veil hiding the face of a woman. The light was snuffed out, leaving only the bright fireflies clustered along the walls. A woman screamed and several sobbed.

Sera kept her expression serene but inside, she congratulated herself on scaring most of the guests. Next, she curled inward over her hands. When she stretched and flung her arms wide, a luminescent half-moon three feet tall rose towards the ceiling. It hovered above them and spun in a slow circle, banishing the deepest dark. Her crows became one with the dark and melted back into the shadow. As the half-moon revolved, stars flew from it and positioned themselves in familiar constellations.

"Apollo, will you save us from Nyx?" the master of ceremonies called out with a note of alarm in his voice. "Light must battle dark. But who will be victorious and have dominion over us?" Then the courtier beat a hasty retreat to an illusionary mountaintop.

Twenty-Four

Lord Tomlin nodded to her and murmured, "You have only to follow my lead and stick to the plan."

Oh, but we won't be doing that, she thought.

They walked in a slow circle, keeping an equal distance from one another. Light and dark butted against one another like oil and water. Once again, Apollo crafted his bright sun and threw it into the air to restore daylight. Then, with a swipe of one arm, he dissolved the walls of the room until it appeared they sat in an endless golden field of wheat. Sparrows perched on the ripening seed heads and chirped to each other.

Sera smiled. Light was far easier to extinguish than create. She flicked one hand and her crows flew down and covered the sun with their midnight feathers. Then they hunted out each glimmering copper sparrow. As a crow's claws wrapped around a sparrow, it burst in a small puff of orange and yellow mist. Then night reigned once more.

Lord Tomlin conjured his luminescent chariot and radiant unicorn. He stepped into the vehicle and took up the reins, sending the unicorn cantering around the room. Light poured from them, bright enough to warn ships away from a rocky coastline during a moonless storm.

From the archway ran an inky black panther. Bunching its powerful hind legs, the cat leapt on the unicorn. The equine screamed as the panther's claws dug into its hindquarters. The chariot came to an abrupt halt and Lord Tomlin leapt free as it tipped to one side while equine battled feline. Lord Tomlin frowned. In his script, the panther died under the unicorn's hooves, except no matter how hard he tried, Tomlin couldn't dislodge the panther from the rear of his creature.

Furniture scraped as some people leapt to their feet, perhaps to run from the room. But Sera wasn't an utter monster—there was no blood or gore in this fight. Her cat's claws delivered a painless death as they unpicked the magic of the unicorn. With each slash, part of the horned horse dissolved until nothing stood in the harness. With a snarl, the panther stalked to the chariot and sat guarding it.

Sera approached and patted the large cat. Then she stepped into the chariot and raised her arms. The vehicle burst apart into a shower of midnight blue sparks, they swirled around her and then the majority winked out of existence. The few that remained settled on her gown and joined the stars.

Her opponent narrowed his gaze at her and whispered ensorcelled words that brushed over her ears. *Remember the directions I gave you.*

Sera plastered a demure smile on her face and nodded to him.

Lord Tomlin's fancy costume wavered as he tried to draw more power to combat her. The climax of the evening was an old-fashioned mage battle. Sera took one side of the room, Tomlin the other. They faced each other like duellists, then began with balls of lightning. Apollo's were bluish-white. Sera threw balls the colour of a raven's wing—black with ripples of deepest green and purple. When the orbs collided, they exploded and showered harmless sparks on those below.

When Tomlin switched to fiery spears, Sera created a spiderweb that caught them and held them aloft.

"You have put up a good display, Lady Winyard, but the time has come for you to concede." Lord Tomlin sent the words along a vibrating spear.

How easy it would be to capitulate. Weariness weighed down Sera's movements and her body and mind longed to curl up in bed and sleep for days. But the spark of stubbornness inside her urged her on. She caught the way Lord Tomlin grimaced with each new casting. Sera gambled that her opponent was consuming his magic at a faster rate than she.

Lord Rowan's question whispered through her mind. *Have you tested your limits?*

She wanted to show everyone what she was capable of—what better time than now?

Bowing her head, Sera dropped her hands to her sides and relaxed her shoulders. Reaching down through the timbers and stonework of the building, she touched the earth far below her feet and burrowed into it. Drawing more magic from the earth that gave them all life.

Silence fell over the room, broken only by a wheeze from Lord Tomlin, who thought her pose signalled defeat. Sera turned her palms outward and in a slow, measured move, she raised her hands. The floor shook and glasses rattled. A rumble rolled through the room and vibrated through every person.

"What is she doing? Make her stop!" a man shrieked.

A shadow undulated across the floor. Then a primal roar made people clap their hands over their ears as a dragon's head made of obsidian emerged. As the beast bellowed, one monstrous forearm pulled itself free of the parquet and slammed down. Then another foot with eight-inch claws joined it. Like a raven's feather, scales shimmered purple, teal, and black in the low light. The dragon hauled its long, sinuous body from the depths of the earth and wound itself in a protective circle around Sera.

Lord Tomlin huffed and glared at her. With a grunt of effort that caused sweat to bead on his forehead, he hunched inward to cast a gold Pegasus that appeared above him. Its wings flapped to hold it aloft as it dove. The dragon snapped its massive jaws, but missed the flying horse. The equine spun up to the ceiling before somersaulting and flying down again. Shafts of sunlight followed in its wake. Golden hooves struck the dragon in the side of the head.

Sera's creature roared a challenge. The obsidian dragon rose on its hind legs, its shoulders pushed against the ceiling of the room. Then it struck out with both front legs, punching the horse with a double-fisted blow.

The Pegasus hurtled towards the far wall and on impact...disappeared in a puff of orange and pink mist like a bursting sunset. Night once more claimed the room.

The guests gasped. Across from Sera, in the soft silver light from a few stars, Lord Tomlin's eyes widened and then rolled back into his head revealing the whites. His limp body thudded to the floor and a shriek came from a woman in the audience.

"Darkness has extinguished the light! Nyx reigns this evening," the master of ceremonies called out, his voice shaking.

Sera released her dragon. It sank back into the floor and vanished. Conversation erupted. What did it mean? How could evil triumph over good? How had that woman defeated a powerful mage in battle?

Men rushed to Lord Tomlin's side. He had not moved.

"He breathes, but has exhausted his magic," Lord Pendlebury said in a loud voice.

Heads turned to Sera, eyes narrowed, and the conversation struck up anew.

"Well played, Nyx." The king stood and raised a glass to Sera. "We salute you. For there could be no day without night."

Sera smiled. She had beaten them at their own game. After tonight, they would not question whether she had power. Nor would they dare try to manipulate or control her. Sparks raced along her skin and leapt to join the remaining stars above. Magic sang through her veins and whispered of all she could do that night. Among the audience were those who would see her brought down and imprisoned. No need to craft facsimiles of their souls. With the power inside her, she could pluck out her enemies one by one and still their hearts.

A warm, firm touch caressed her knuckles. "You are victorious, Lady Winyard, and can stop now. The king has spoken."

Hugh bent over her hand and kissed her skin, sending a different sort of spark tingling along her veins.

Surplus energy jumped from her arm to his hand and bounced along his jacket sleeve. Not wanting to set fire to him, she drew a ragged breath. *No*, she commanded the magic, calling it back to her core.

The crescent moon shimmered and dissolved, along with all the stars that fell to the ground as glittering fluff. The candles relit themselves and flared brightly, bathing the room in their glow. Fear ebbed from the guests once light was restored, and conversation calmed.

"Let us go," Hugh murmured, tucking her hand into the crook of his elbow and keeping her close to his side.

The crowd parted to let them pass. Through the

double doors and out into the corridor they walked. Kitty and Lieutenant Powers joined them.

"You were amazing!" Kitty kissed her cheek.

With each step Sera took, her body grew weaker and she placed more weight on Hugh's muscular arm. Defeating Tomlin had used all her magic—only a faint trickle now remained to keep her enchantments active until she recalled them.

"Take me home," she whispered, entrusting herself to her friends.

Instead of leaving through the main palace entrance, Kitty ushered them along a long corridor. Sera stumbled and Hugh wrapped an arm around her waist. Her vision narrowed as blackness nibbled at the edges. The twists and turns of the hall soon terminated at a side door that appeared to be used by tradespeople accessing the kitchens. At this hour of the night, it stood quiet and deserted—except for the waiting carriage.

A footman jumped down from his perch beside the driver and pulled the door open.

"You did it," Hugh said, placing a kiss on her temple.

"We did it," Sera breathed, each word forming mist on the chill air.

Relief flowed through her body and with it, the last tiny bit of magic that had kept her ambulatory. Sera looked up at the night sky decorated with a sliver of moon and thousands of stars. Her mind spun upward to join the darkness and it folded her in a warm embrace.

Or it might have been Hugh's strong arms catching her as her body tumbled into unconsciousness.

The pounding against her skull pulled Sera from sleep. She tried to call forth her magic to fend off her attacker, but her sluggish blood had none to offer. Pressing a hand to her forehead, she cracked her eyes open. Light filtered through partly closed curtains and shadows moved back and forth.

"How long?" she rasped. From the dryness of her throat, she wondered if she had been unconscious for weeks.

"Two days. Kitty, could you ask Vicky for hot water and broth, please? I have white willow bark ready to brew a tea. It will help with the headache you no doubt have." Hugh picked up Sera's hand and held his pocket watch in the other. He took her pulse, felt either side of her neck, pulled up her eyelids, and checked inside her mouth. Only once he was satisfied did his features soften. "You had us all worried."

"Magic demands its price, but I refused to let Tomlin win." She struggled to sit up. Hugh assisted and fussed with the placement of the pillows behind her.

"You have defeated him twice," Kitty said on re-entering the room. "Once in the banquet room, and again now. He is still in an enforced slumber and hasn't awakened yet."

Elliot leaned against a wall, his usual jaunty expression more serious. "You've had a number of callers, milady."

"What did you tell them?" Sera took the glass from Hugh, and held it in two hands to take a cautious sip.

"To sod off," Elliot said.

Sera nearly snorted cool lemonade out her nose. No doubt Elliot had been none too subtle in telling visitors that she could not be disturbed.

"Lord Ormsby came. Your aunt Natalie met him on the doorstep and refused to let him in. It would take a much braver man than the Speaker to try to barge past that one." Only now did Elliot's familiar grin return.

"Nat is here?" Sera took another drink and wondered when the gargoyle had arrived.

"She's keeping watch up on the roof with our friendly crow. I'll go tell her you're awake." Elliot winked and left her crowded bedchamber.

Hugh hovered at Sera's side and dragged over a ladderback chair to sit near her. "The battle caused a panic among those gathered along the Thames to watch it. A dragon the size of a building emerging from the water made many run. Sadly, dozens were injured but none fatally."

Kitty sat on a corner of the bed, worry etched between her eyes. "We have put it about that, inspired by Nyx, you have been locked in your study writing spells and incantations she whispered to you and you could not be disturbed while working. Lady Tinwald paid a call and left this for you." Kitty reached into a pocket of her gown and pulled out a brown velvet purse. She took the glass from Sera's hand and placed the purse in it instead.

Sera bounced its weight in her palm and something clinked. "The potions worked?"

"Obviously." Kitty grinned like a proud parent. "I suspect you will soon have more business than an apothecary when the dysentery hits town."

Hugh took the purse and deposited it on the table beside the bed. "As Lady Winyard's attending surgeon, I decree that she needs to rest now. We have all reassured ourselves that she appears unharmed. After some willow bark tea and a bowl of bone broth, she is going to sleep for a few more hours."

Sera wanted to argue, but her small amount of energy seemed to flow out her toes even as Hugh spoke.

Kitty patted her hand. "Rest. I will be downstairs when the dragon here lets us back in."

Sera settled down under the blankets and let Hugh fuss over her. He fed her the tasty soup and the willow bark tea, then drew the curtains to enclose the room in darkness.

When she awoke some time later, Sera found him dozing in the chair at her side. In the dim light, she studied his square jaw and the breadth of his shoulders. His hands clutched a book that even in sleep he hadn't let go. She would have watched him sleep, but her stomach rumbled loudly enough to disturb him.

He opened his eyes and smiled at her. "Hungry?"

She returned his smile. "Famished. It's like I haven't eaten for days."

"I'll tell Rosie you are allowed a small meal." He lit

a lantern by the bed and then another on the mantel before leaving her room.

When he returned, he read to her from the newspaper and caught her up on events that had happened while she was unconscious. Riots had broken out when she won. Some panicked that the handmaiden of death would come for them. Others defended her, saying she fought for the common people.

"At titles go, I prefer *handmaiden of death* over *mistress of drains.*"

One by one, the rest of her found family entered the room. Kitty claimed a corner of the bed. Elliot carried a pitcher. Rosie bustled over and threw her arms around her, then kissed her forehead before letting her go. Nat cast her a grin and a nod before taking up a position by the window. Gargoyles really were creatures of few words.

Vicky clutched a tray. "Oh, milady, I was ever so relieved to hear you were awake."

Sera smiled at the nervous maid. She must have been worried, to speak out in company. "Thank you, Vicky. I am sorry we had to delay our celebratory dinner, but we have all the more reason for one now."

A delicious aroma wafted from the tray. It reminded Sera of rainy days in the kitchen, when Rosie would take leftover bread, soak it in whisked egg, and then fry it in butter.

"Oh, that smells so good." Sera smoothed the blankets over her lap in anticipation.

"Miss Wassler and Lord Zedlitz gave us the recipe. Rosie wanted to make it special for you when you woke." Vicky placed the tray on Sera's knees and lifted the silver dome. On the plate sat golden triangles of *weiner schnitzel.*

"There was some argument over slicing the meat thinly enough." Elliot's shoulders heaved in laughter.

"And how was that resolved?" Sera picked up a piece and nibbled the fried veal.

Divine.

Rosie nodded to Hugh. "Mr Miles cut it up."

The large surgeon shrugged his shoulders. "I have some skill with a knife and the patience required to meet Miss Wassler's exacting standards."

Sera consumed the tasty dish. Now she had no need to find an Austrian noble when she wanted schnitzel delights. Not when there was a very able Englishman who could deliver the goods.

"Wasn't Miss Wassler he was trying to impress when he spent all afternoon getting it just right," Elliot murmured as he poured a glass of lemonade for Sera.

Laughter broke out and Sera leaned against the pillows as the conversation of her found family and friends flowed around her. She soaked it in, and considered herself blessed for the good people in her life.

The next day, Sera managed to leave her nest of blankets and retrieve the ensorcelled piece of paper she had found under Lord Branvale's bed. Elbows on her desk, she stared at the sheet. No matter how many revelation spells she had cast over the page, it remained stubbornly blank and gave up no more of the secret correspondence. She had only the one tantalising message to dissect and aid her search for the truth.

"Damn. With Branvale dead, I will never know who holds this page's counterpart." Then the blindingly obvious solution smacked into her brain and she sucked in a breath. "I don't need Branvale."

She reached for the pen and dipped its nib into the ink. What to write? The unknown correspondent could be next door or on the other side of the world. They could be friend or foe. Had they conspired with her guardian to protect her, suppress her, or use her for their own ends?

The time had come to grasp opportunity and throw down a gauntlet. In a neat hand, she wrote:

I am free of your shackle. No man will ever govern me.
I will find you.

There. Now she had only to wait and see what answer her message might provoke.

———◆———

SERAPHINA'S JOURNEY TO uncover the secrets around her continues in Shadow Schemes...

**Tournament of Shadows
Book 3: Shadow Schemes**

A lost child will uncover old secrets....

After her triumphant performance as Queen of the Night, Sera is instructed to stay out of public sight by the Mage Council. She is tasked with settling a restless spirit, roused by the fate of a descendant. A noblewoman stands accused of orchestrating the sad fate of her daughter, and the ghoul will not return to her grave until Sera does *something*.

Sera journeys to the countryside in pursuit of evidence to free the woman, but finds a gothic manor harbouring secrets within its walls, and a lord intent on being rid of his troublesome wife. Did the noblewoman truly do away with her daughter, or was a more sinister hand responsible?

As Sera struggles to reveal the truth, doubts invade her mind. Will her efforts see the mother walk free, or to the gallows?

A historical fantasy novel set in Georgian England where magic is real and creatures from myth walk the streets. Grab the next instalment of your favourite mage's adventures now.

Buy: Shadow Schemes

https://tillywallace.com/books/tournament-of-shadows/shadow-schemes/

History. Magic. Family.

I do hope you enjoyed Seraphina's adventure. If you would like to dive deeper into the world, or learn more about the odd assortment of characters that populate it, you can join the community by signing up at:
https://www.tillywallace.com/newsletter

Also by Tilly Wallace

For the most complete and up to date list of books, please visit:

https://tillywallace.com/books/

Available series:

Tournament of Shadows

Manner and Monsters

Highland Wolves

About the Author

Tilly drinks entirely too much coffee and is obsessed with hats. When not scouring vintage stores for her next chapeau purchase, she writes whimsical historical fantasy novels, set in a bygone time where magic is real. With a quirky and loveable cast, her books combine vintage magic and gentle humour.

Through loyal friendships, her characters discover that in an uncertain world, the strongest family is the one you create.

To be the first to hear about new releases and special offers sign up at:
https://www.tillywallace.com/newsletter

Tilly would love to hear from you:
https://www.tillywallace.com
tilly@tillywallace.com

facebook.com/tillywallaceauthor
bookbub.com/authors/tilly-wallace
goodreads.com/tillywallace